itty bitty
HELLBOY ™

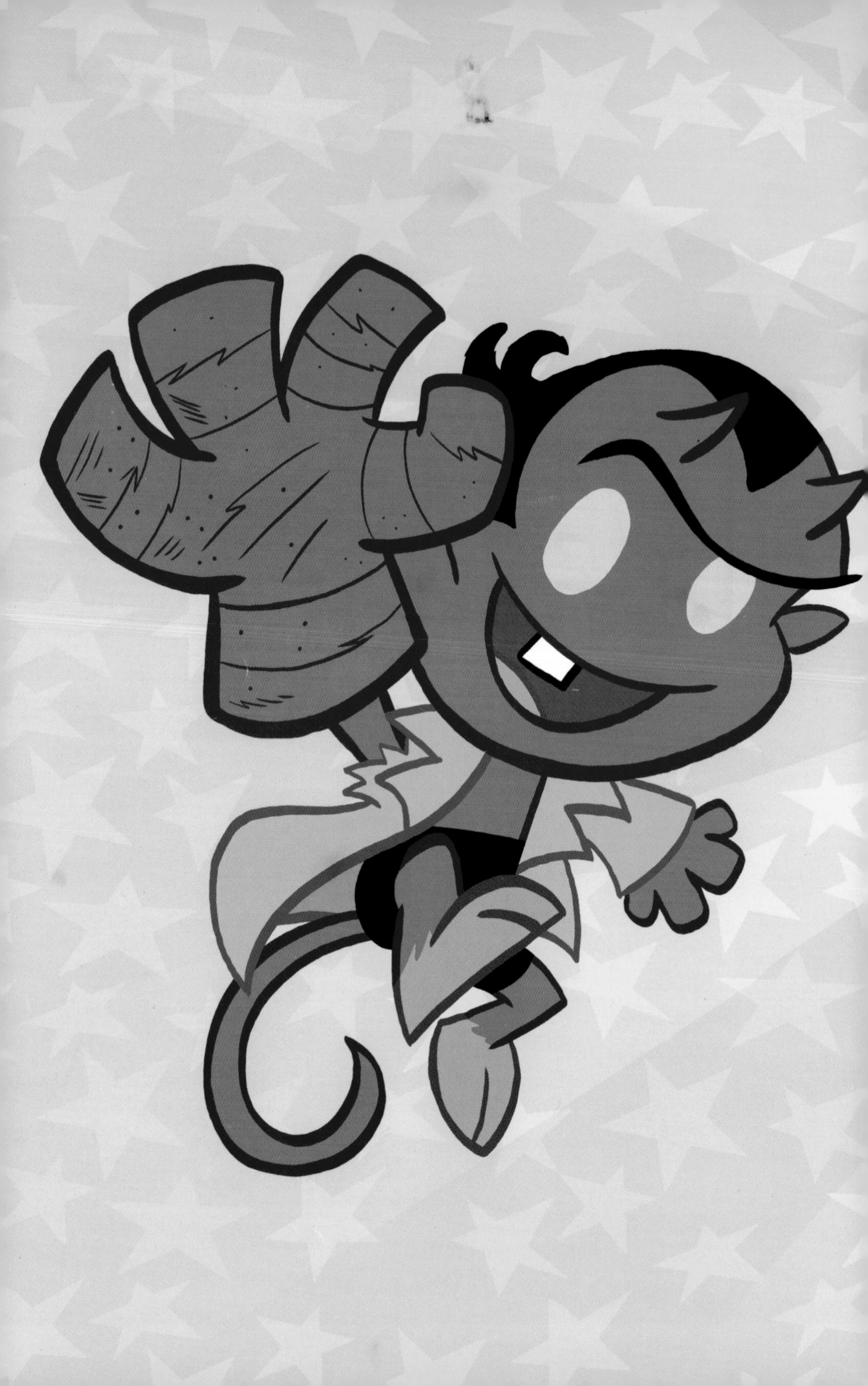

itty bitty HELLBOY™

The Search for the Were-Jaguar!

ART BALTAZAR & FRANCO

WRITER & ARTIST · WRITER

HELLBOY CREATED BY MIKE MIGNOLA

Publisher MIKE RICHARDSON

Original Series Editors SHANTEL LaROCQUE
& BRENDAN WRIGHT

Original Series Assistant Editor JEMIAH JEFFERSON

Collection Editor SHANTEL LaROCQUE

Collection Assistant Editor KATII O'BRIEN

Designer ETHAN KIMBERLING

Digital Art Technician CHRISTINA McKENZIE

Dark Horse Books

MIKE RICHARDSON President and Publisher • NEIL HANKERSON Executive Vice President TOM WEDDLE Chief Financial Officer • RANDY STRADLEY Vice President of Publishing MICHAEL MARTENS Vice President of Book Trade Sales • MATT PARKINSON Vice President of Marketing • DAVID SCROGGY Vice President of Product Development • DALE LaFOUNTAIN Vice President of Information Technology • CARA NIECE Vice President of Production and Scheduling • KEN LIZZI General Counsel • DAVEY ESTRADA Editorial Director • DAVE MARSHALL Editor in Chief • SCOTT ALLIE Executive Senior Editor • CHRIS WARNER Senior Books Editor • CARY GRAZZINI Director of Print and Development LIA RIBACCHI Art Director • MARK BERNARDI Director of Digital Publishing

Published by
Dark Horse Books
A division of Dark Horse Comics, Inc.
10956 SE Main Street
Milwaukie, OR 97222

First edition: May 2016 • ISBN 978-1-61655-801-7

This volume collects Itty Bitty Hellboy: The Search for the Were-Jaguar! #1–#4, originally published by Dark Horse Comics.

1 3 5 7 9 10 8 6 4 2
Printed in China

Library of Congress Cataloging-in-Publication Data

Names: Baltazar, Art, author, artist. | Aureliani, Franco, author.
Title: Itty Bitty Hellboy. Volume 2, The search for the were-jaguar! / story
  by Art Baltazar and Franco ; art by Art Baltazar.
Other titles: Search for the were-jaguar!
Description: First edition. | Milwaukie, OR : Dark Horse Books, [2016] |
  Summary: "Itty Bitty Hellboy and his friends hear a rumor of an island
  populated by creatures like their pal Roger, but the problem is there is
  only one pair of underwear to share between everyone. So the gang embarks
  on a special mission to deliver underwear to the Island of Rogers, but
  their mission is suddenly interrupted by the discovery of the strange
  mysterious beast known as . . . the Were-Jaguar!"-- Provided by publisher.
  | "Hellboy created by Mike Mignola" | "Collecting Itty Bitty Comics:
  Hellboy #9-#12"
Identifiers: LCCN 2015042955 | ISBN 9781616558017 (paperback)
Subjects: LCSH: Graphic novels. | CYAC: Graphic novels. | Underwear--Fiction.
  | Shapeshifting--Fiction. | Humorous stories. | BISAC: JUVENILE FICTION /
  Comics & Graphic Novels / General.
Classification: LCC PZ7.7.B33 Itd 2016 | DDC 741.5/973--dc23
LC record available at http://lccn.loc.gov/2015042955

CHAPTER ONE

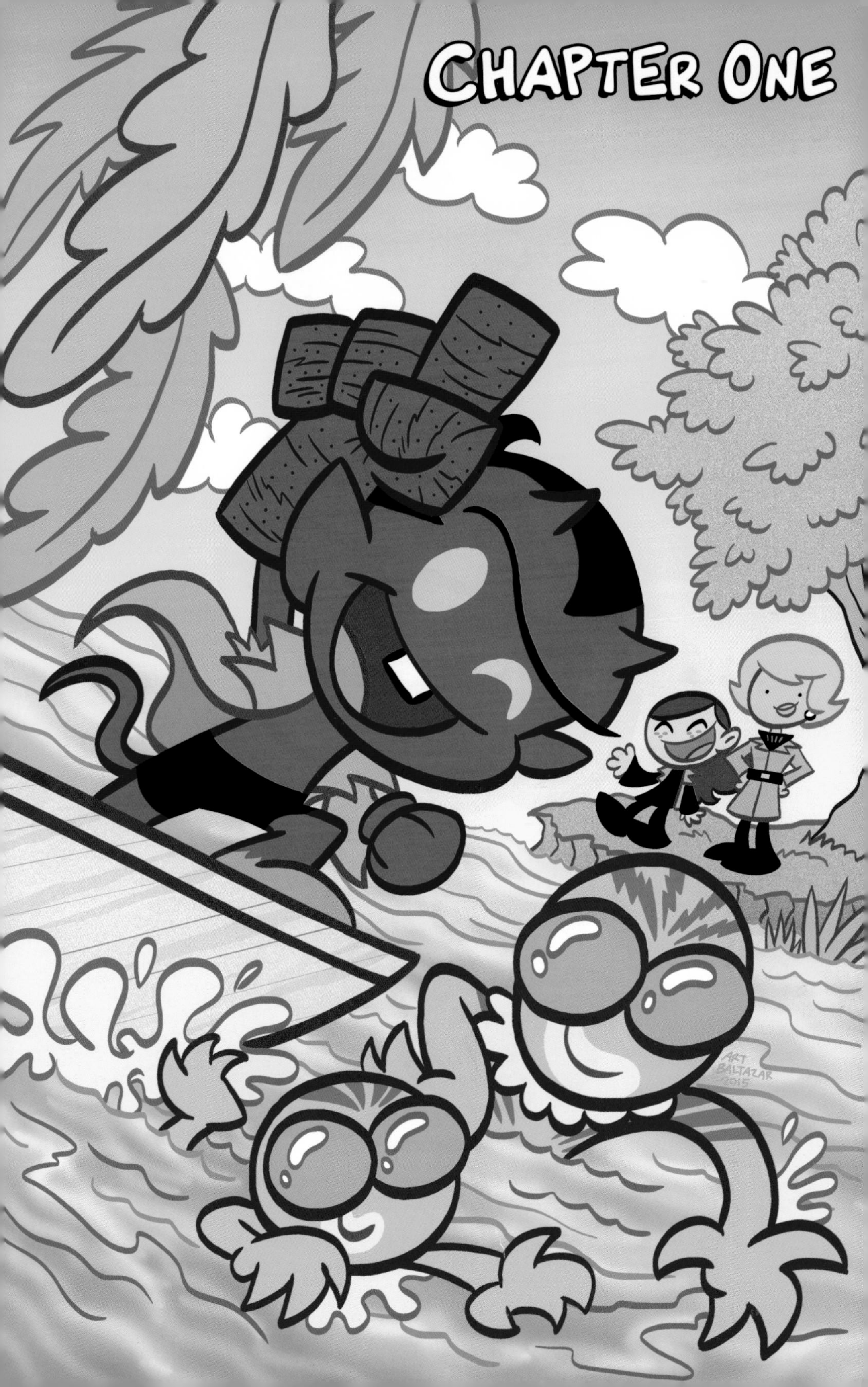

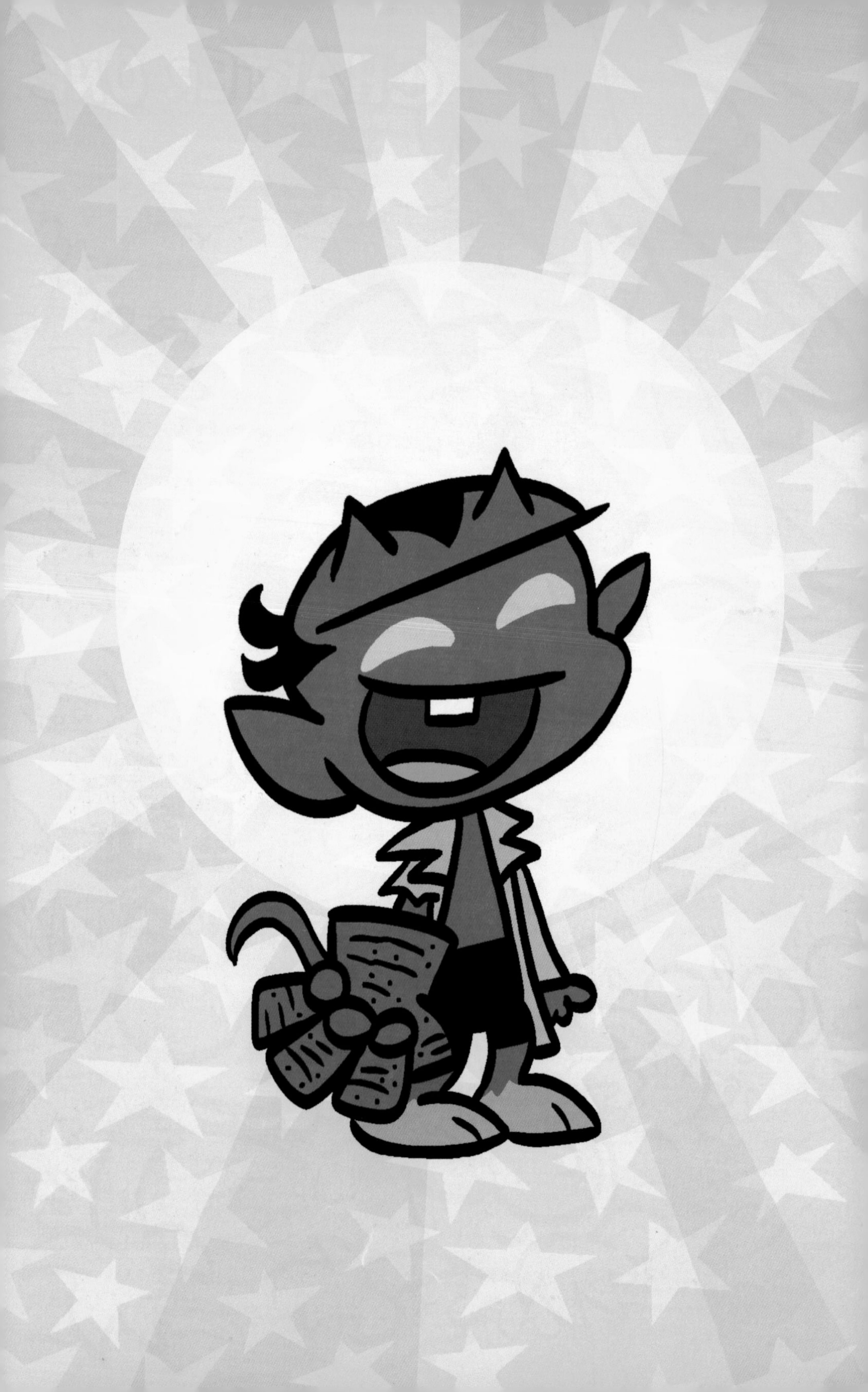

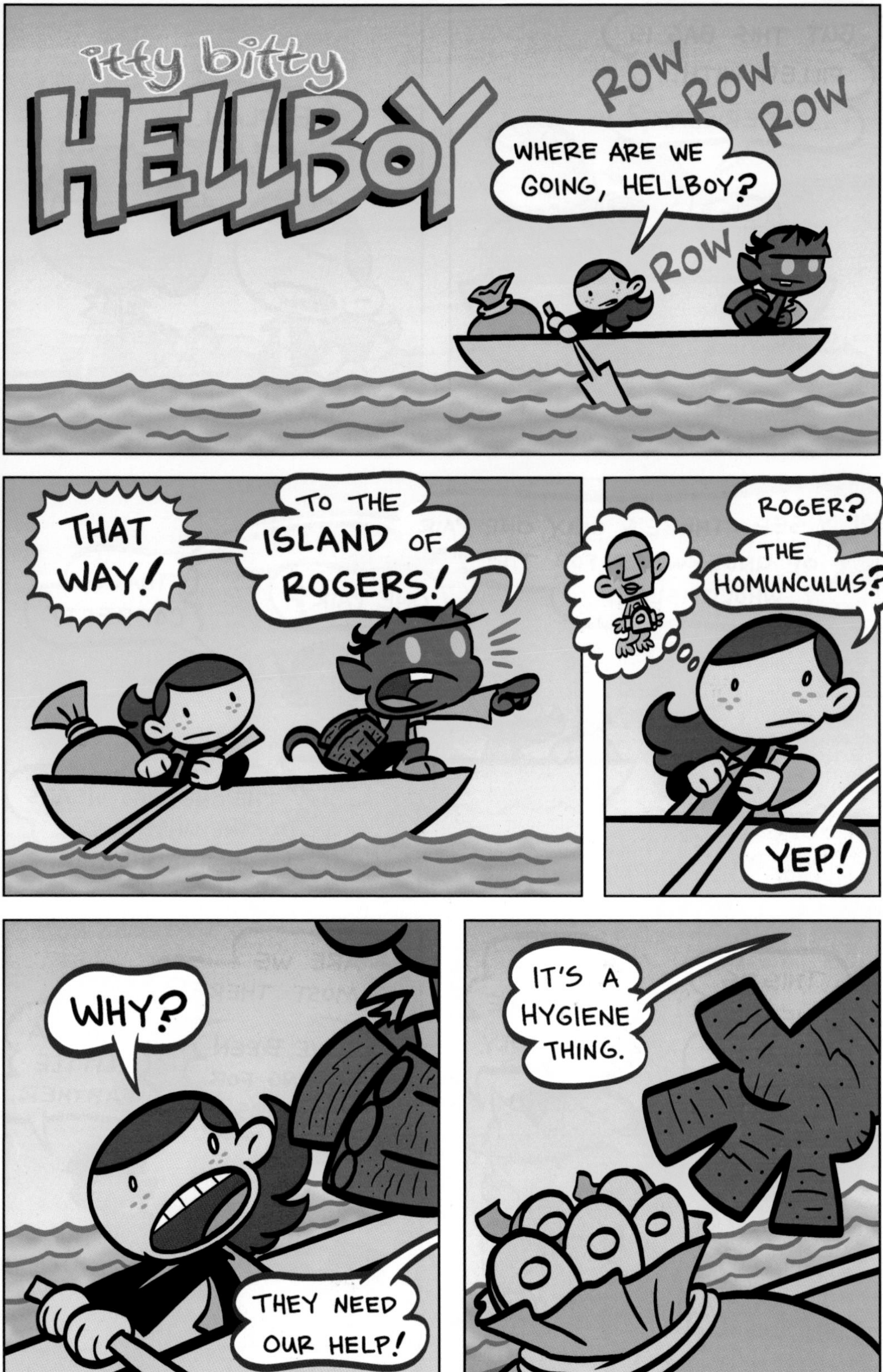
itty bitty HELLBOY
ROW ROW ROW
WHERE ARE WE GOING, HELLBOY?
ROW
THAT WAY!
TO THE ISLAND OF ROGERS!
ROGER?
THE HOMUNCULUS?
YEP!
WHY?
THEY NEED OUR HELP!
IT'S A HYGIENE THING.

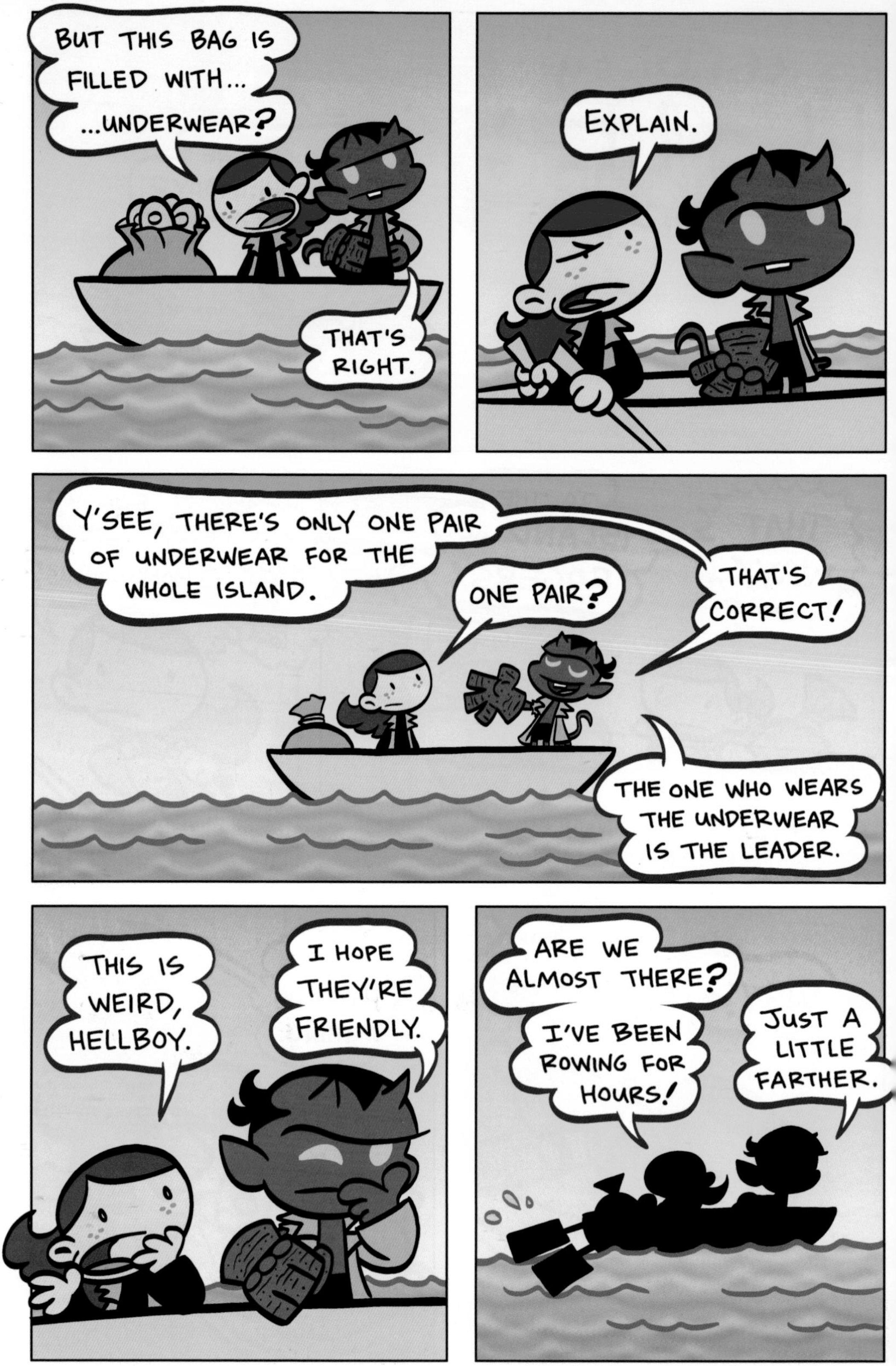
BUT THIS BAG IS FILLED WITH... ...UNDERWEAR?
THAT'S RIGHT.
EXPLAIN.
Y'SEE, THERE'S ONLY ONE PAIR OF UNDERWEAR FOR THE WHOLE ISLAND.
ONE PAIR?
THAT'S CORRECT!
THE ONE WHO WEARS THE UNDERWEAR IS THE LEADER.
THIS IS WEIRD, HELLBOY.
I HOPE THEY'RE FRIENDLY.
ARE WE ALMOST THERE?
I'VE BEEN ROWING FOR HOURS!
JUST A LITTLE FARTHER.

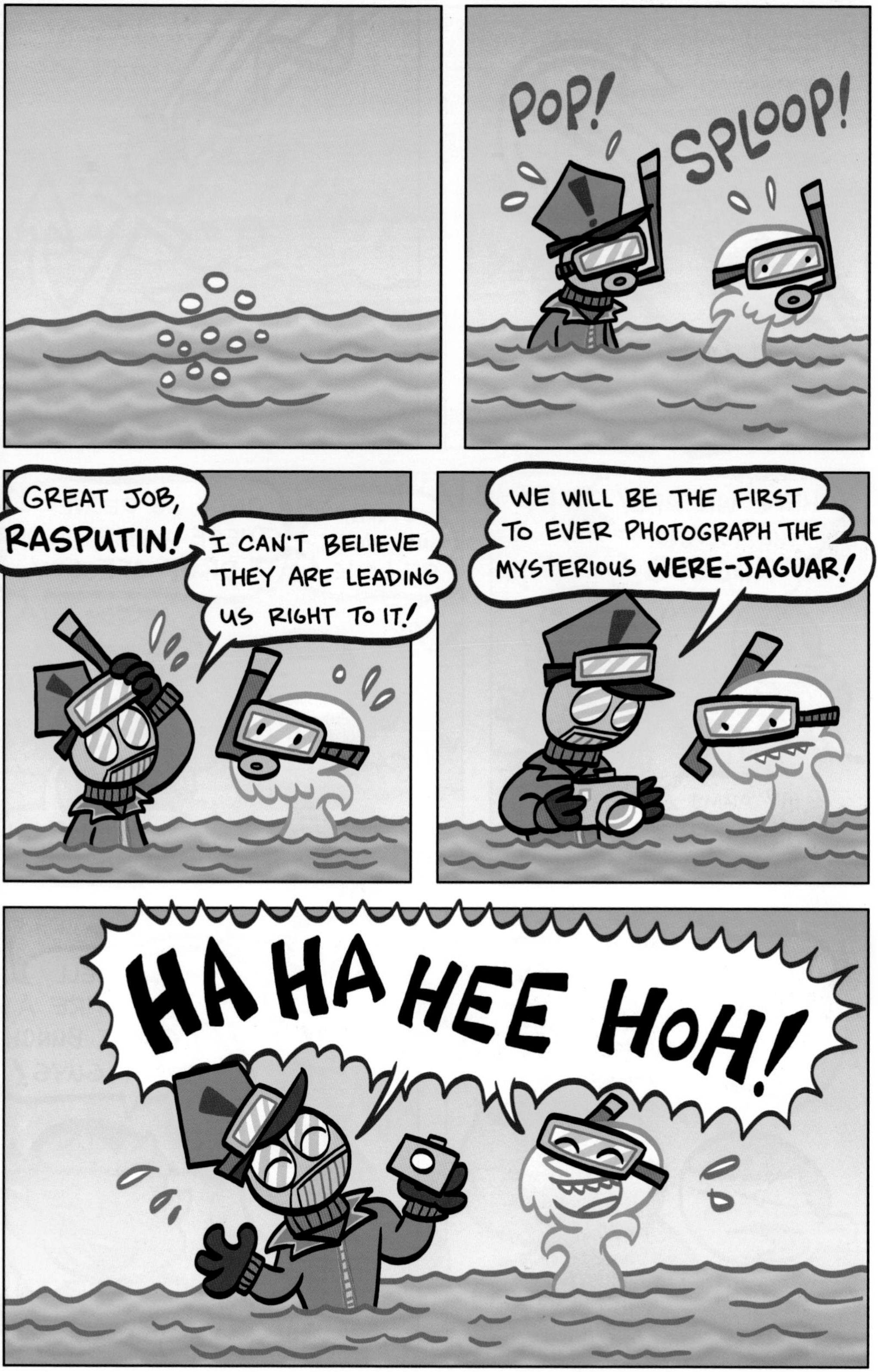
POP!
SPLOOP!
GREAT JOB, RASPUTIN!
I CAN'T BELIEVE THEY ARE LEADING US RIGHT TO IT!
WE WILL BE THE FIRST TO EVER PHOTOGRAPH THE MYSTERIOUS WERE-JAGUAR!
HA HA HEE HOH!

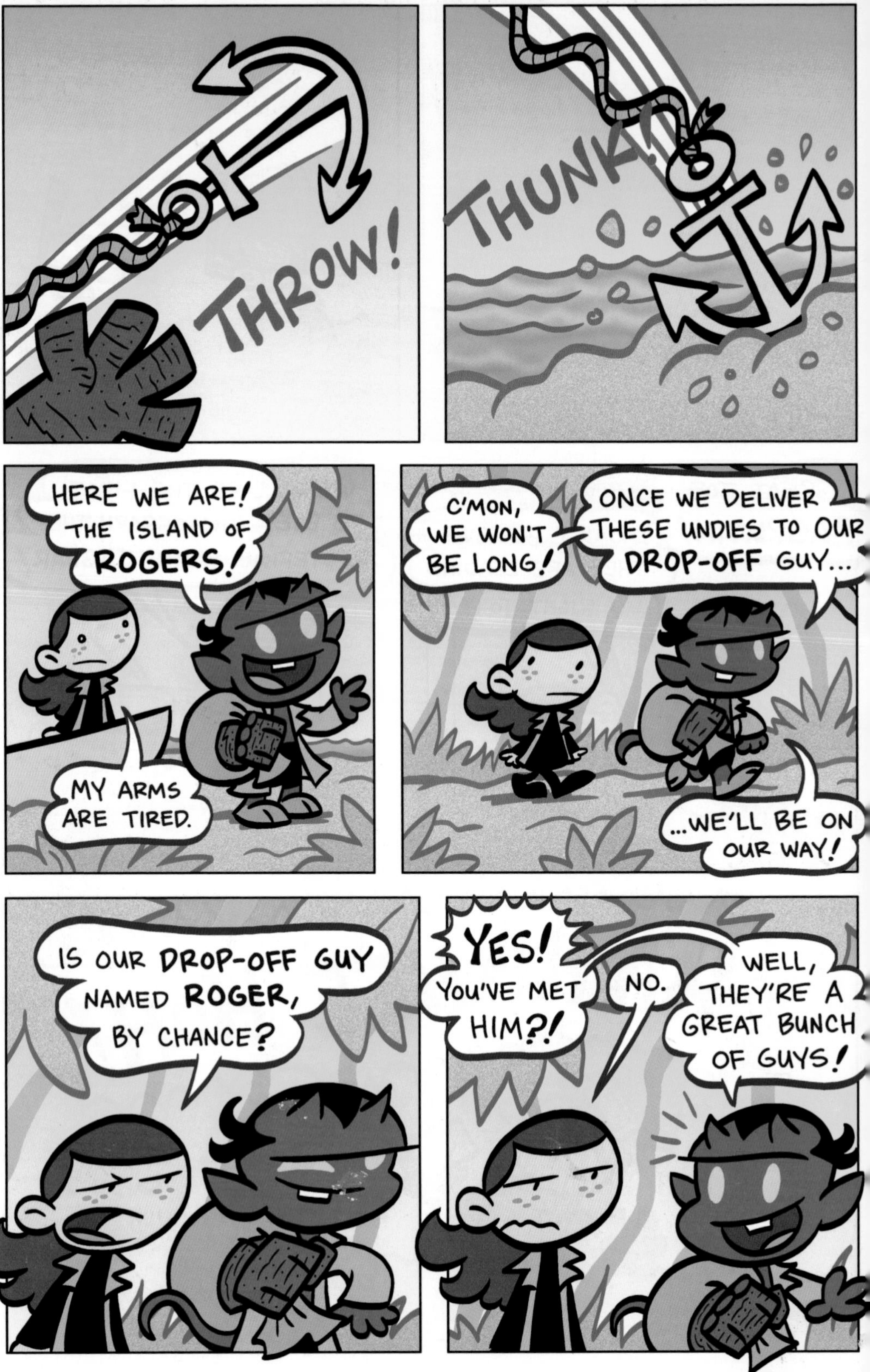
THROW!
THUNK!
HERE WE ARE! THE ISLAND OF ROGERS!
MY ARMS ARE TIRED.
C'MON, WE WON'T BE LONG!
ONCE WE DELIVER THESE UNDIES TO OUR DROP-OFF GUY...
...WE'LL BE ON OUR WAY!
IS OUR DROP-OFF GUY NAMED ROGER, BY CHANCE?
YES! YOU'VE MET HIM?!
NO.
WELL, THEY'RE A GREAT BUNCH OF GUYS!

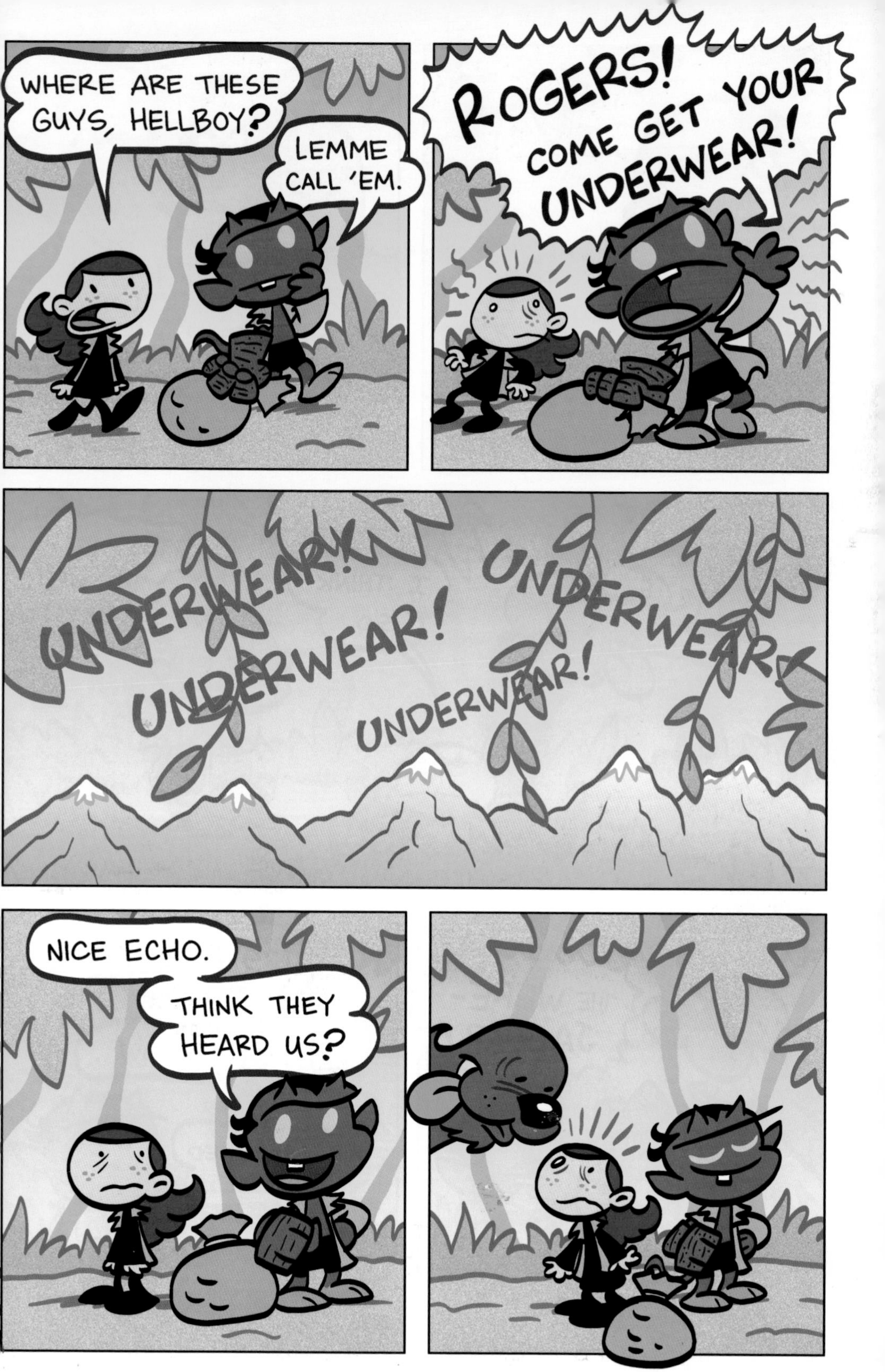
WHERE ARE THESE GUYS, HELLBOY?
LEMME CALL 'EM.
ROGERS! COME GET YOUR UNDERWEAR!
UNDERWEAR!
UNDERWEAR!
UNDERWEAR!
UNDERWEAR!
NICE ECHO.
THINK THEY HEARD US?

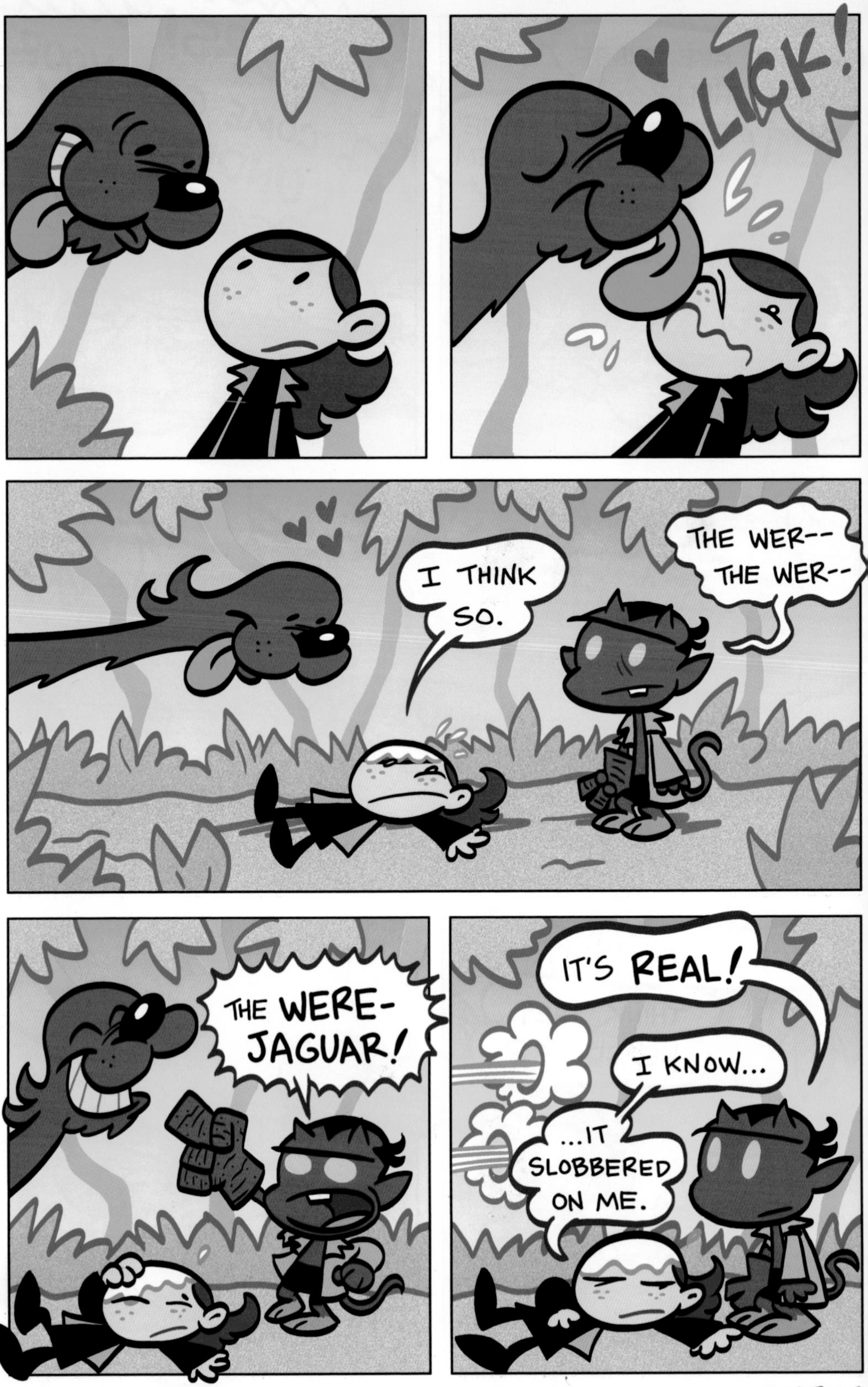
LICK!
I THINK SO.
THE WER-- THE WER--
THE WERE-JAGUAR!
IT'S REAL!
I KNOW...
...IT SLOBBERED ON ME.

—COOTIES.

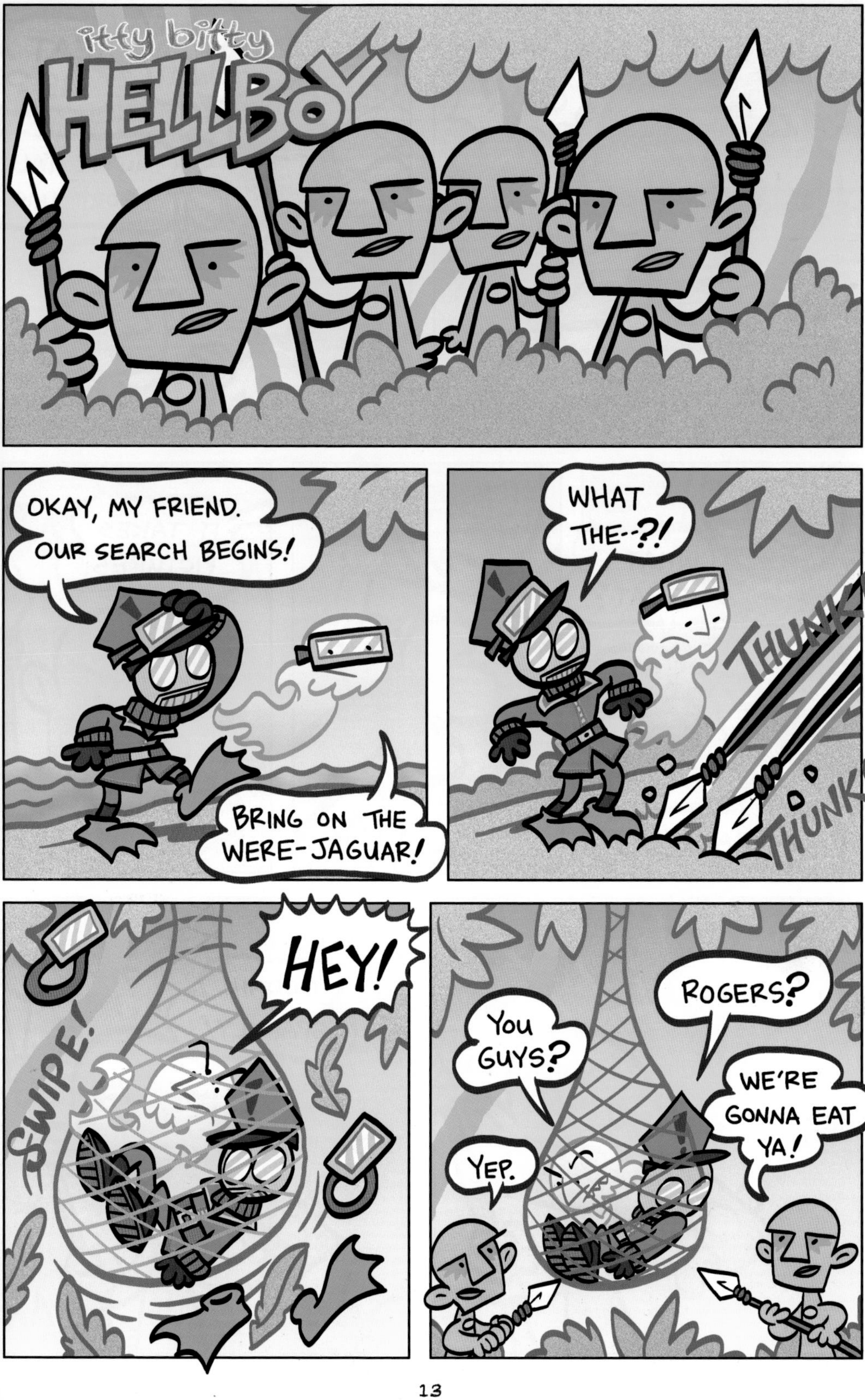
itty bitty
HELLBOY
OKAY, MY FRIEND. OUR SEARCH BEGINS!
BRING ON THE WERE-JAGUAR!
WHAT THE--?!
THUNK!
THUNK!
HEY!
SWIPE!
ROGERS?
YOU GUYS?
WE'RE GONNA EAT YA!
YEP.

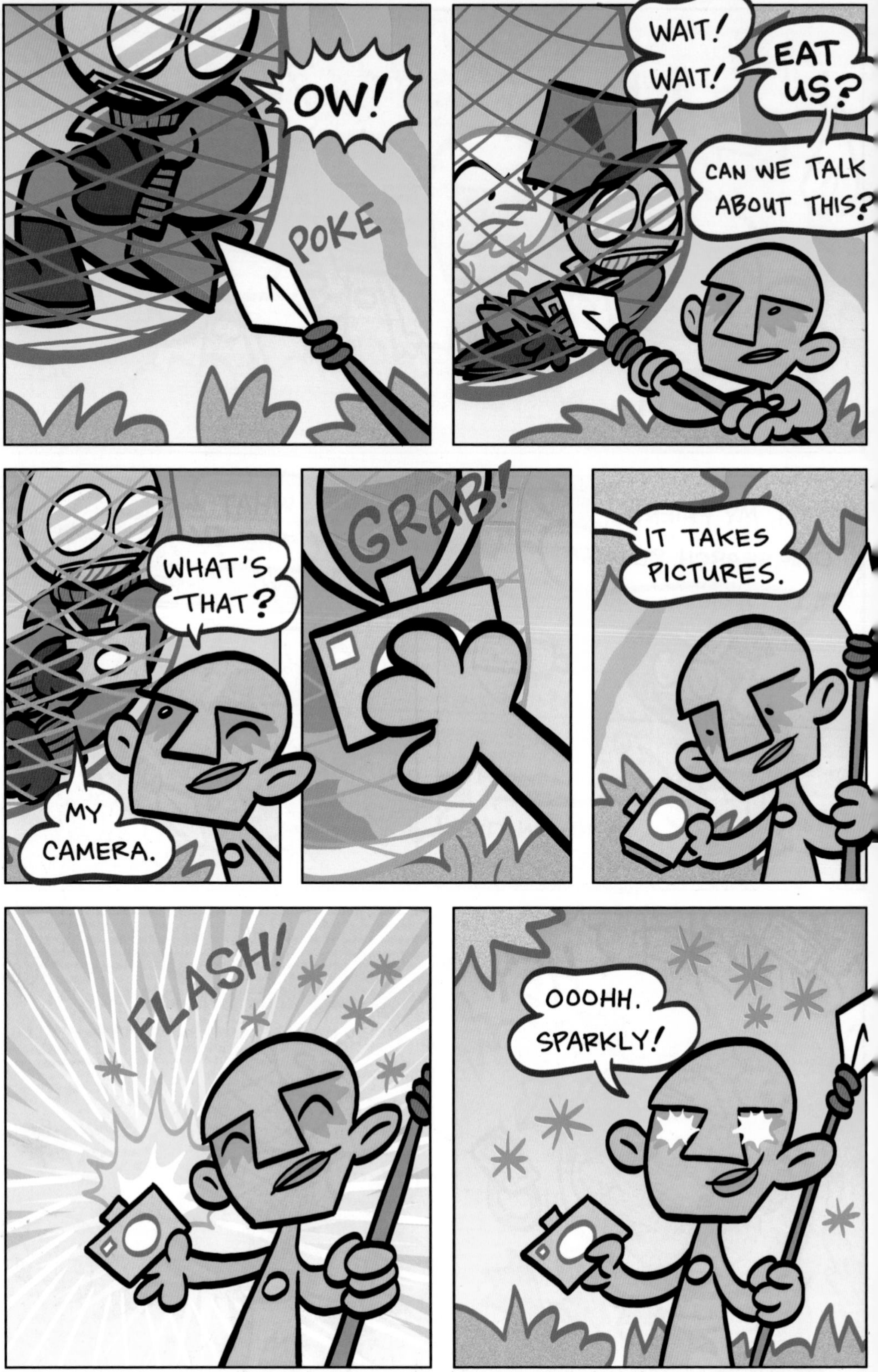
OW!
POKE
WAIT! WAIT!
EAT US?
CAN WE TALK ABOUT THIS?
WHAT'S THAT?
MY CAMERA.
GRAB!
IT TAKES PICTURES.
FLASH!
OOOHH. SPARKLY!

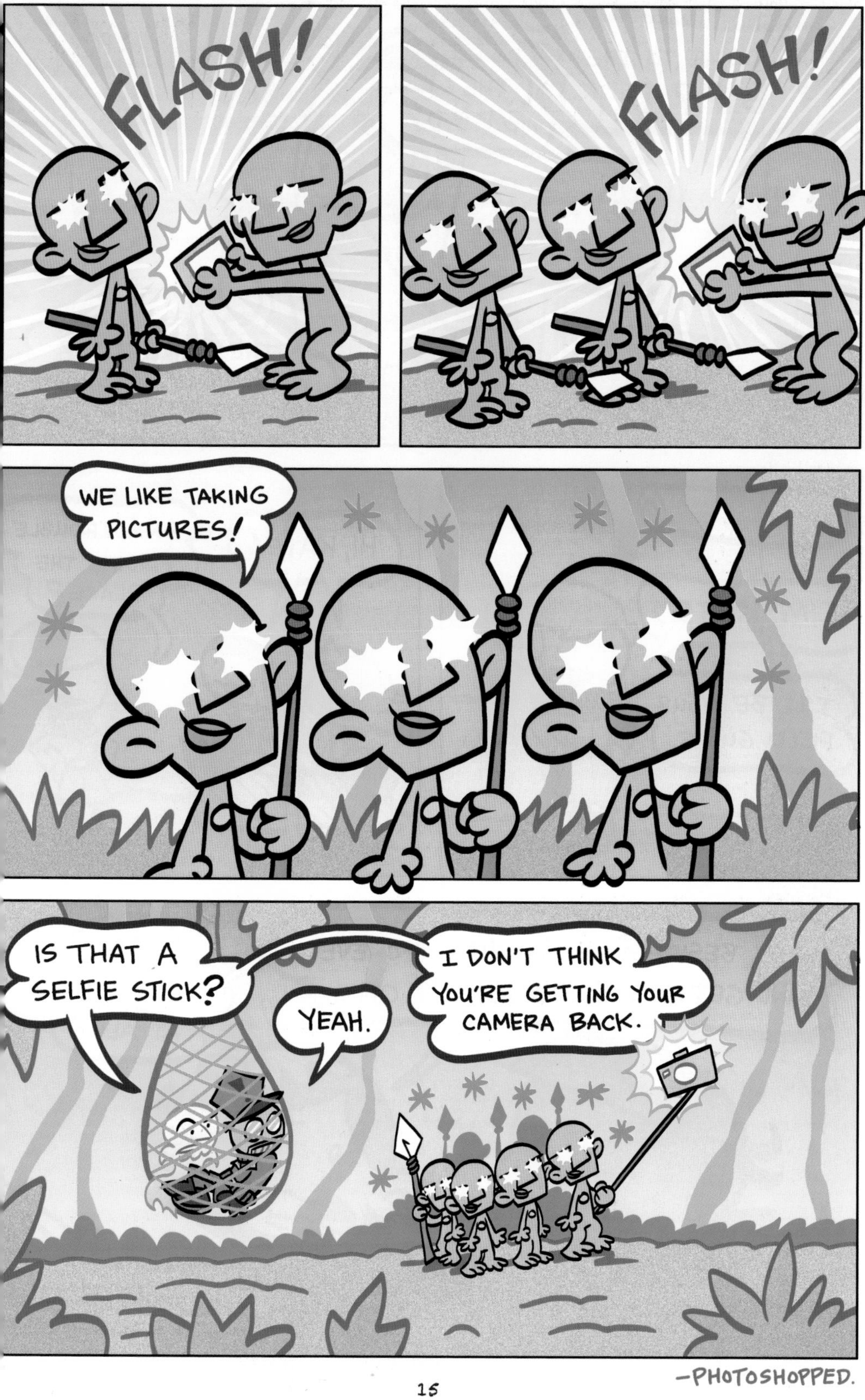
FLASH!
FLASH!
WE LIKE TAKING PICTURES!
IS THAT A SELFIE STICK?
YEAH.
I DON'T THINK YOU'RE GETTING YOUR CAMERA BACK.

—PHOTOSHOPPED.

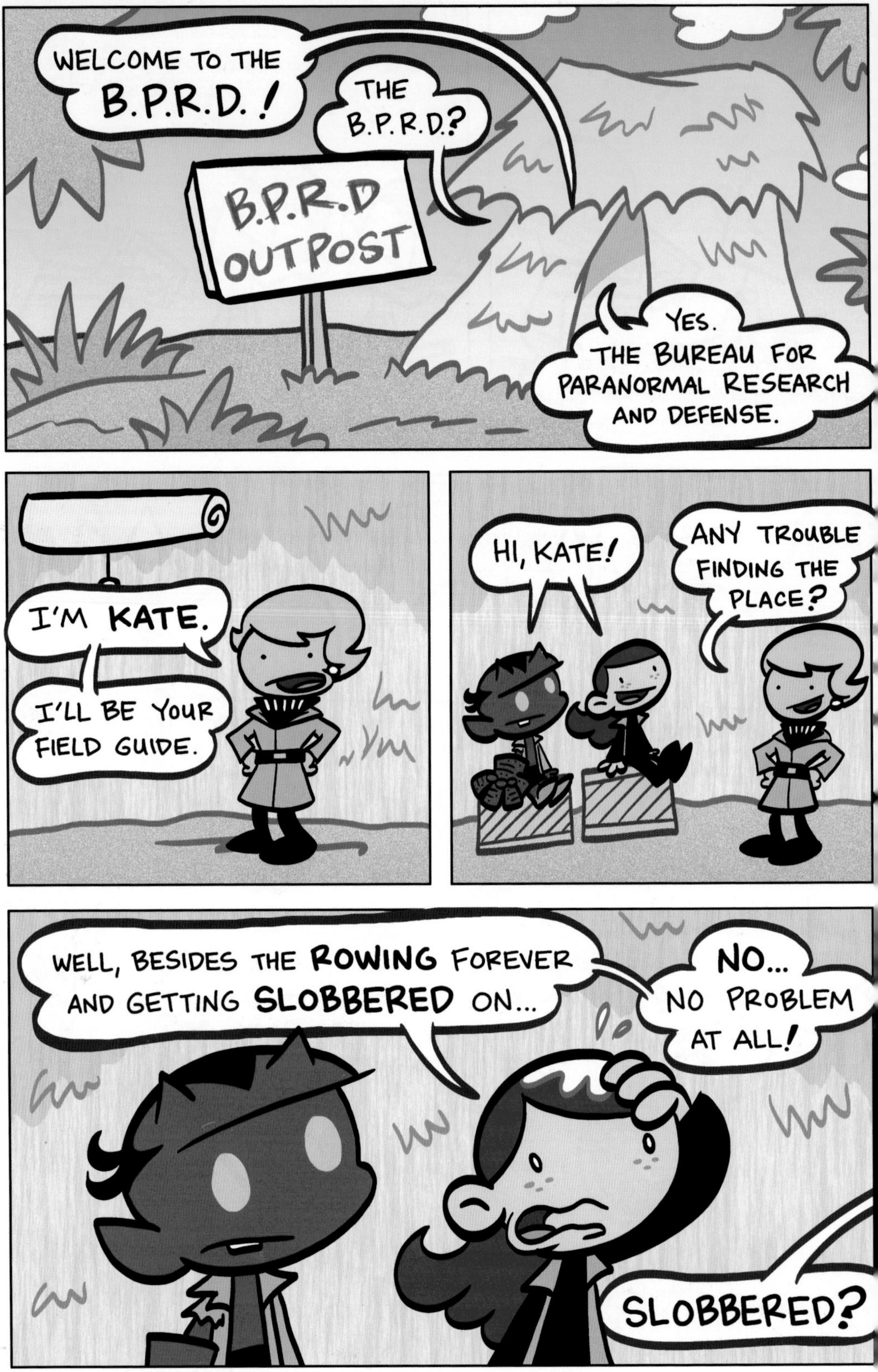
WELCOME TO THE B.P.R.D.!
THE B.P.R.D.?
B.P.R.D OUTPOST
YES. THE BUREAU FOR PARANORMAL RESEARCH AND DEFENSE.
I'M KATE.
I'LL BE YOUR FIELD GUIDE.
HI, KATE!
ANY TROUBLE FINDING THE PLACE?
WELL, BESIDES THE ROWING FOREVER AND GETTING SLOBBERED ON...
NO... NO PROBLEM AT ALL!
SLOBBERED?

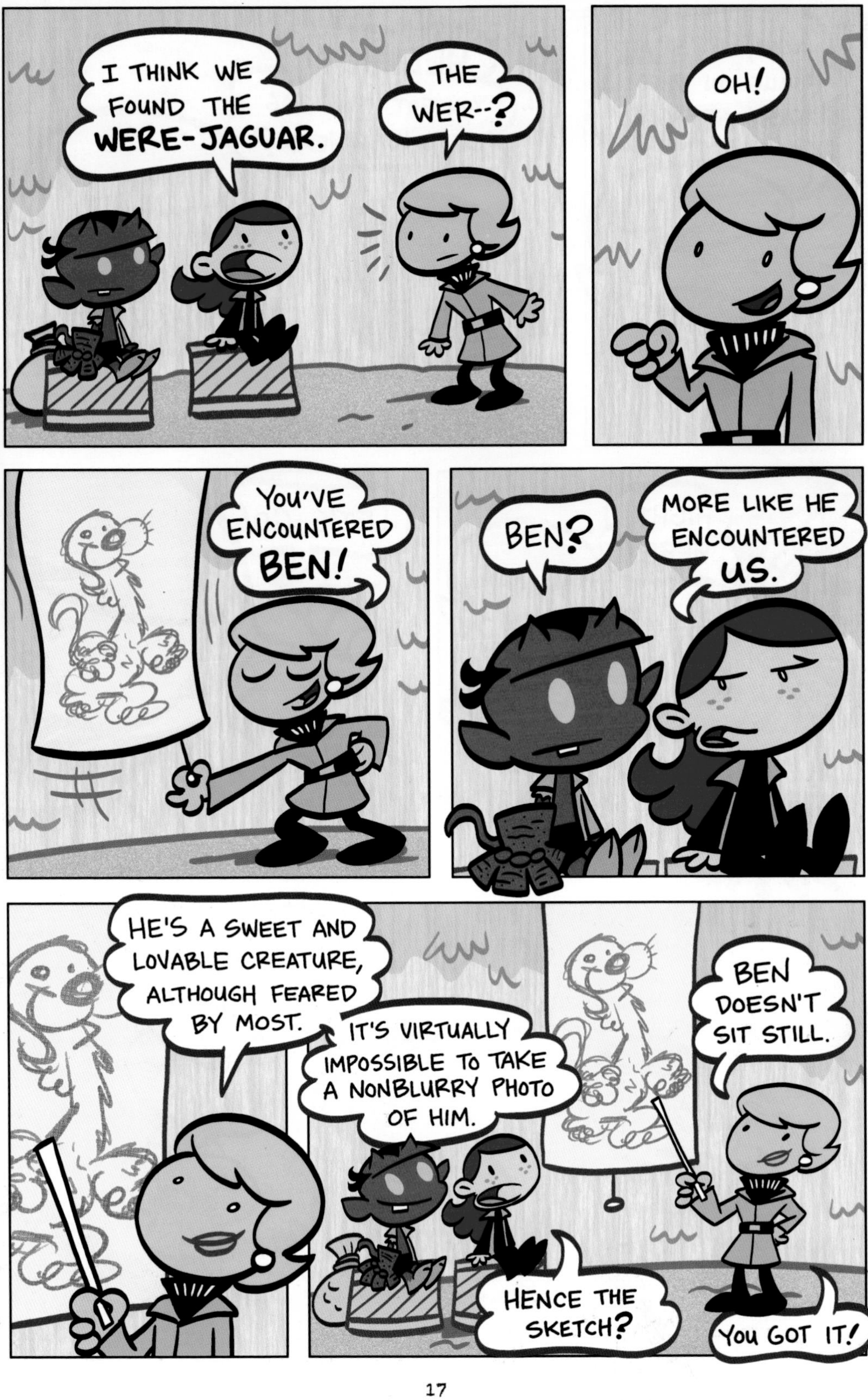
I THINK WE FOUND THE WERE-JAGUAR.
THE WER--?
OH!
YOU'VE ENCOUNTERED BEN!
BEN?
MORE LIKE HE ENCOUNTERED US.
HE'S A SWEET AND LOVABLE CREATURE, ALTHOUGH FEARED BY MOST.
IT'S VIRTUALLY IMPOSSIBLE TO TAKE A NONBLURRY PHOTO OF HIM.
BEN DOESN'T SIT STILL.
HENCE THE SKETCH?
YOU GOT IT!

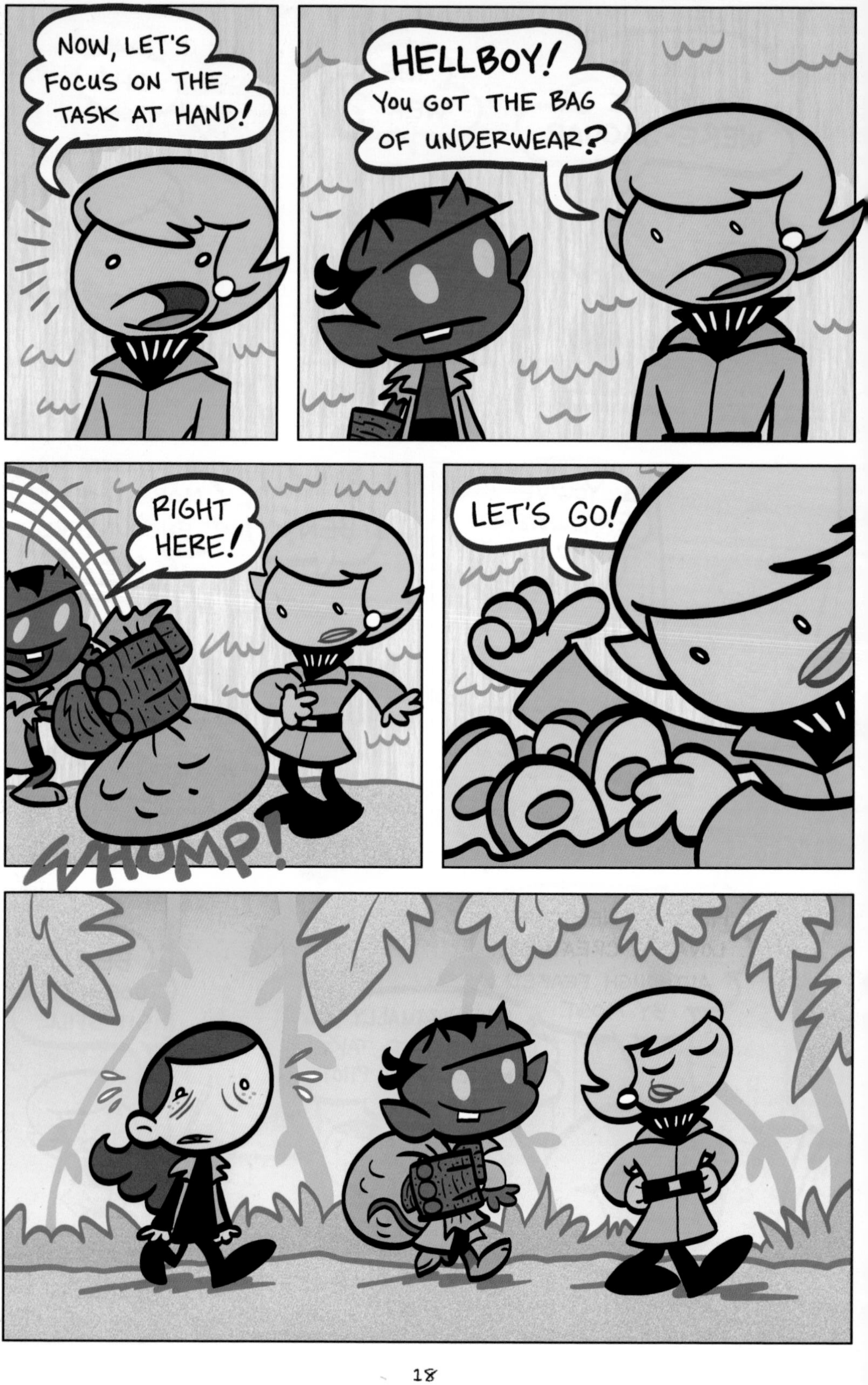
NOW, LET'S FOCUS ON THE TASK AT HAND!
HELLBOY! YOU GOT THE BAG OF UNDERWEAR?
RIGHT HERE!
WHOMP!
LET'S GO!

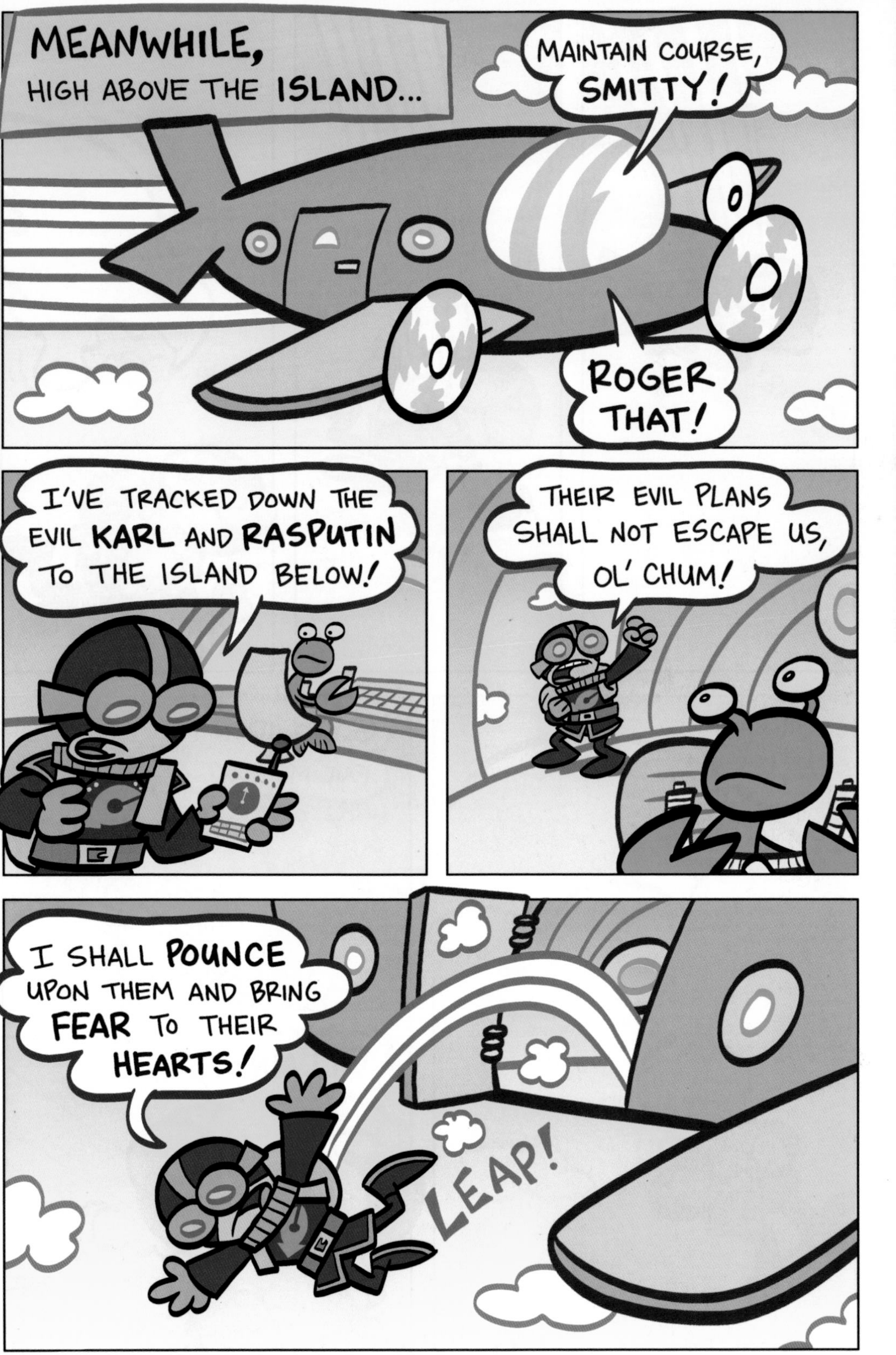
MEANWHILE, HIGH ABOVE THE ISLAND...
MAINTAIN COURSE, SMITTY!
ROGER THAT!
I'VE TRACKED DOWN THE EVIL KARL AND RASPUTIN TO THE ISLAND BELOW!
THEIR EVIL PLANS SHALL NOT ESCAPE US, OL' CHUM!
I SHALL POUNCE UPON THEM AND BRING FEAR TO THEIR HEARTS!
LEAP!

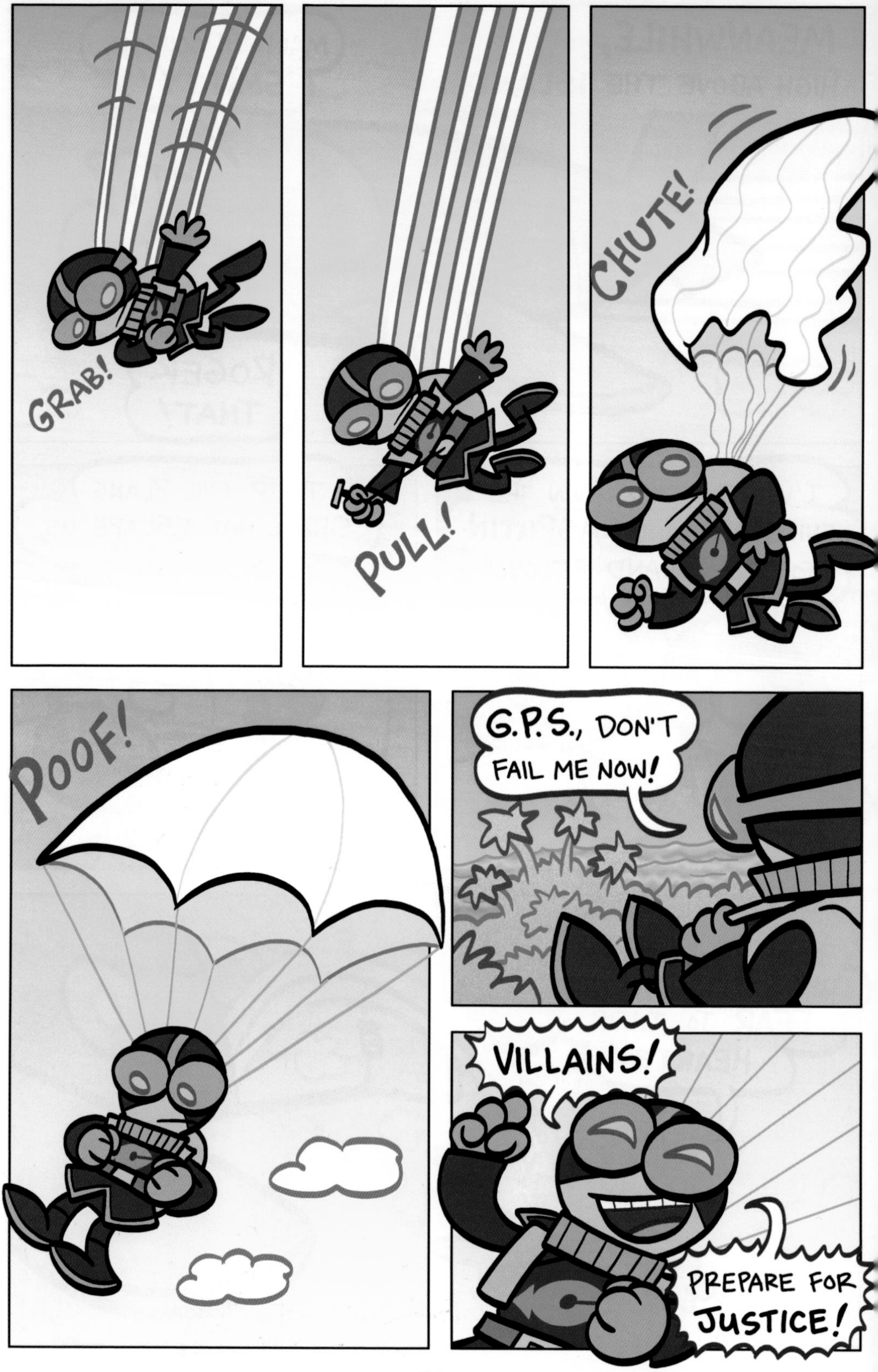
GRAB!
PULL!
CHUTE!
POOF!
G.P.S., DON'T FAIL ME NOW!
VILLAINS!
PREPARE FOR JUSTICE!

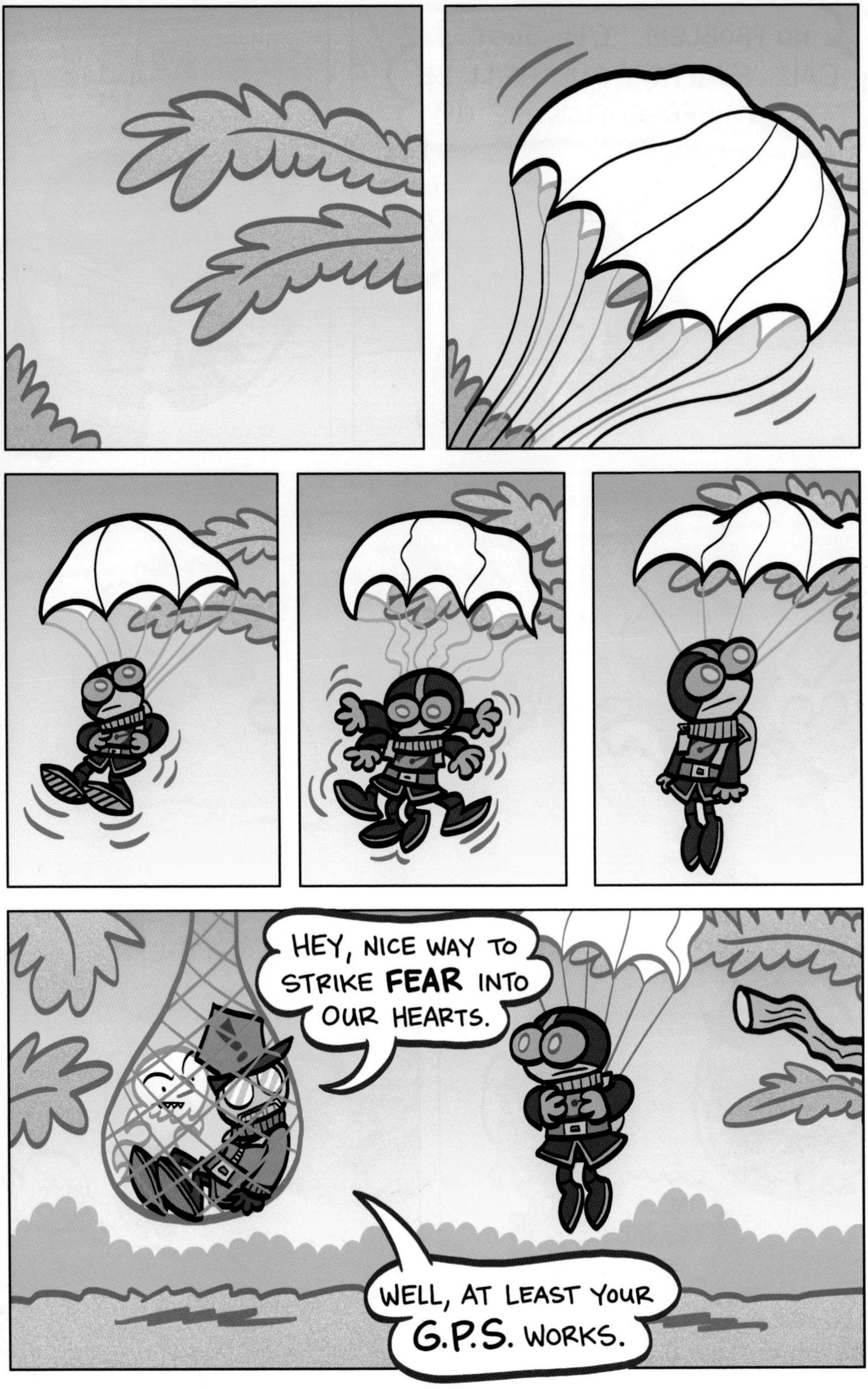
HEY, NICE WAY TO STRIKE **FEAR** INTO OUR HEARTS.
WELL, AT LEAST YOUR G.P.S. WORKS.

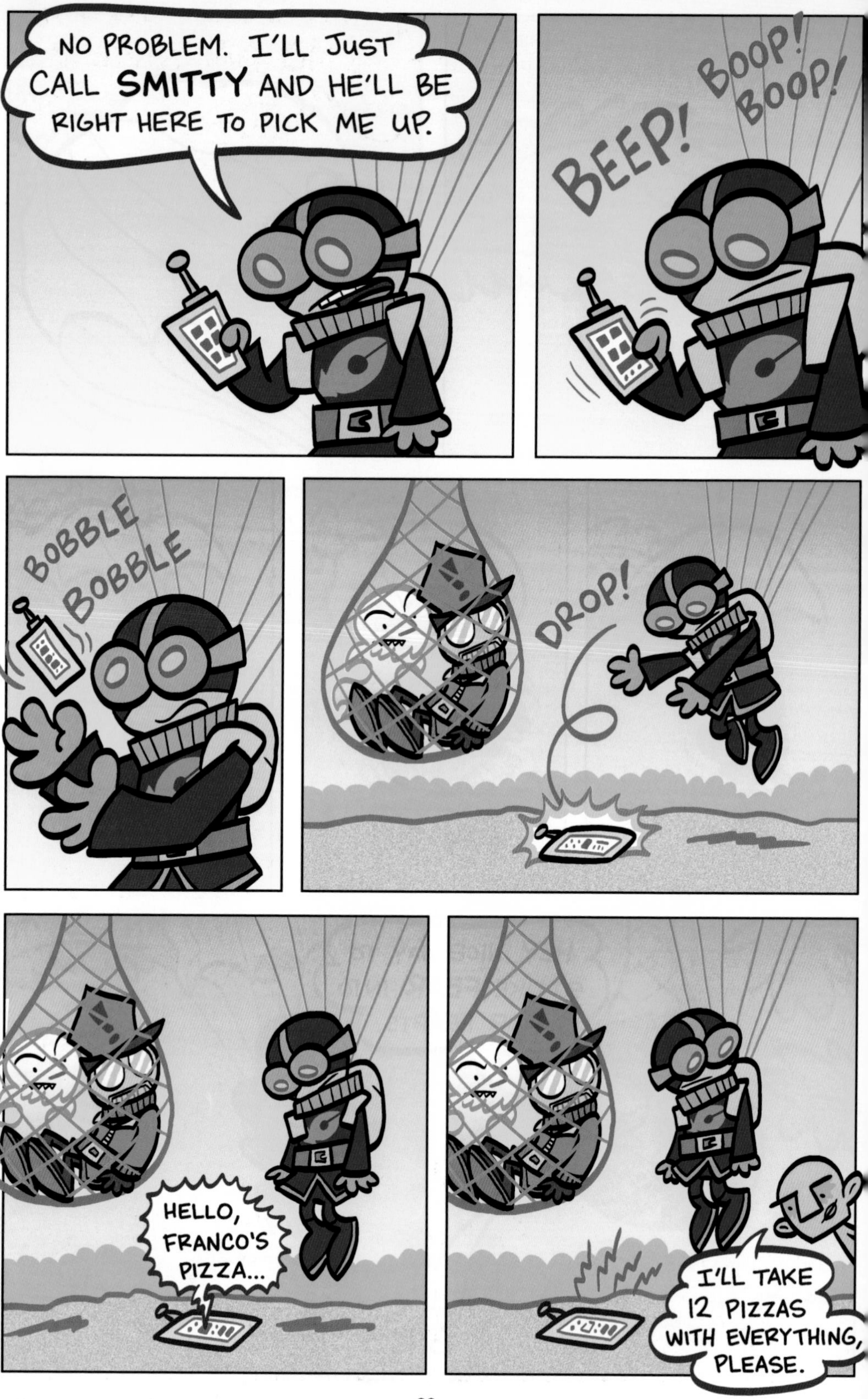
NO PROBLEM. I'LL JUST CALL SMITTY AND HE'LL BE RIGHT HERE TO PICK ME UP.
BEEP!
BOOP! BOOP!
BOBBLE BOBBLE
DROP!
HELLO, FRANCO'S PIZZA...
I'LL TAKE 12 PIZZAS WITH EVERYTHING, PLEASE.

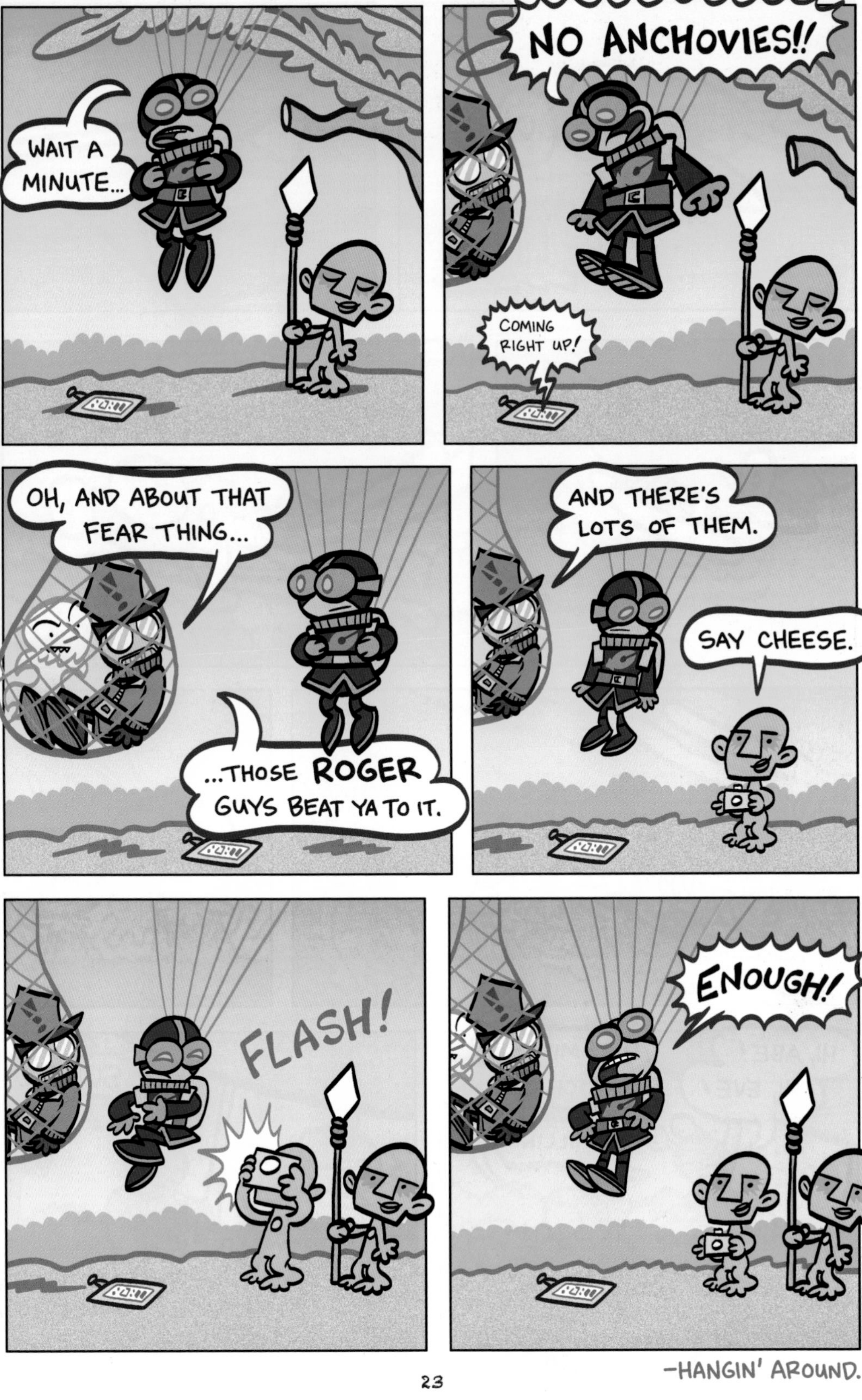
WAIT A MINUTE...
NO ANCHOVIES!!
COMING RIGHT UP!
OH, AND ABOUT THAT FEAR THING...
...THOSE ROGER GUYS BEAT YA TO IT.
AND THERE'S LOTS OF THEM.
SAY CHEESE.
FLASH!
ENOUGH!

–HANGIN' AROUND.

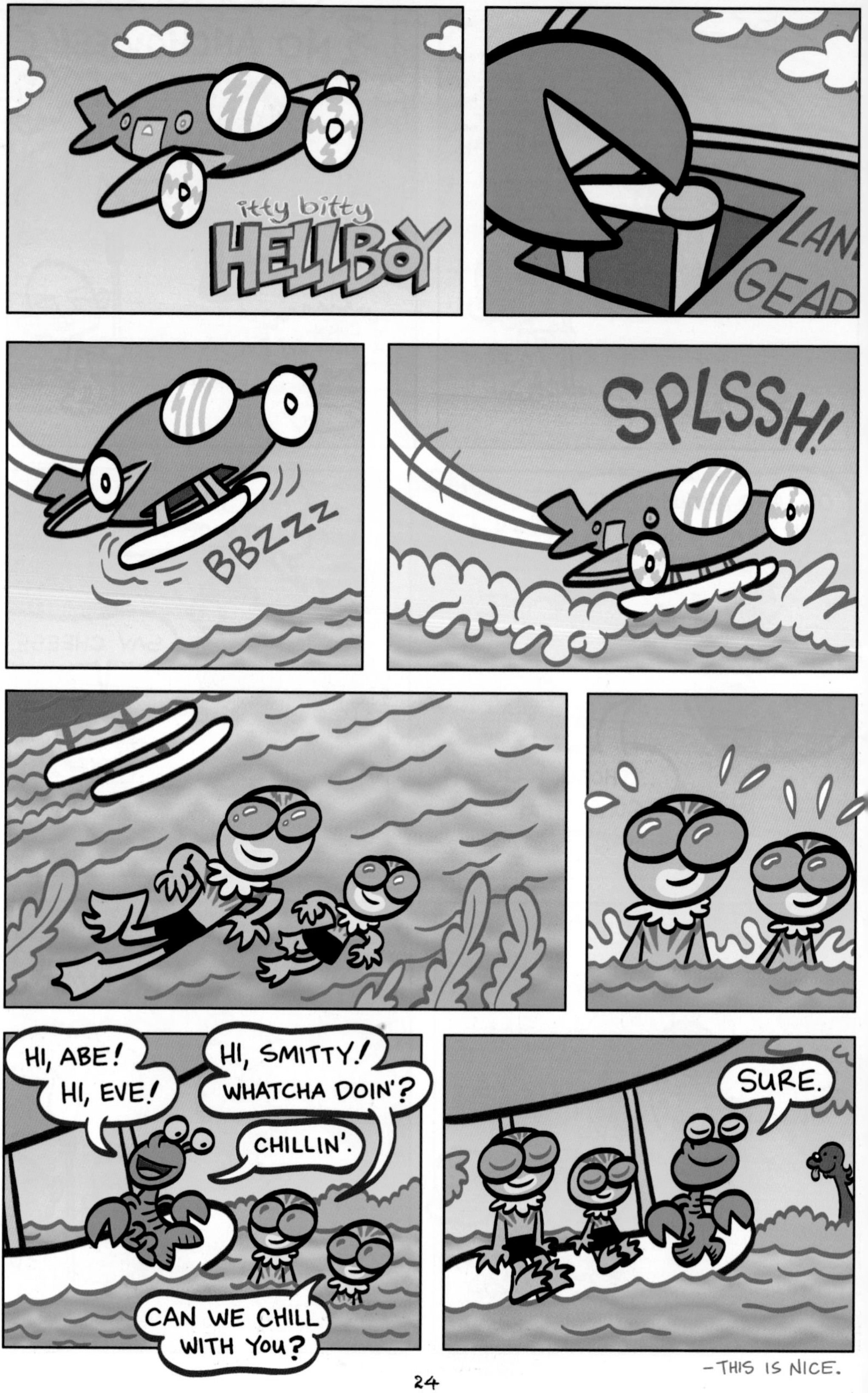
itty bitty
HELLBOY
LAN
GEAR
BBZZZ
SPLSSH!
HI, ABE!
HI, EVE!
HI, SMITTY! WHATCHA DOIN'?
CHILLIN'.
CAN WE CHILL WITH YOU?
SURE.

—THIS IS NICE.

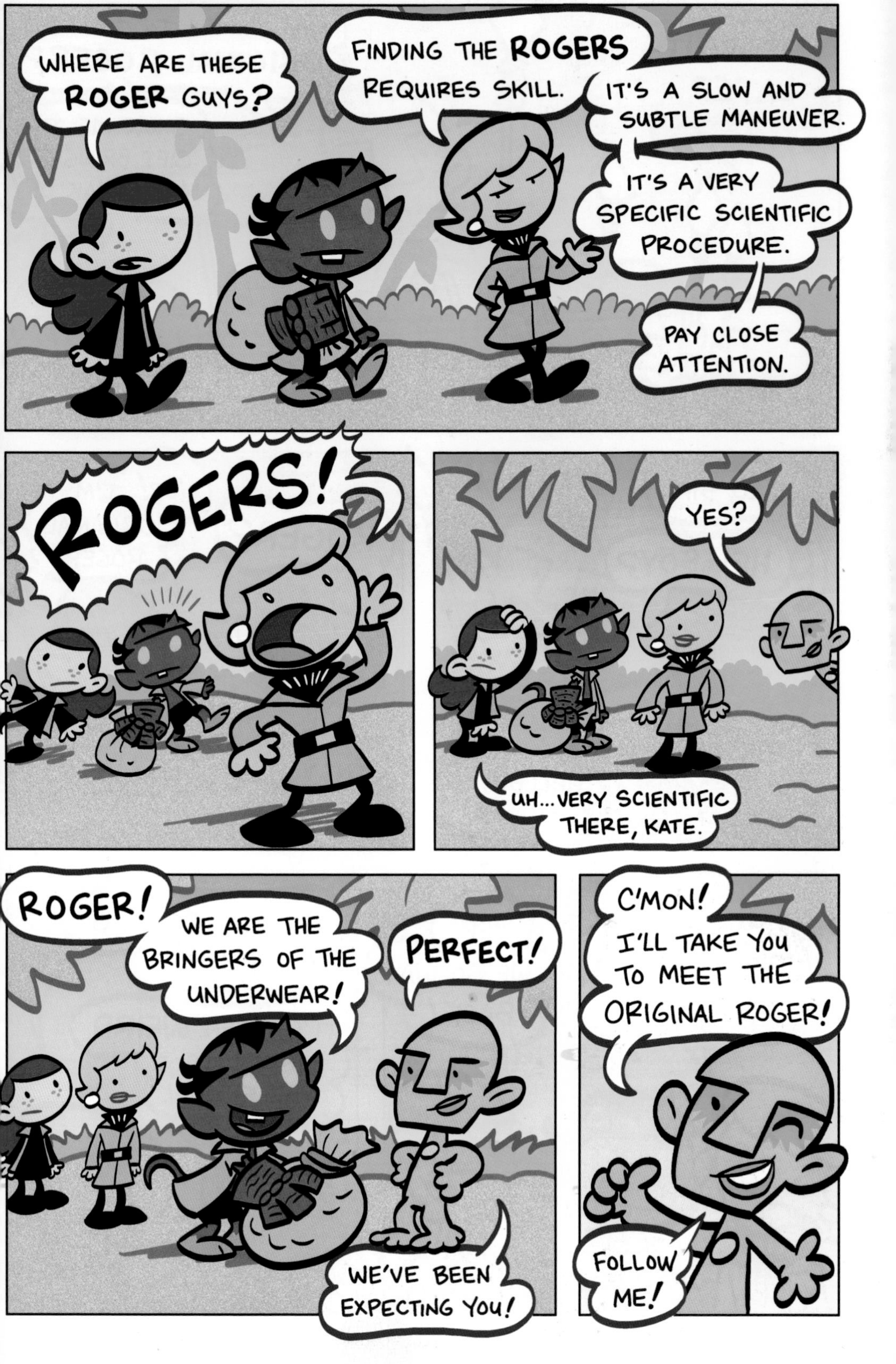
WHERE ARE THESE ROGER GUYS?
FINDING THE ROGERS REQUIRES SKILL.
IT'S A SLOW AND SUBTLE MANEUVER.
IT'S A VERY SPECIFIC SCIENTIFIC PROCEDURE.
PAY CLOSE ATTENTION.
ROGERS!
YES?
UH... VERY SCIENTIFIC THERE, KATE.
ROGER!
WE ARE THE BRINGERS OF THE UNDERWEAR!
PERFECT!
WE'VE BEEN EXPECTING YOU!
C'MON!
I'LL TAKE YOU TO MEET THE ORIGINAL ROGER!
FOLLOW ME!

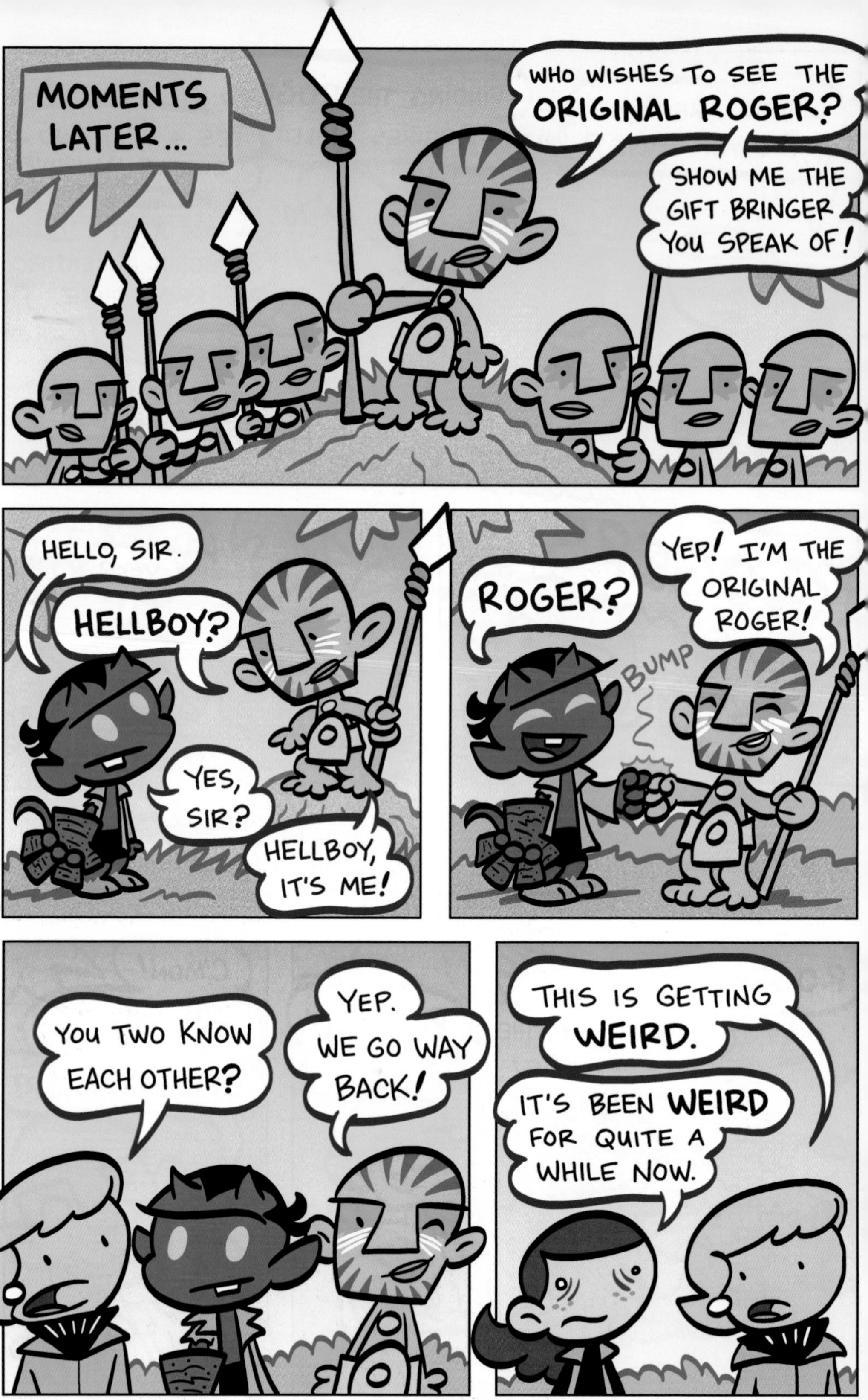
MOMENTS LATER...
WHO WISHES TO SEE THE ORIGINAL ROGER?
SHOW ME THE GIFT BRINGER YOU SPEAK OF!
HELLO, SIR.
HELLBOY?
YES, SIR?
HELLBOY, IT'S ME!
ROGER?
YEP! I'M THE ORIGINAL ROGER!
BUMP
YOU TWO KNOW EACH OTHER?
YEP. WE GO WAY BACK!
THIS IS GETTING WEIRD.
IT'S BEEN WEIRD FOR QUITE A WHILE NOW.

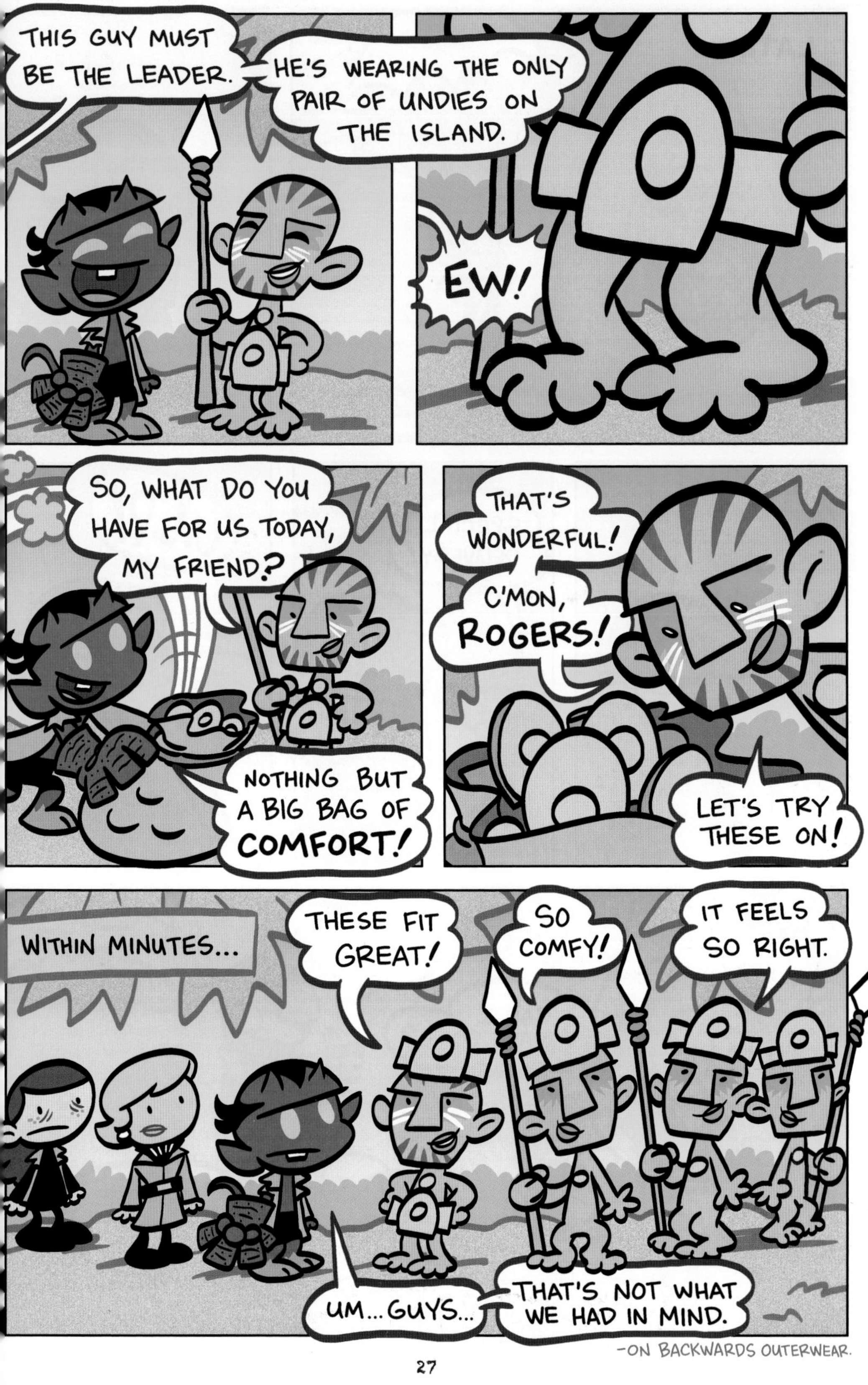
THIS GUY MUST BE THE LEADER.
HE'S WEARING THE ONLY PAIR OF UNDIES ON THE ISLAND.
EW!
SO, WHAT DO YOU HAVE FOR US TODAY, MY FRIEND?
NOTHING BUT A BIG BAG OF COMFORT!
THAT'S WONDERFUL!
C'MON, ROGERS!
LET'S TRY THESE ON!
WITHIN MINUTES...
THESE FIT GREAT!
SO COMFY!
IT FEELS SO RIGHT.
UM... GUYS...
THAT'S NOT WHAT WE HAD IN MIND.

-ON BACKWARDS OUTERWEAR.

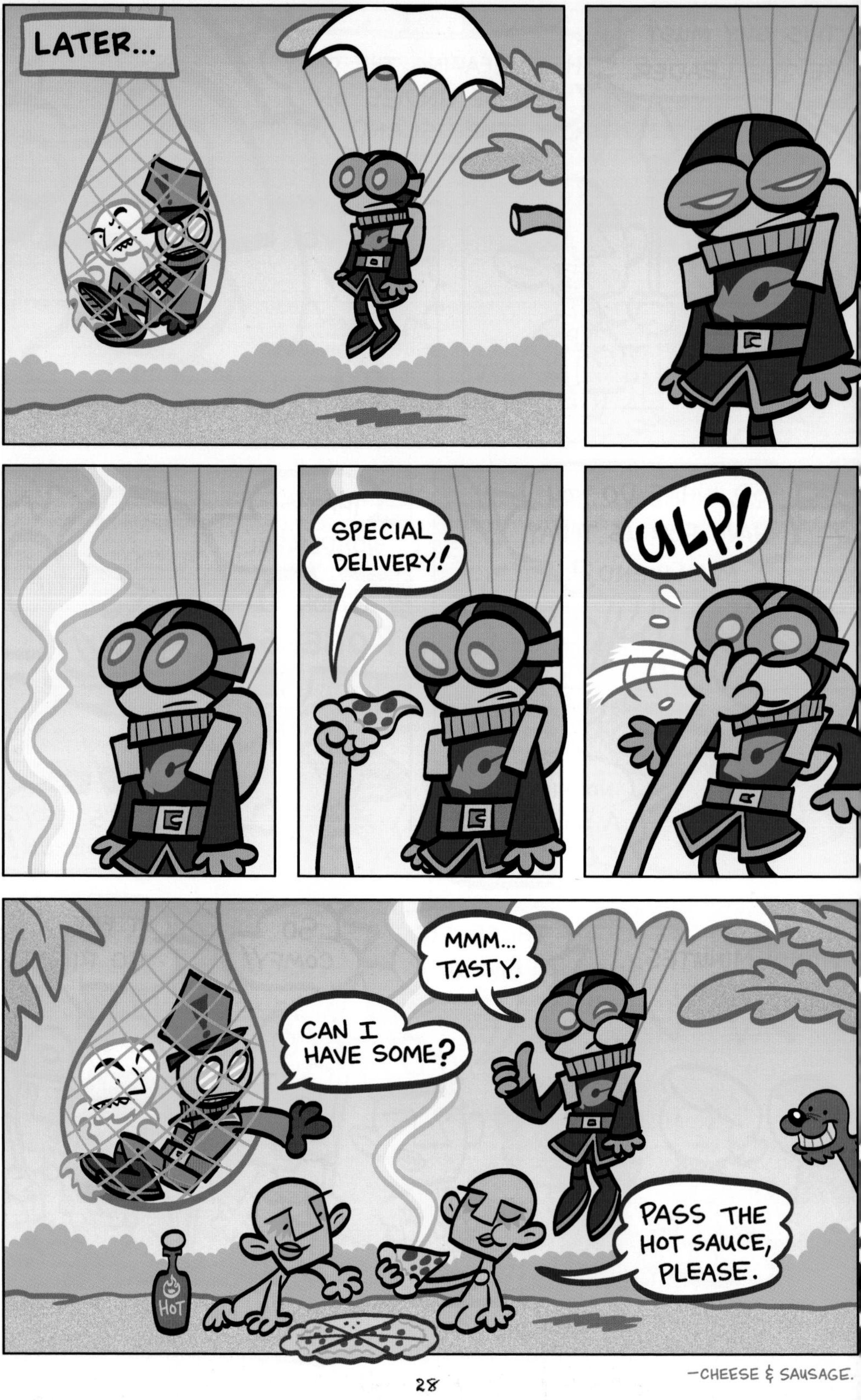
LATER...
SPECIAL DELIVERY!
ULP!
MMM... TASTY.
CAN I HAVE SOME?
PASS THE HOT SAUCE, PLEASE.
HOT

—CHEESE & SAUSAGE.

CHAPTER TWO

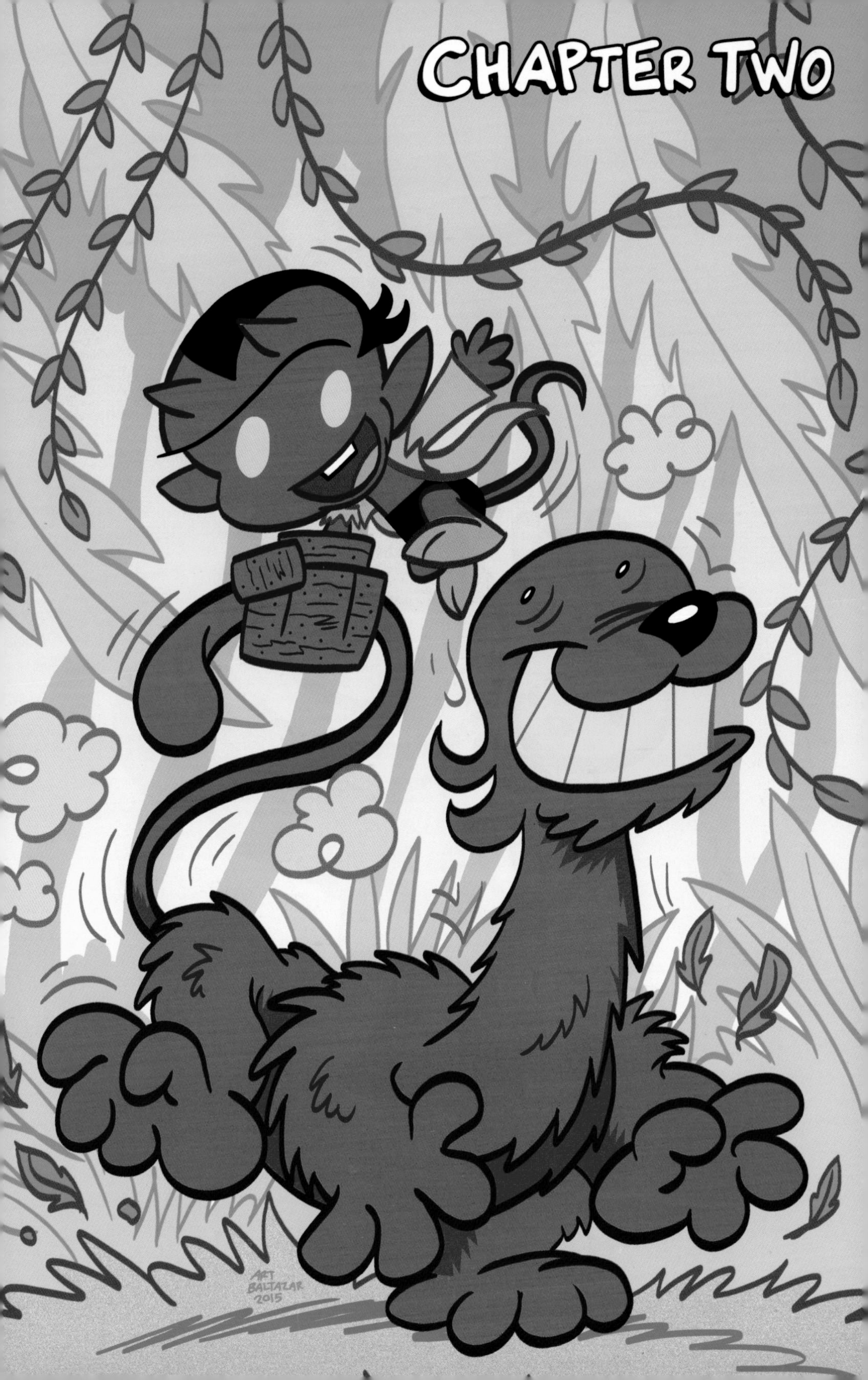

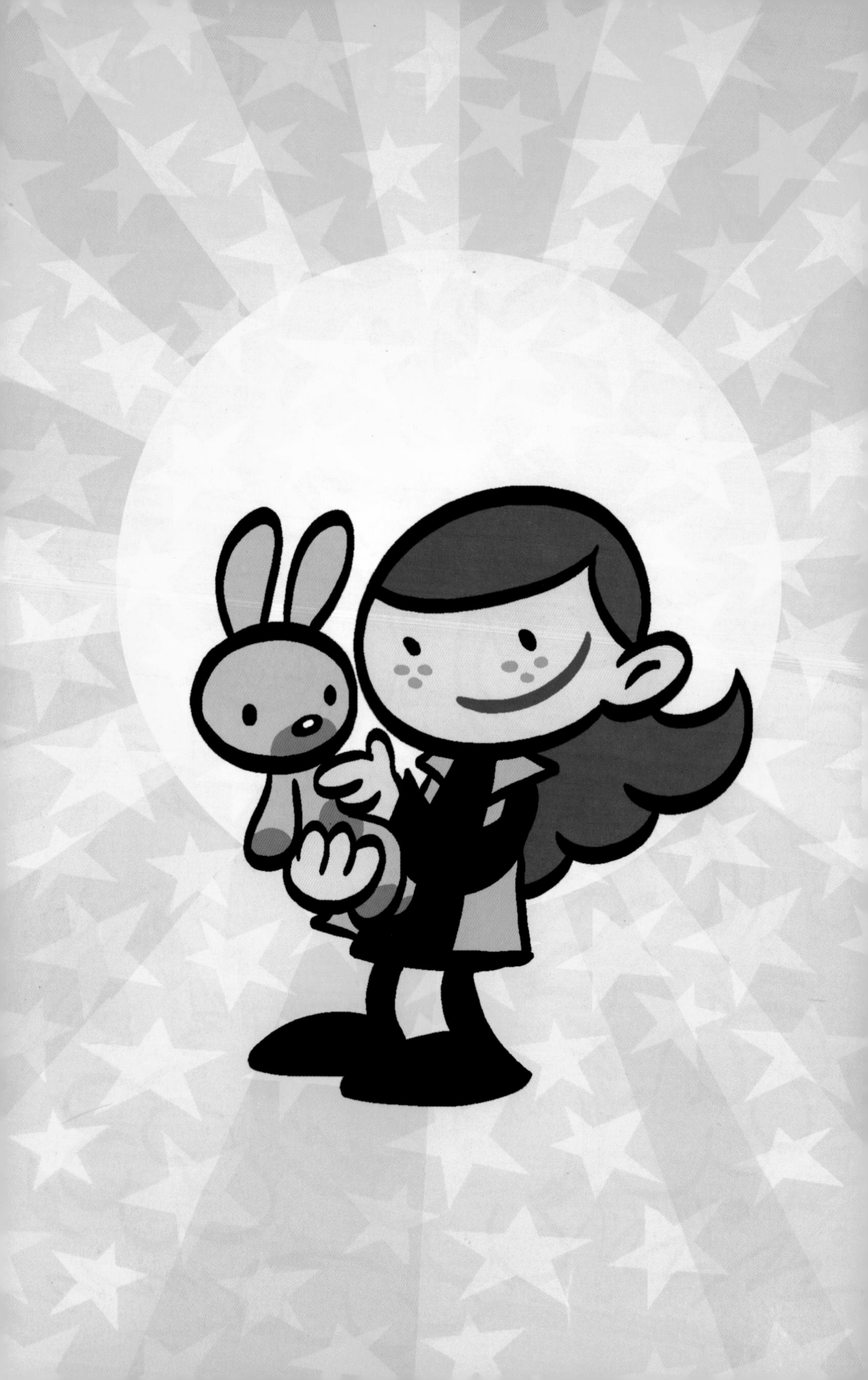

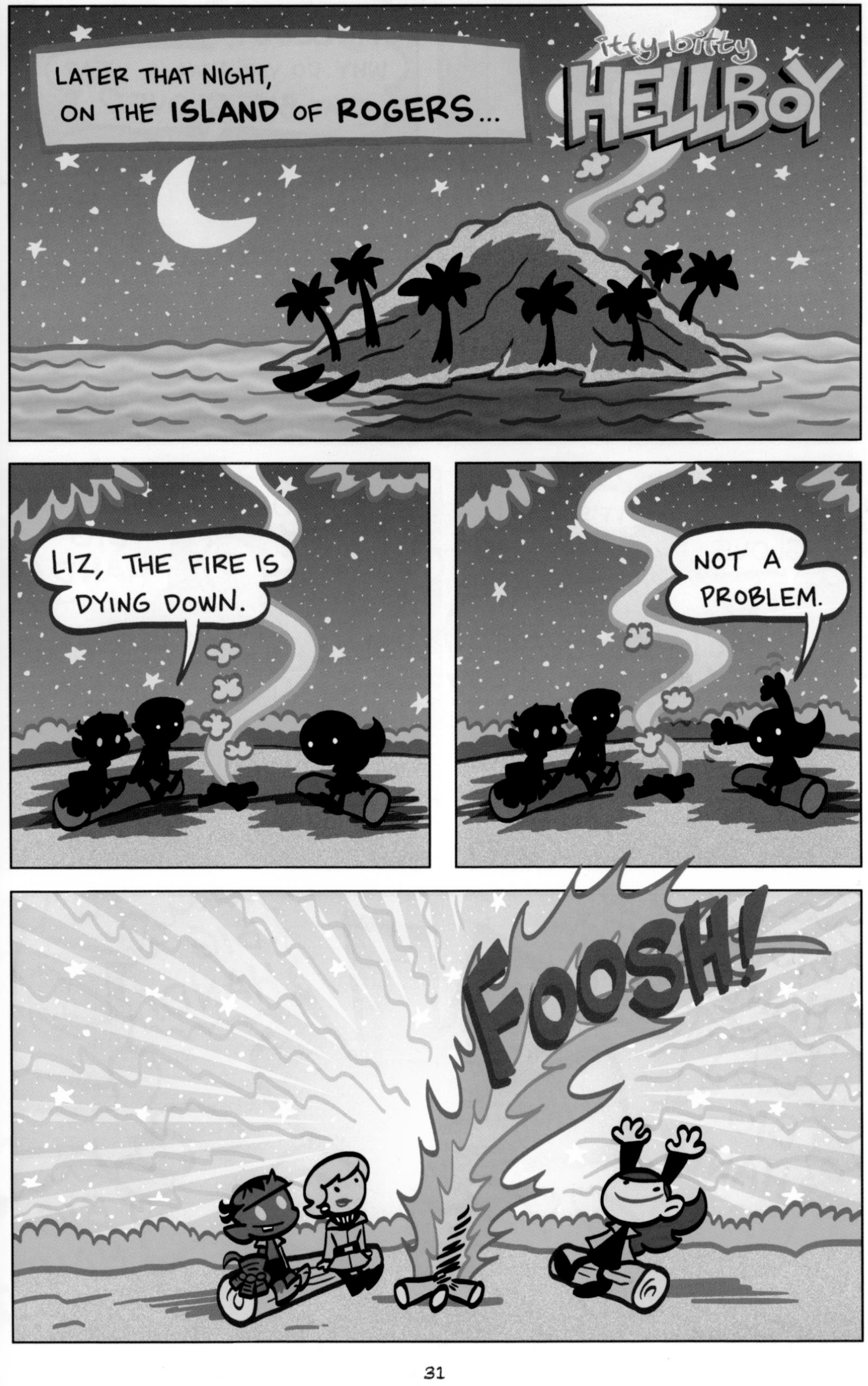
LATER THAT NIGHT, ON THE ISLAND OF ROGERS...
itty bitty HELLBOY
LIZ, THE FIRE IS DYING DOWN.
NOT A PROBLEM.
FOOSH!

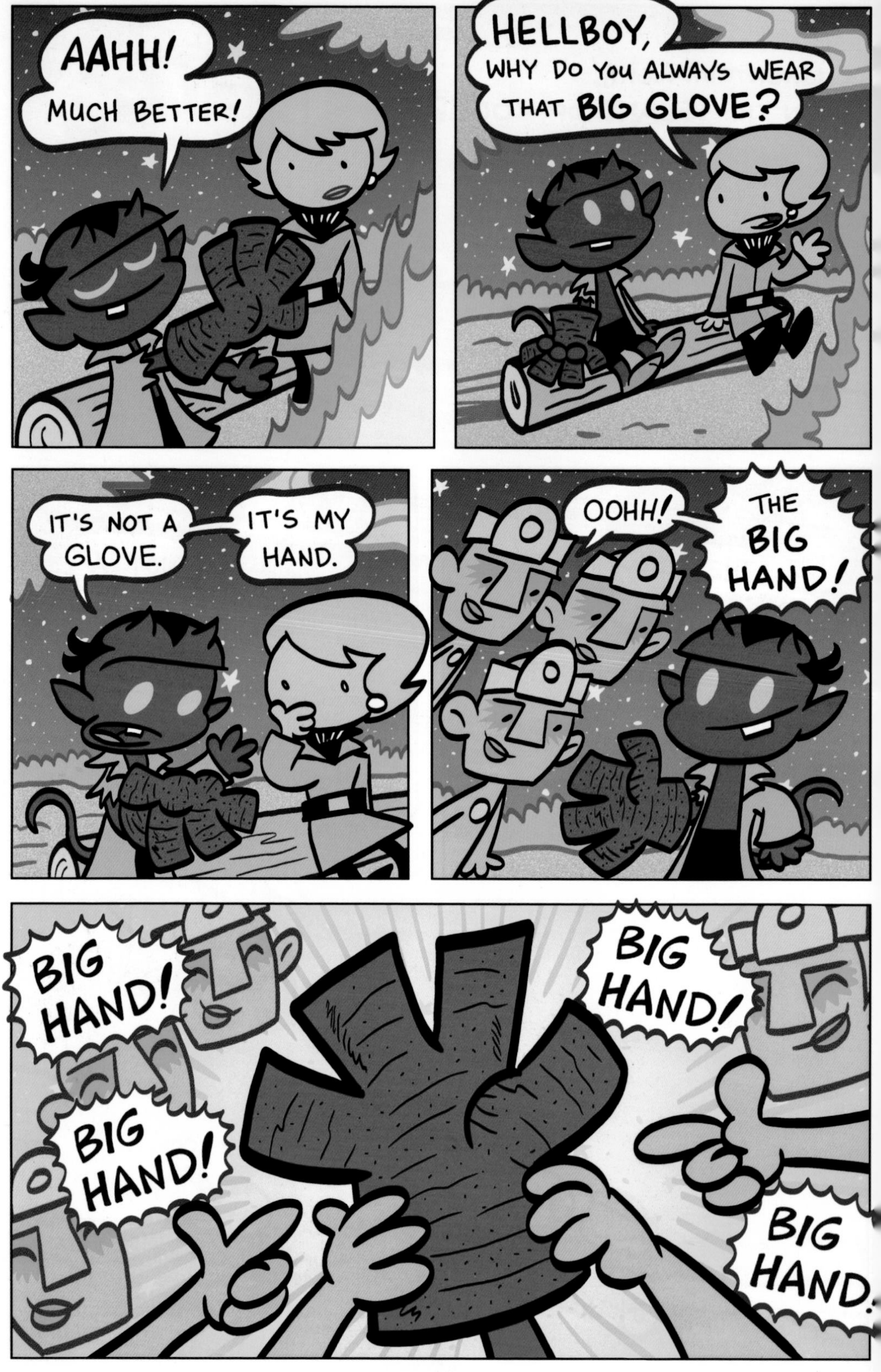
AAHH!
MUCH BETTER!
HELLBOY,
WHY DO YOU ALWAYS WEAR
THAT BIG GLOVE?
IT'S NOT A
GLOVE.
IT'S MY
HAND.
OOHH!
THE
BIG
HAND!
BIG
HAND!
BIG
HAND!
BIG
HAND!
BIG
HAND!

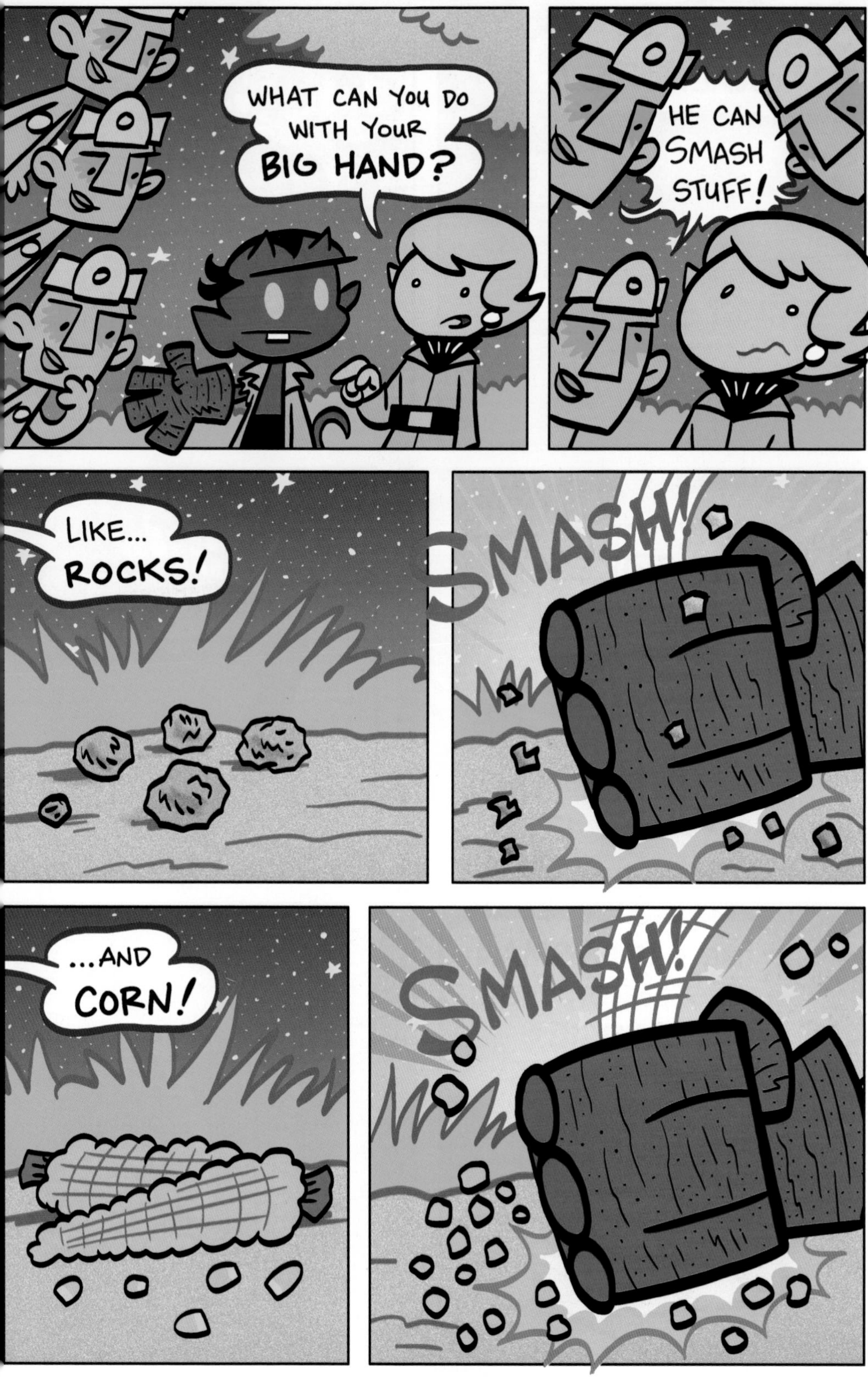
WHAT CAN YOU DO WITH YOUR BIG HAND?
HE CAN SMASH STUFF!
LIKE... ROCKS!
SMASH!
...AND CORN!
SMASH!

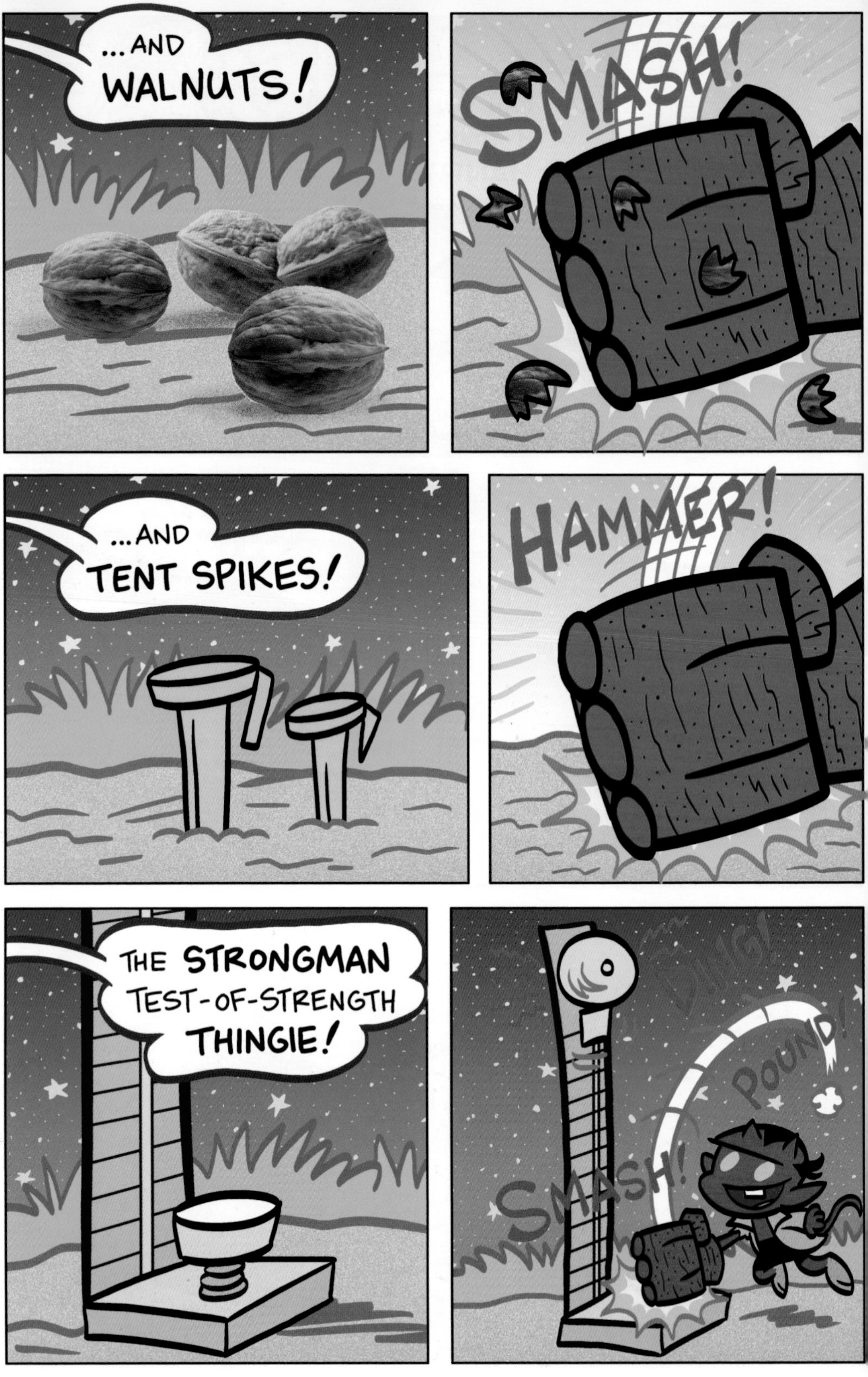
...AND WALNUTS!
SMASH!
...AND TENT SPIKES!
HAMMER!
THE STRONGMAN TEST-OF-STRENGTH THINGIE!
DING!
POUND!
SMASH!

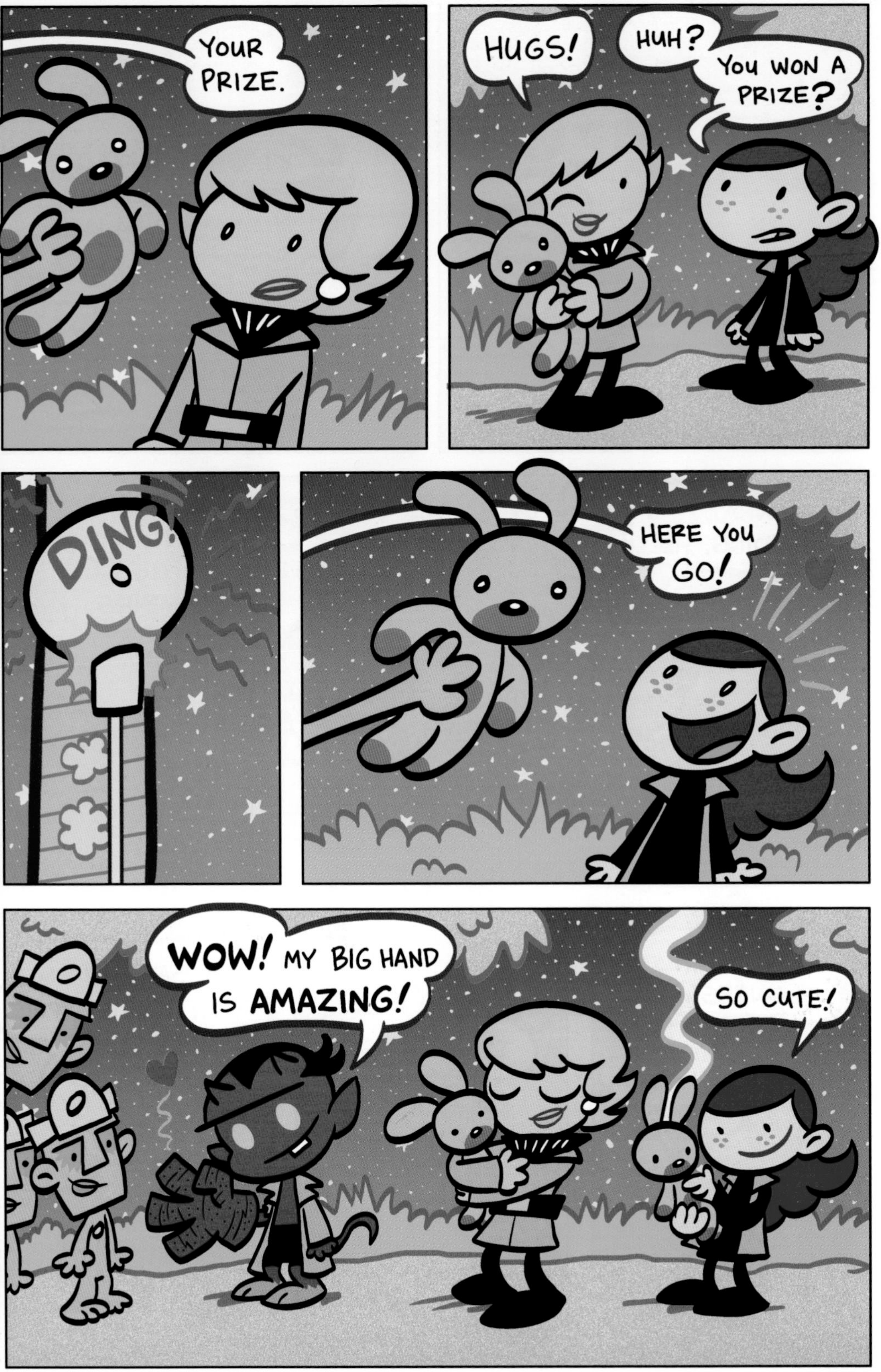
YOUR PRIZE.
HUGS!
HUH?
YOU WON A PRIZE?
DING!
HERE YOU GO!
WOW! MY BIG HAND IS AMAZING!
SO CUTE!

-DING!

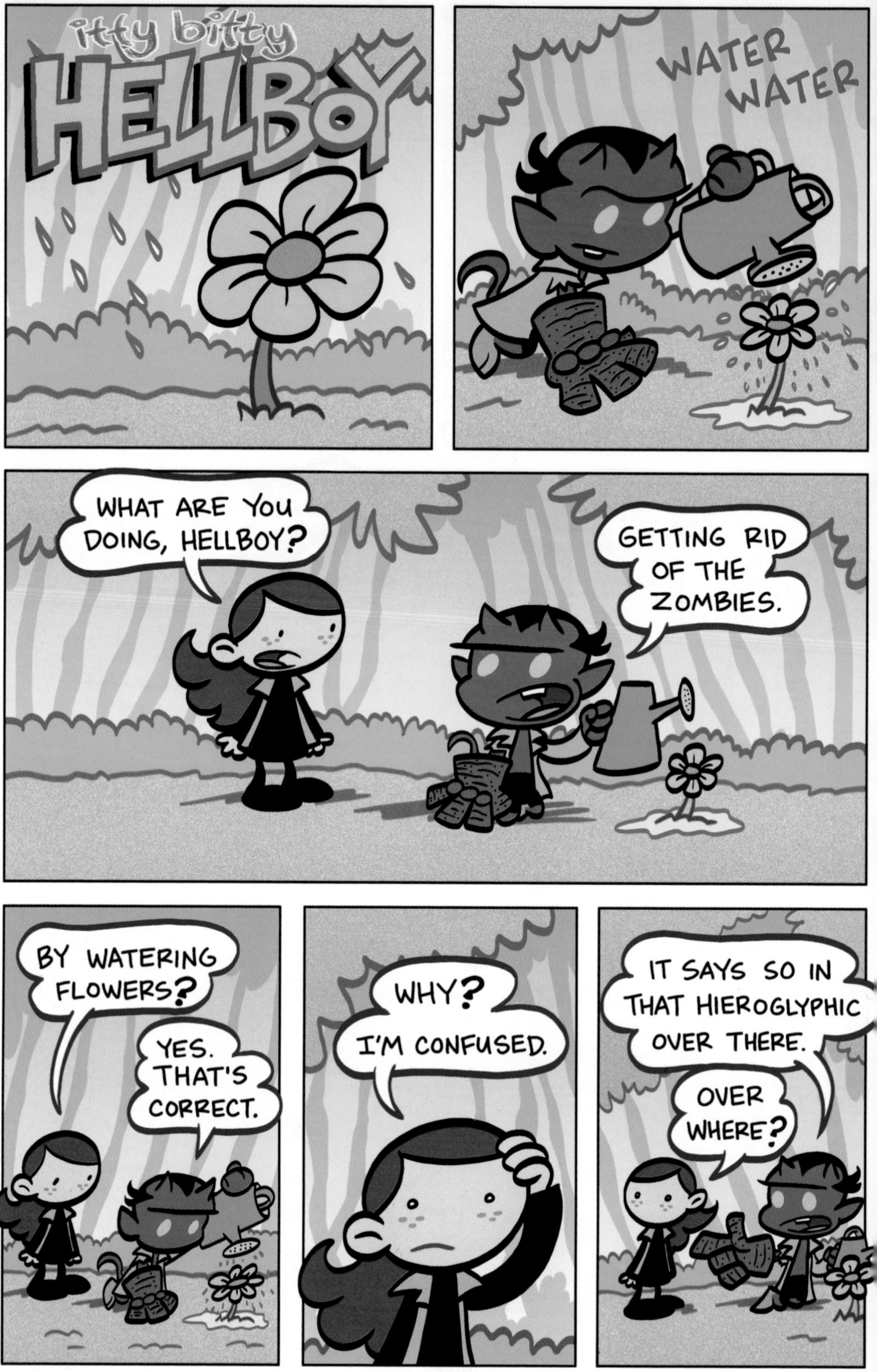
itty bitty
HELLBOY
WATER WATER
WHAT ARE YOU DOING, HELLBOY?
GETTING RID OF THE ZOMBIES.
BY WATERING FLOWERS?
YES. THAT'S CORRECT.
WHY? I'M CONFUSED.
IT SAYS SO IN THAT HIEROGLYPHIC OVER THERE.
OVER WHERE?

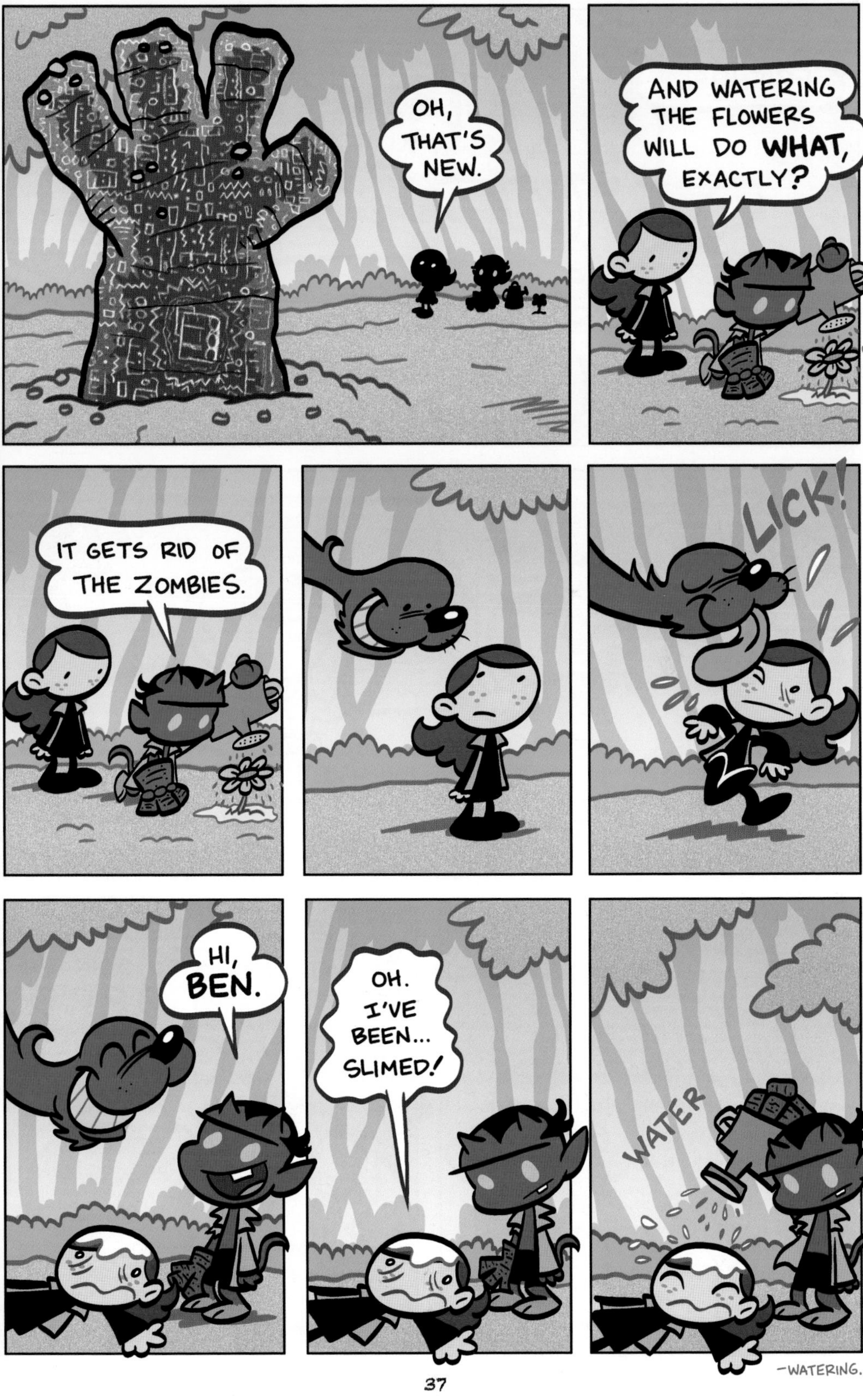
OH, THAT'S NEW.
AND WATERING THE FLOWERS WILL DO **WHAT**, EXACTLY?
IT GETS RID OF THE ZOMBIES.
LICK!
HI, **BEN.**
OH. I'VE BEEN... SLIMED!
WATER

—WATERING.

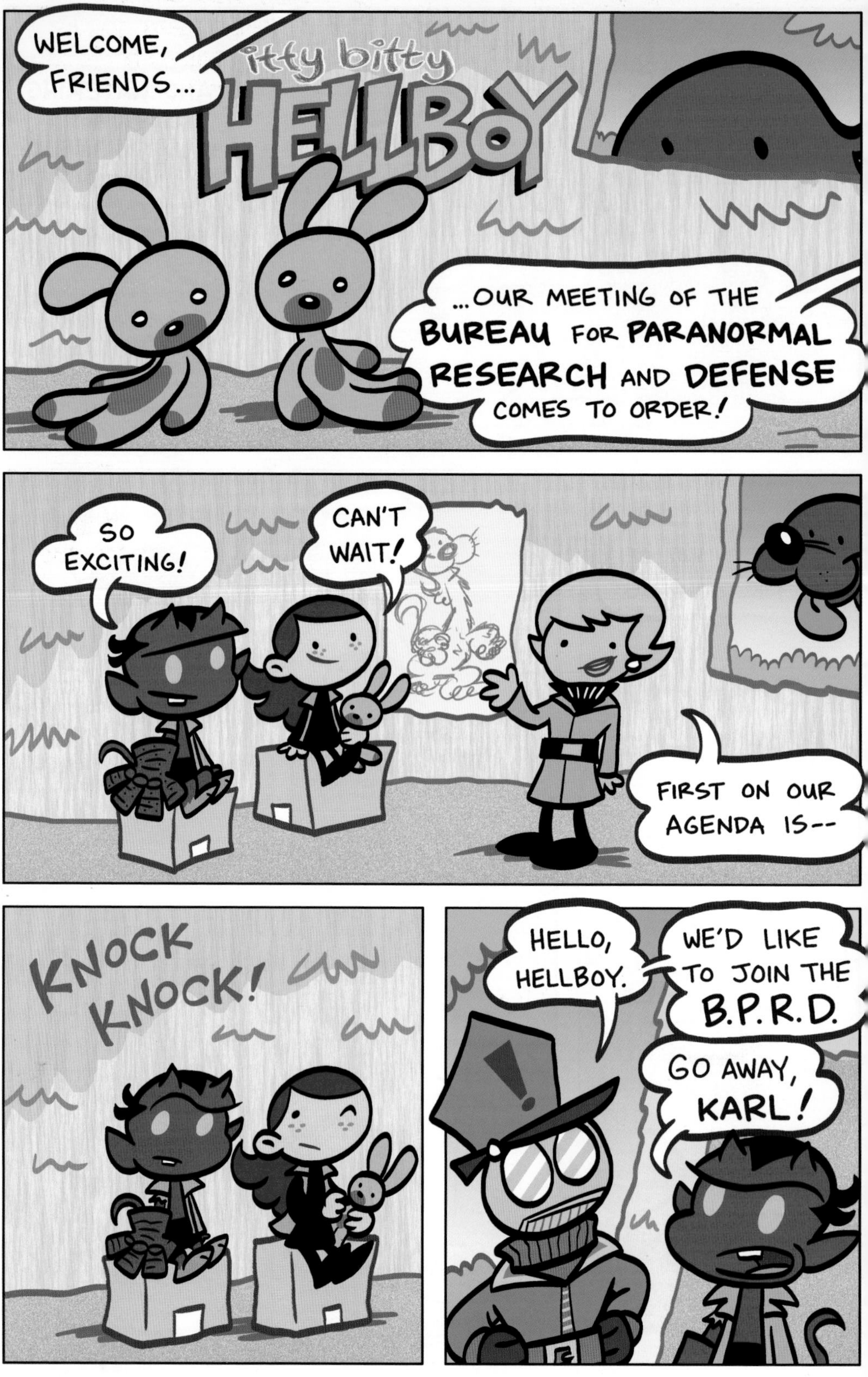
WELCOME, FRIENDS...
itty bitty HELLBOY
...OUR MEETING OF THE BUREAU FOR PARANORMAL RESEARCH AND DEFENSE COMES TO ORDER!
SO EXCITING!
CAN'T WAIT!
FIRST ON OUR AGENDA IS--
KNOCK KNOCK!
HELLO, HELLBOY.
WE'D LIKE TO JOIN THE B.P.R.D.
GO AWAY, KARL!

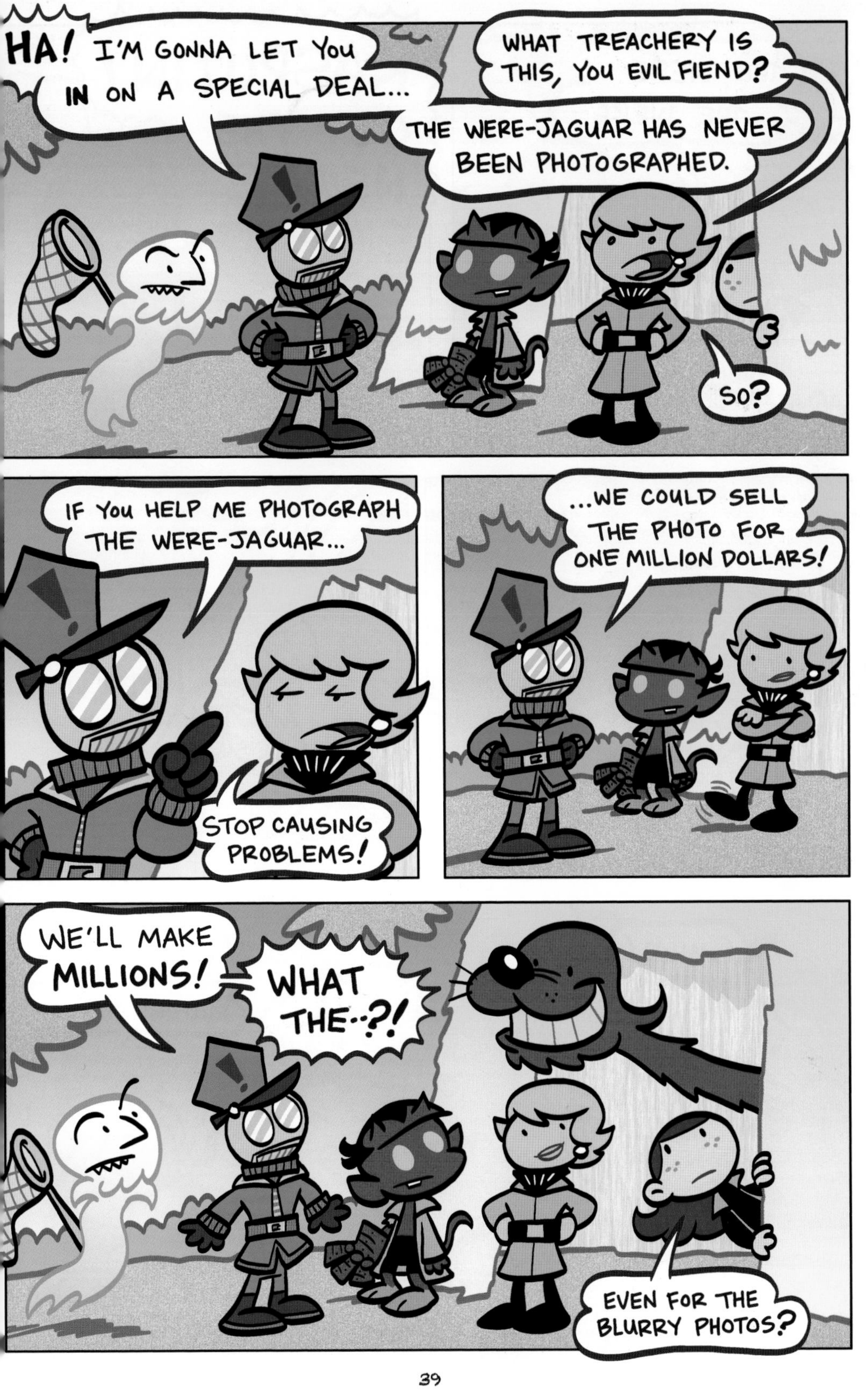
HA! I'M GONNA LET YOU IN ON A SPECIAL DEAL...
WHAT TREACHERY IS THIS, YOU EVIL FIEND?
THE WERE-JAGUAR HAS NEVER BEEN PHOTOGRAPHED.
SO?
IF YOU HELP ME PHOTOGRAPH THE WERE-JAGUAR...
STOP CAUSING PROBLEMS!
...WE COULD SELL THE PHOTO FOR ONE MILLION DOLLARS!
WE'LL MAKE MILLIONS!
WHAT THE··?!
EVEN FOR THE BLURRY PHOTOS?

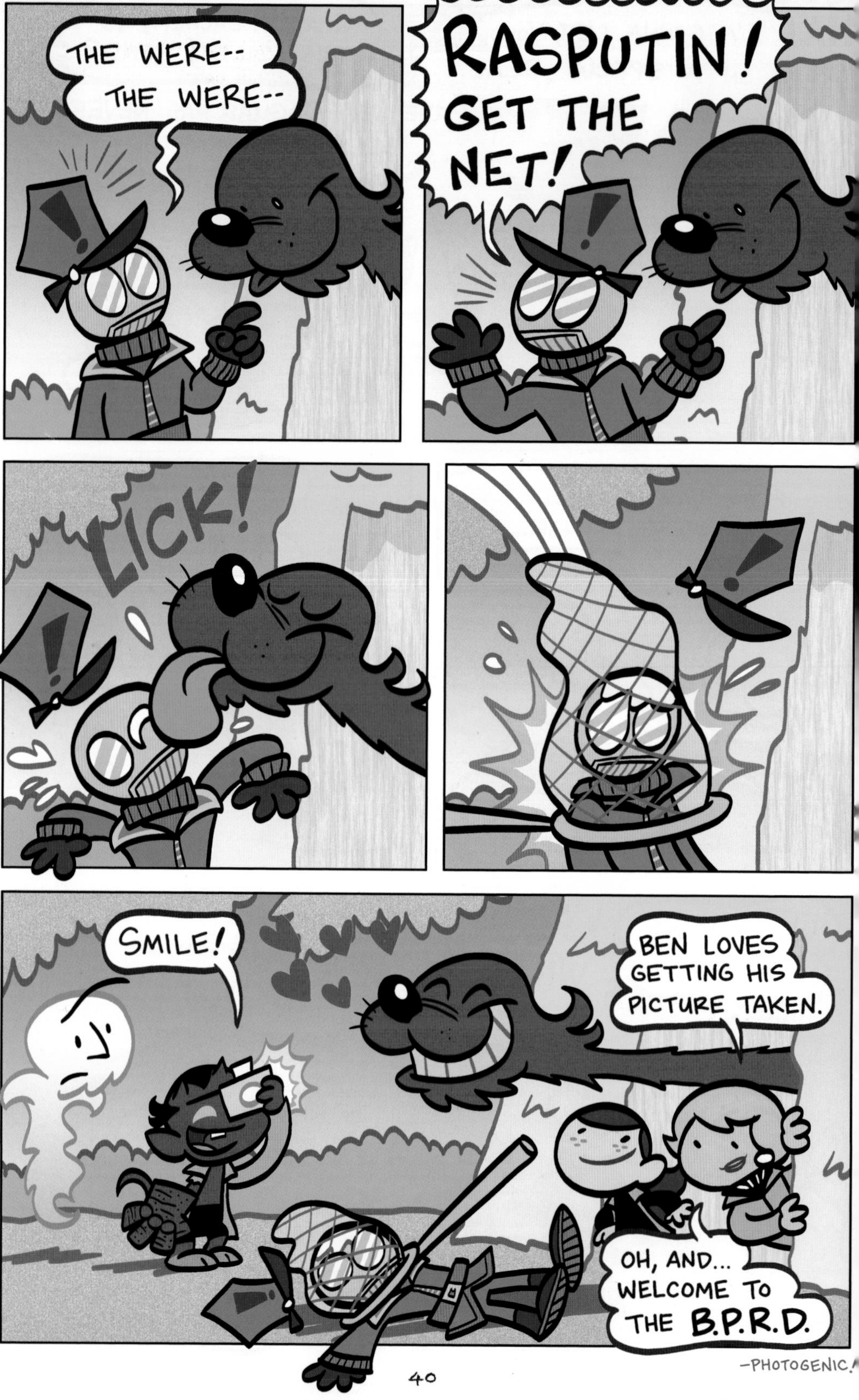
THE WERE--
THE WERE--
RASPUTIN! GET THE NET!
LICK!
SMILE!
BEN LOVES GETTING HIS PICTURE TAKEN.
OH, AND... WELCOME TO THE B.P.R.D.

-PHOTOGENIC!

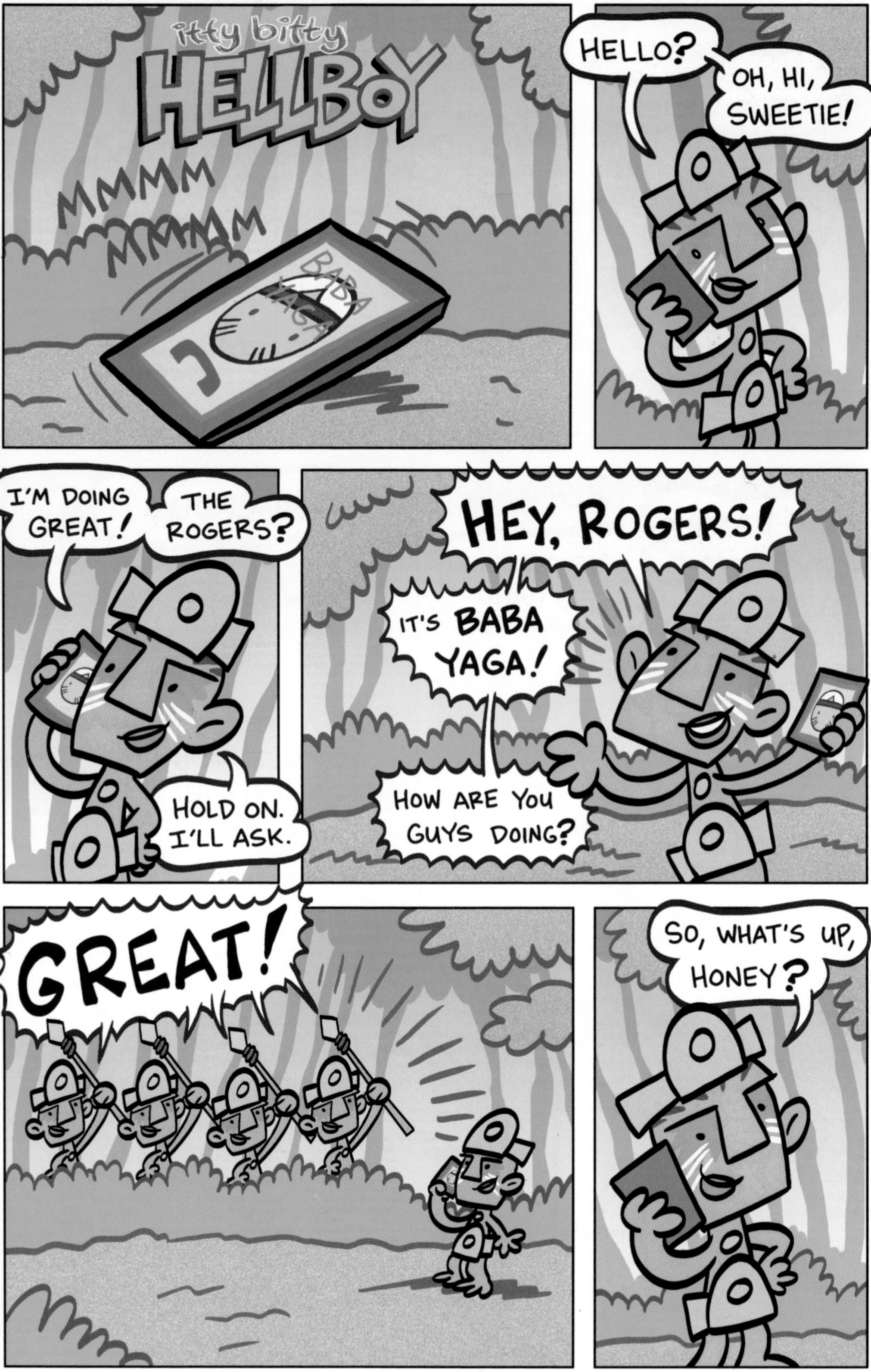
itty bitty
HELLBOY
MMMM MMMM
BABA YAGA
HELLO?
OH, HI, SWEETIE!
I'M DOING GREAT!
THE ROGERS?
HOLD ON. I'LL ASK.
HEY, ROGERS!
IT'S BABA YAGA!
HOW ARE YOU GUYS DOING?
GREAT!
SO, WHAT'S UP, HONEY?

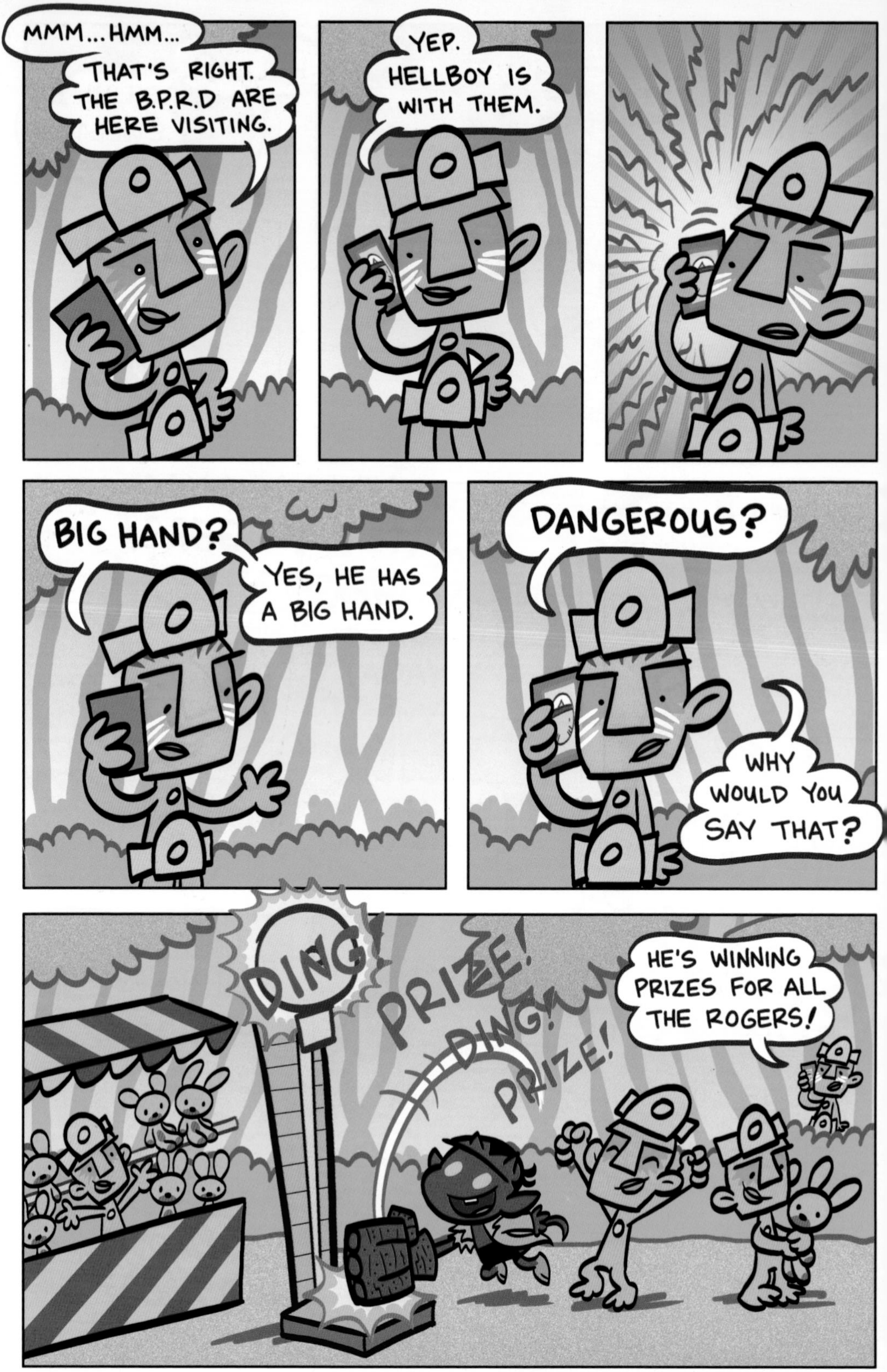
MMM... HMM...
THAT'S RIGHT. THE B.P.R.D ARE HERE VISITING.
YEP. HELLBOY IS WITH THEM.
BIG HAND?
YES, HE HAS A BIG HAND.
DANGEROUS?
WHY WOULD YOU SAY THAT?
DING!
PRIZE!
DING!
PRIZE!
HE'S WINNING PRIZES FOR ALL THE ROGERS!

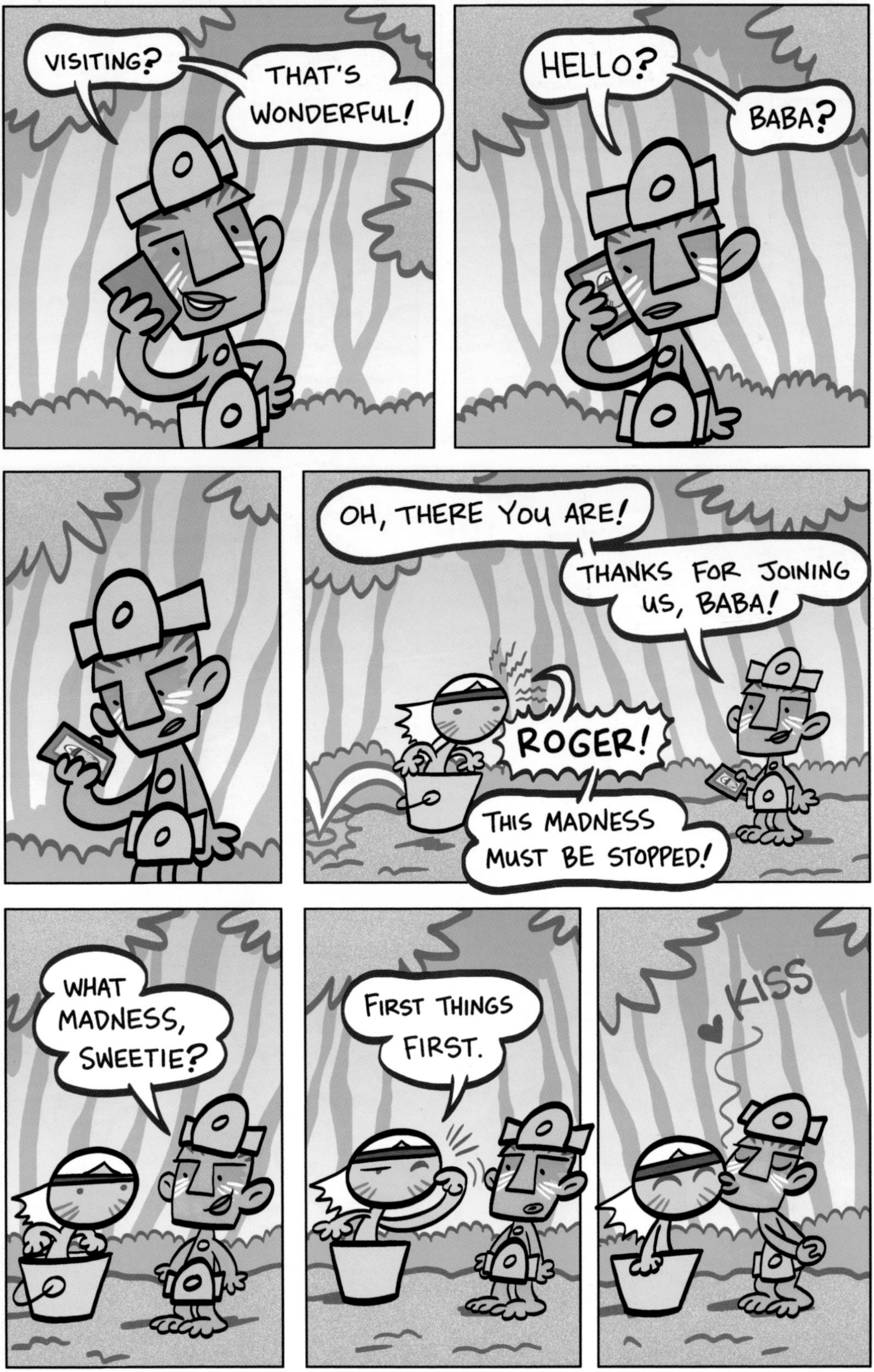
VISITING?
THAT'S WONDERFUL!
HELLO?
BABA?
OH, THERE YOU ARE!
THANKS FOR JOINING US, BABA!
ROGER!
THIS MADNESS MUST BE STOPPED!
WHAT MADNESS, SWEETIE?
FIRST THINGS FIRST.
KISS

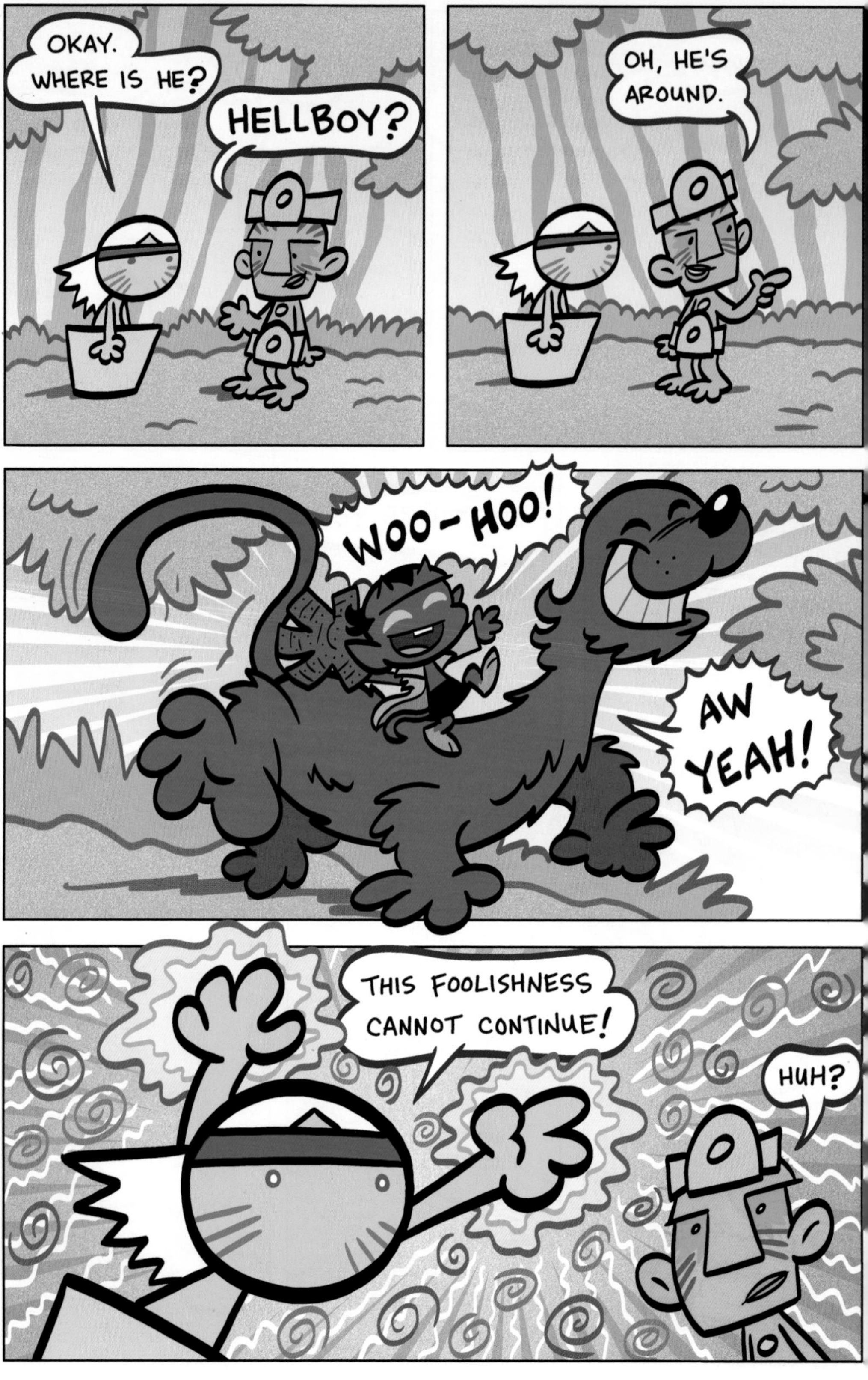
OKAY. WHERE IS HE?
HELLBOY?
OH, HE'S AROUND.
WOO-HOO!
AW YEAH!
THIS FOOLISHNESS CANNOT CONTINUE!
HUH?

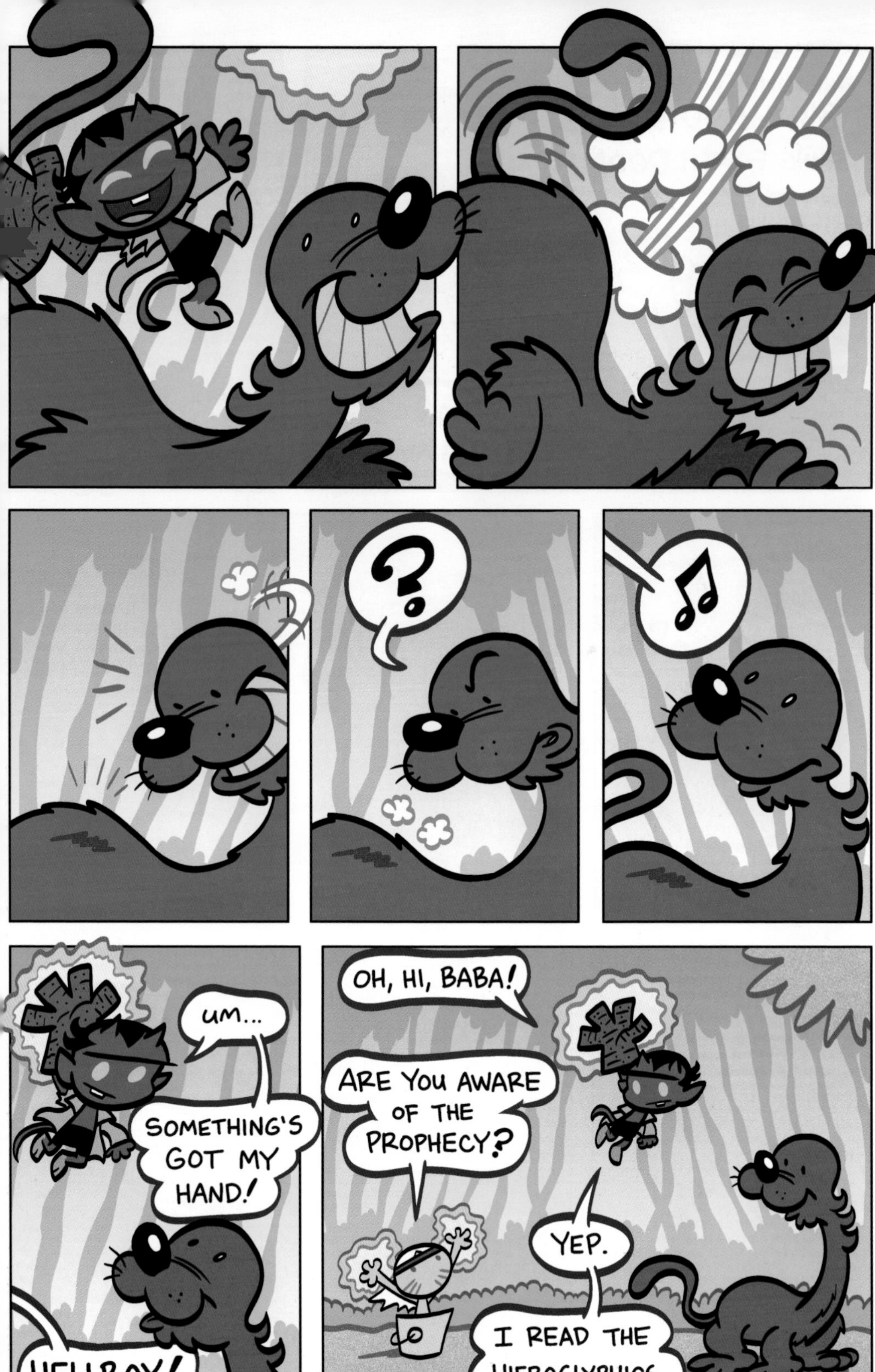
?
♫
UM...
SOMETHING'S GOT MY HAND!
HELLBOY!
OH, HI, BABA!
ARE YOU AWARE OF THE PROPHECY?
YEP.
I READ THE HIEROGLYPHICS.

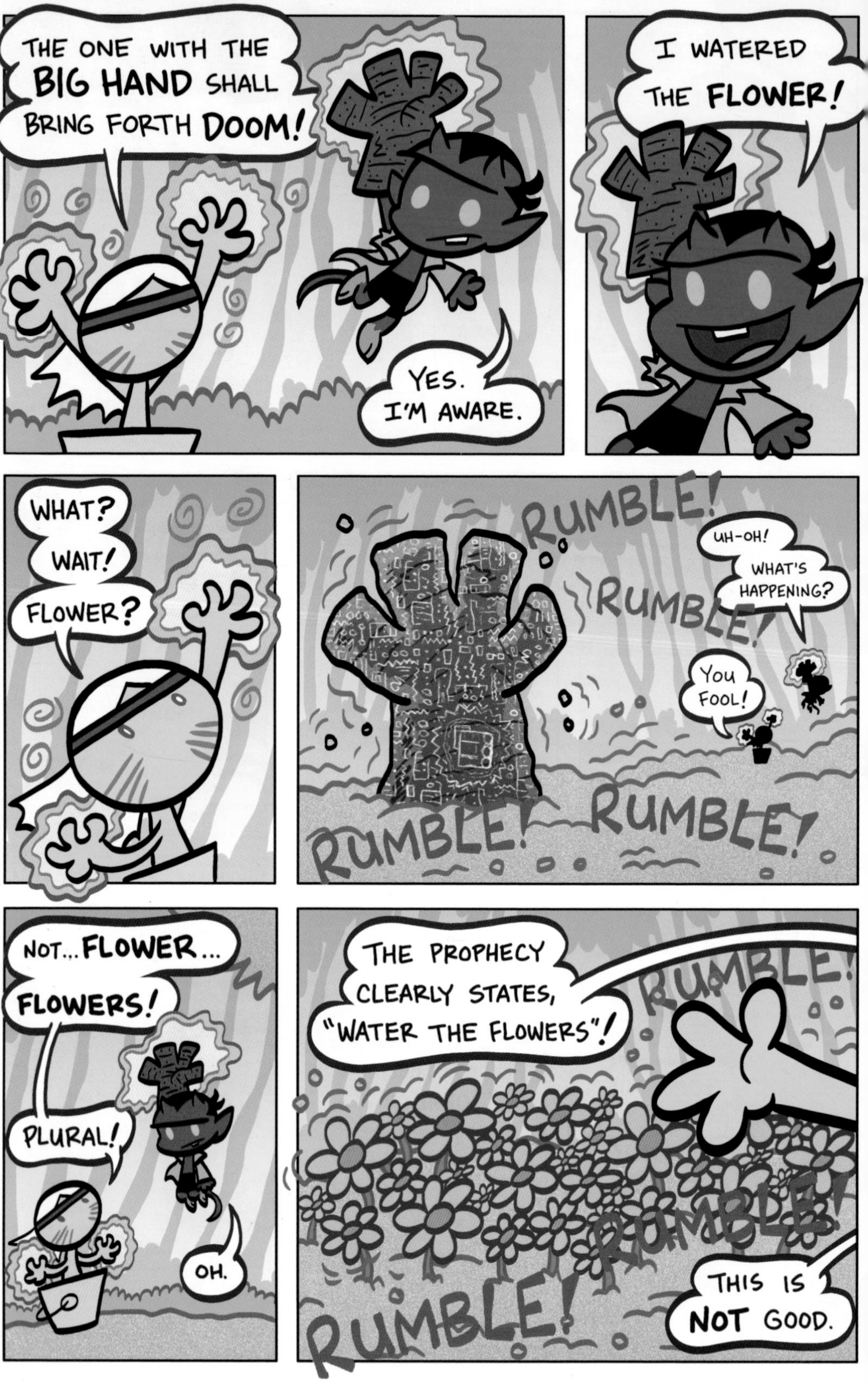
THE ONE WITH THE BIG HAND SHALL BRING FORTH DOOM!
YES. I'M AWARE.
I WATERED THE FLOWER!
WHAT?
WAIT!
FLOWER?
RUMBLE!
UH-OH!
WHAT'S HAPPENING?
RUMBLE!
YOU FOOL!
RUMBLE!
RUMBLE!
NOT... FLOWER...
FLOWERS!
PLURAL!
OH.
THE PROPHECY CLEARLY STATES, "WATER THE FLOWERS"!
RUMBLE!
RUMBLE!
RUMBLE!
THIS IS NOT GOOD.

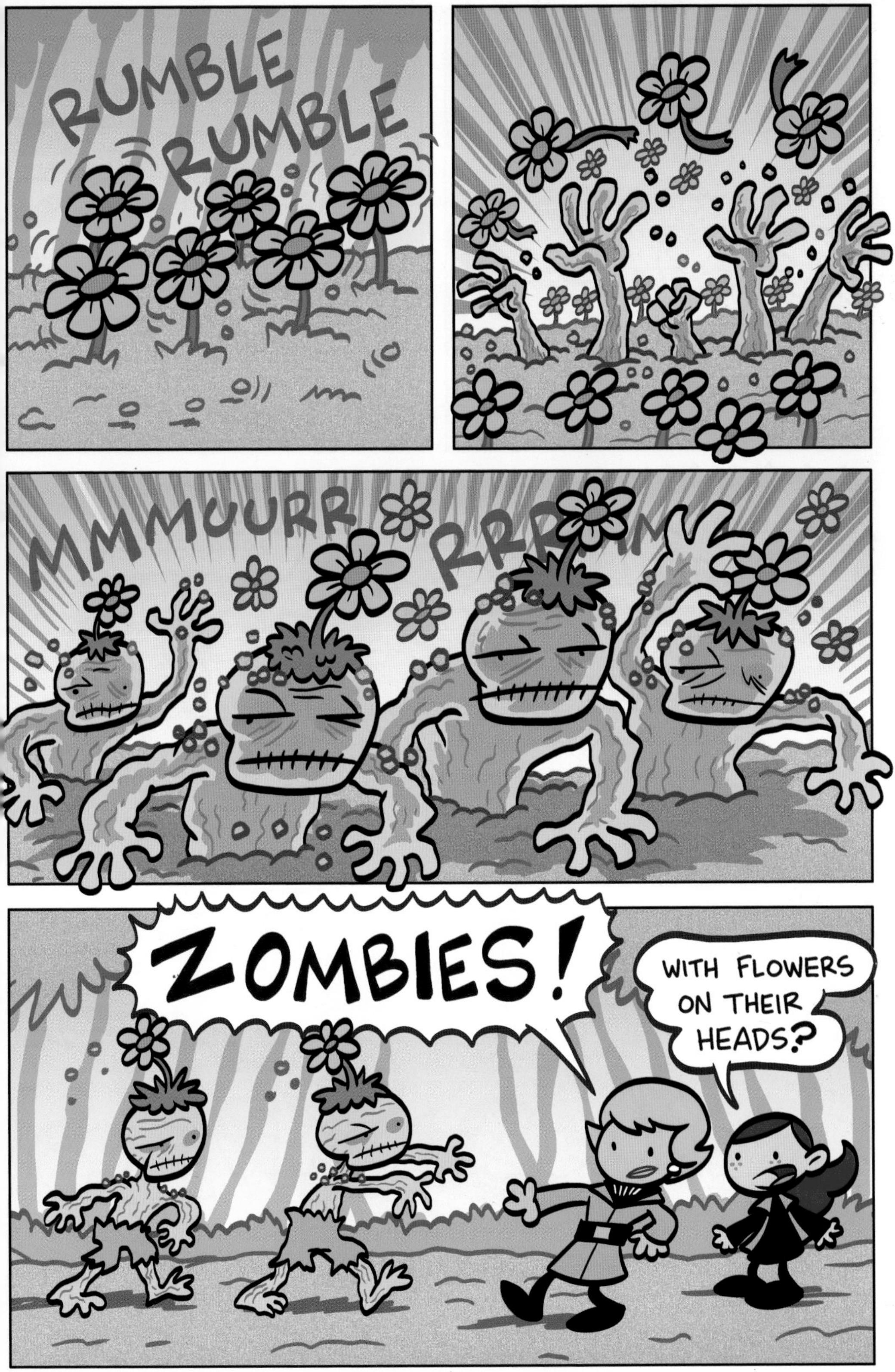
RUMBLE RUMBLE
MMMUURR RRR
ZOMBIES!
WITH FLOWERS ON THEIR HEADS?

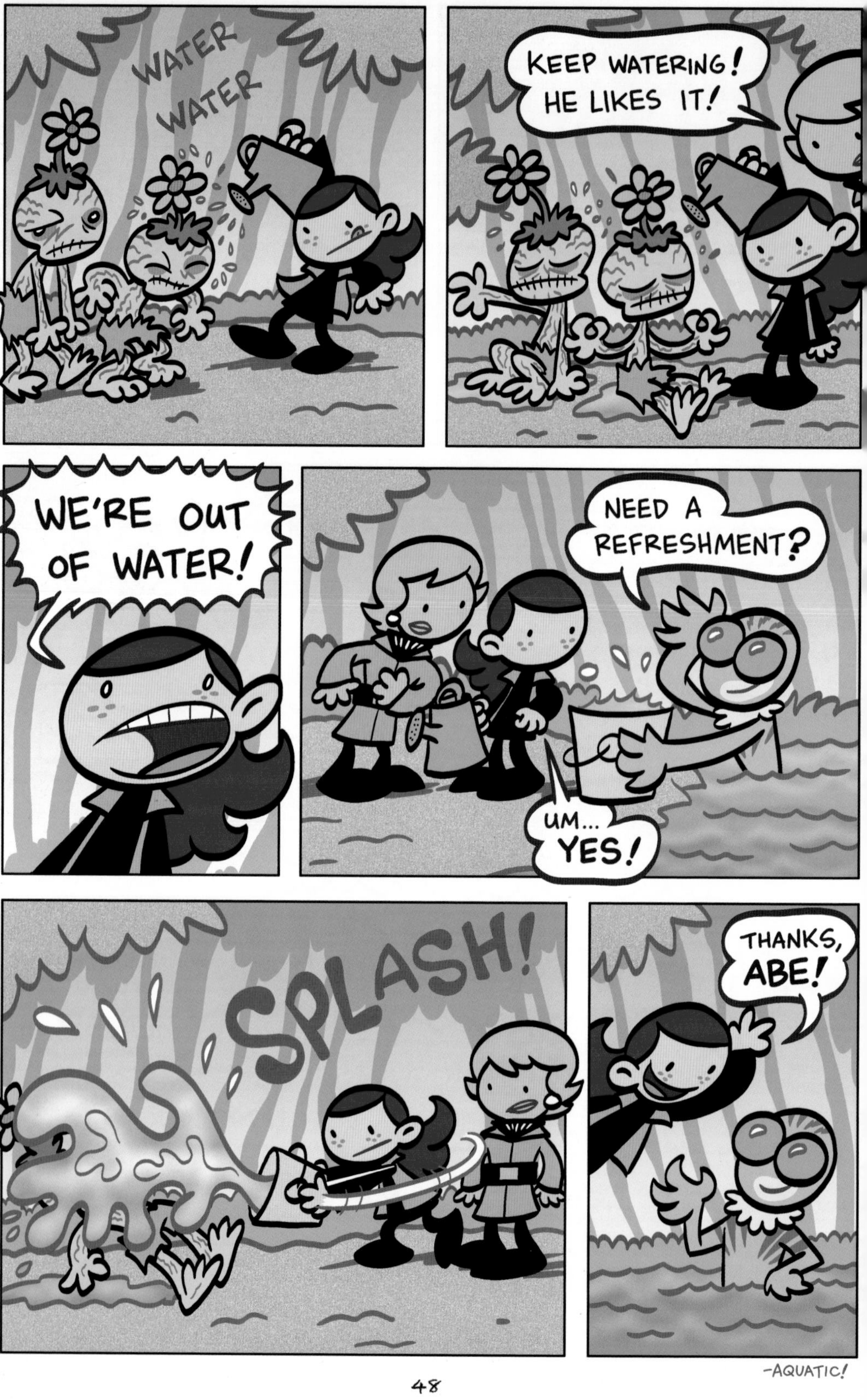
WATER
WATER
KEEP WATERING! HE LIKES IT!
WE'RE OUT OF WATER!
NEED A REFRESHMENT?
UM... YES!
SPLASH!
THANKS, ABE!

-AQUATIC!

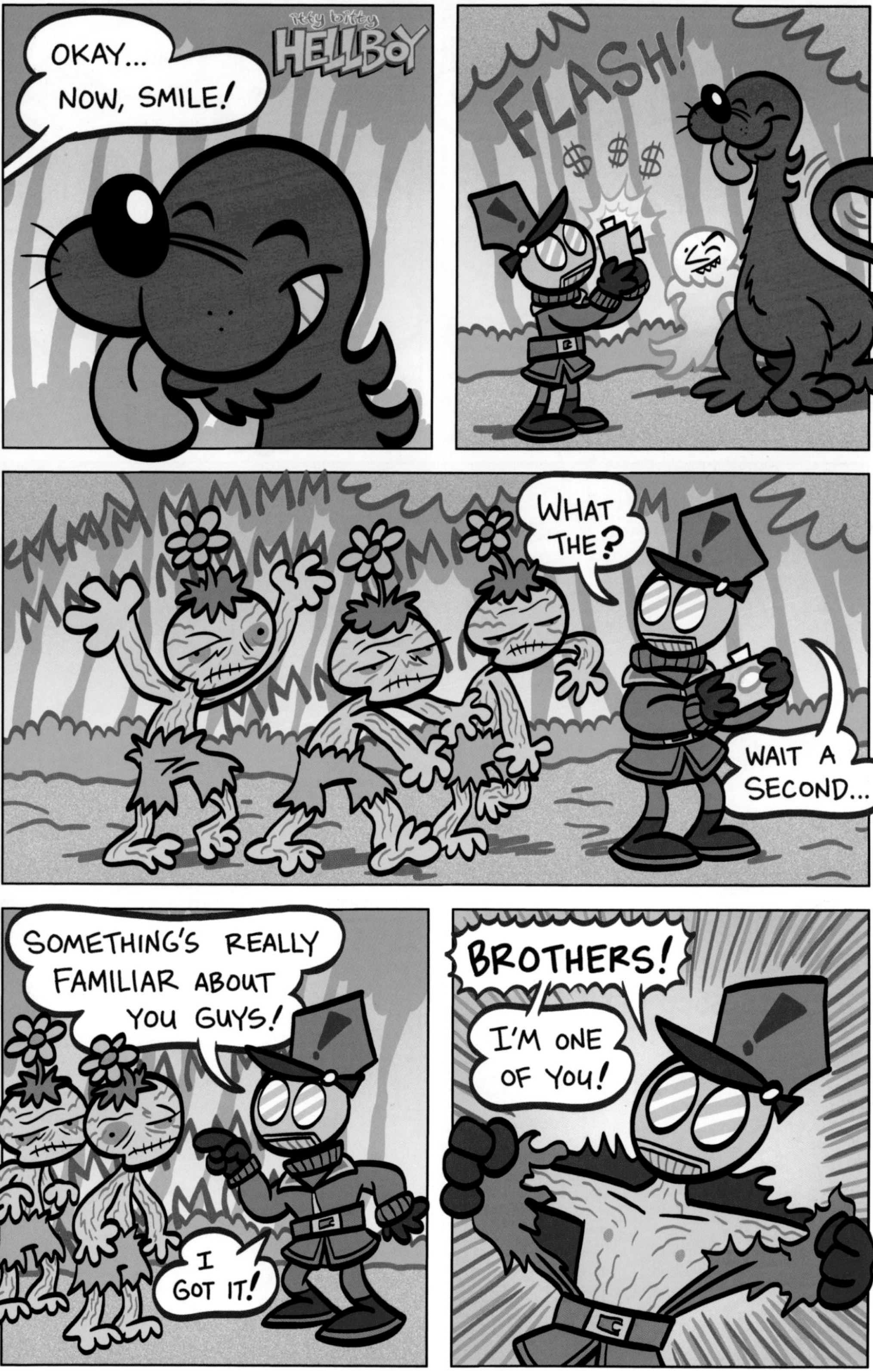
itty bitty HELLBOY
OKAY... NOW, SMILE!
FLASH!
$ $ $
MMMMMMMMM
WHAT THE?
WAIT A SECOND...
SOMETHING'S REALLY FAMILIAR ABOUT YOU GUYS!
I GOT IT!
BROTHERS!
I'M ONE OF YOU!

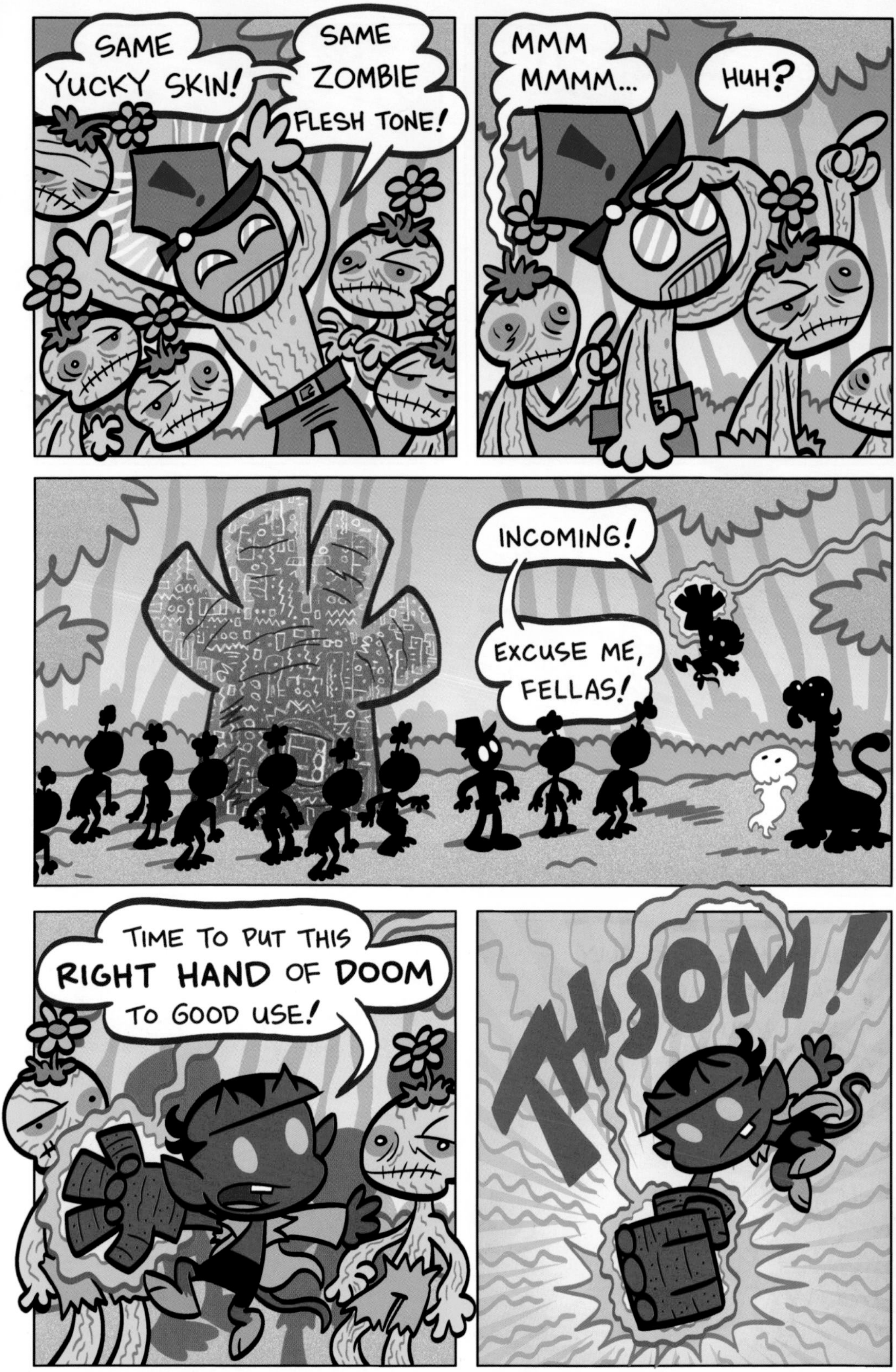
SAME YUCKY SKIN!
SAME ZOMBIE FLESH TONE!
MMM MMMM...
HUH?
INCOMING!
EXCUSE ME, FELLAS!
TIME TO PUT THIS RIGHT HAND OF DOOM TO GOOD USE!
THSOOM!

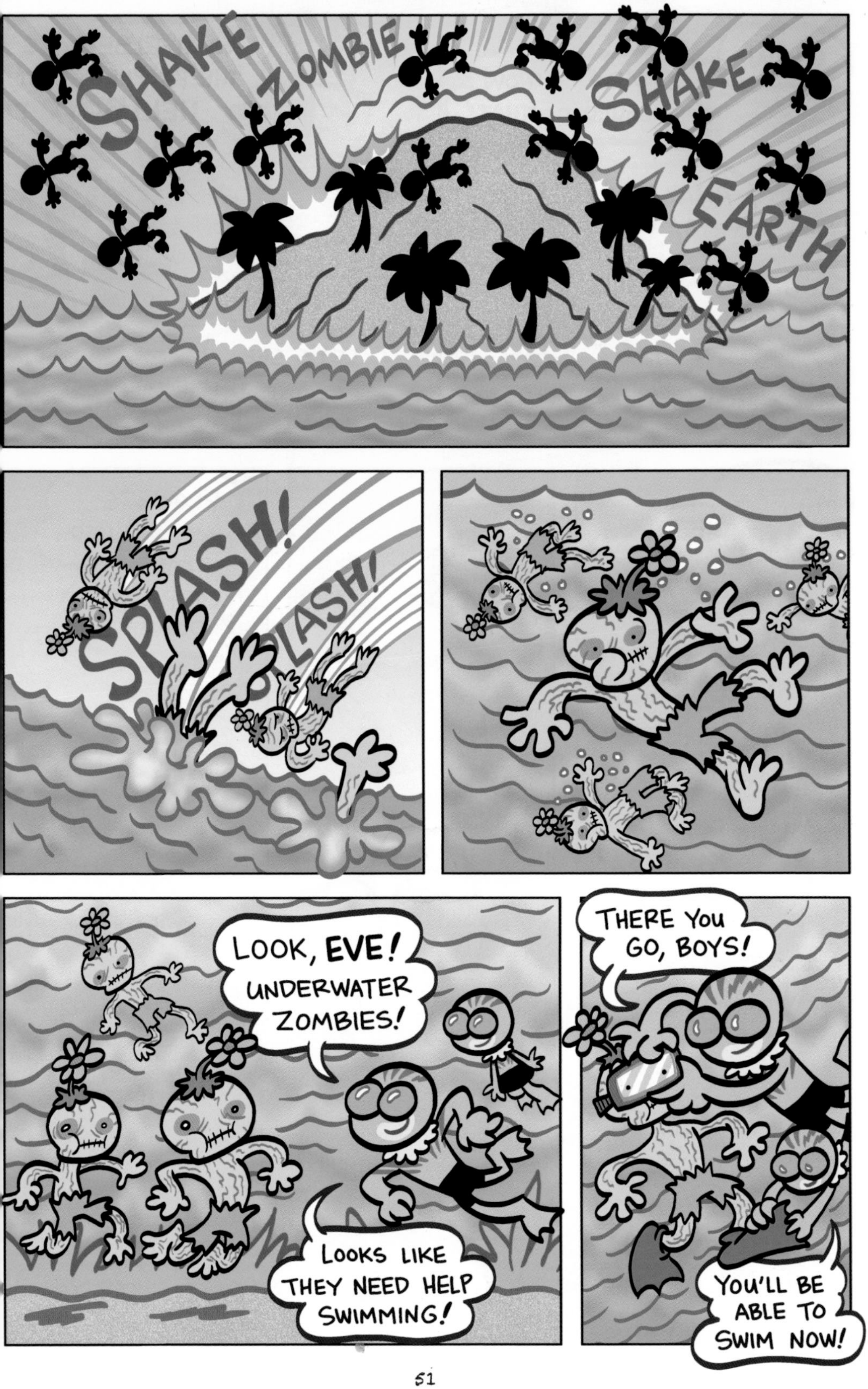
SHAKE
ZOMBIE
SHAKE
EARTH
SPLASH!
SPLASH!
LOOK, **EVE**! UNDERWATER ZOMBIES!
LOOKS LIKE THEY NEED HELP SWIMMING!
THERE YOU GO, BOYS!
YOU'LL BE ABLE TO SWIM NOW!

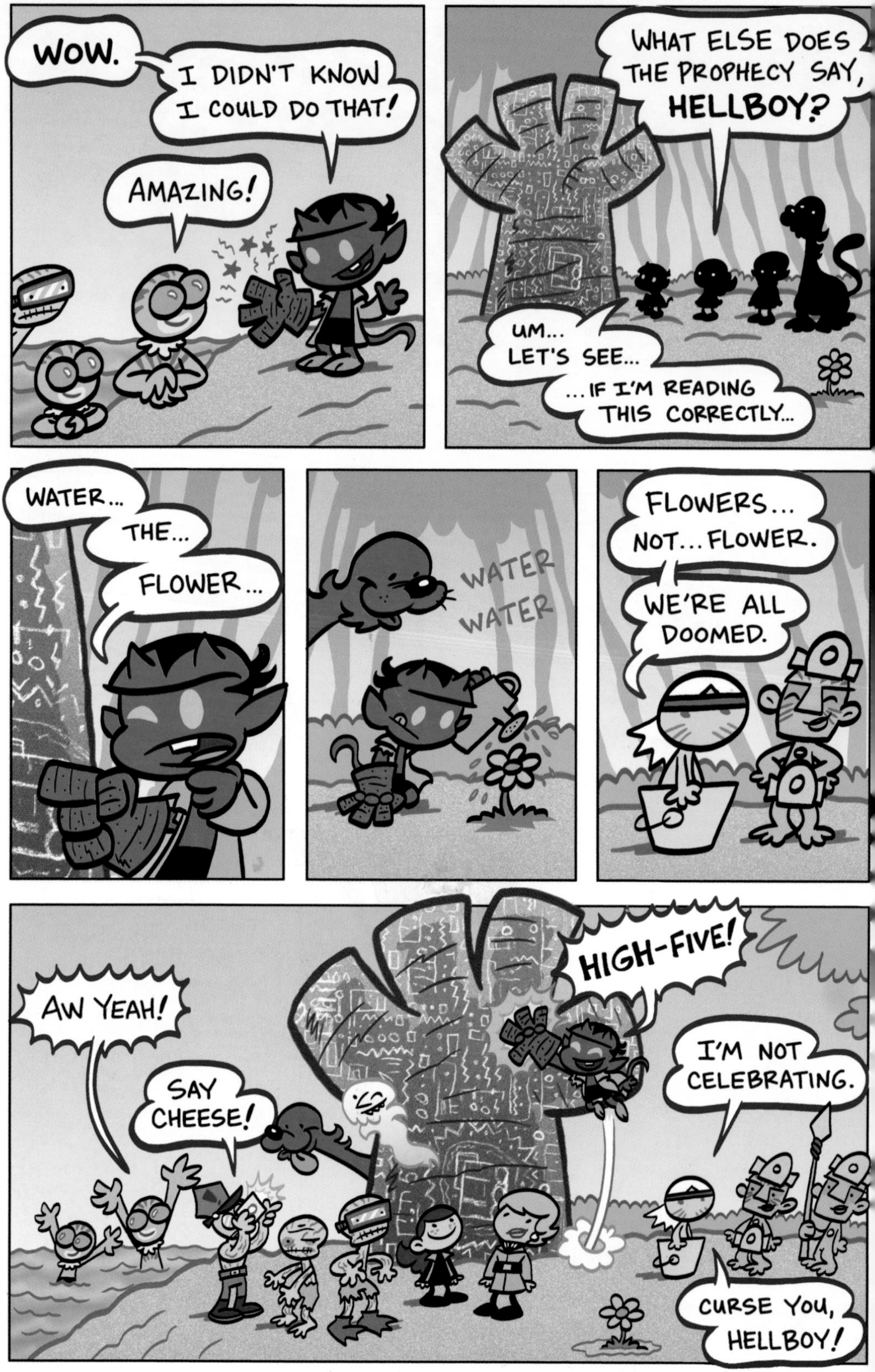
WOW.
I DIDN'T KNOW I COULD DO THAT!
AMAZING!
WHAT ELSE DOES THE PROPHECY SAY, HELLBOY?
UM... LET'S SEE...
...IF I'M READING THIS CORRECTLY...
WATER...
THE...
FLOWER...
WATER WATER
FLOWERS... NOT... FLOWER.
WE'RE ALL DOOMED.
HIGH-FIVE!
AW YEAH!
SAY CHEESE!
I'M NOT CELEBRATING.
CURSE YOU, HELLBOY!

–HIEROGLYPHICAL!

CHAPTER THREE

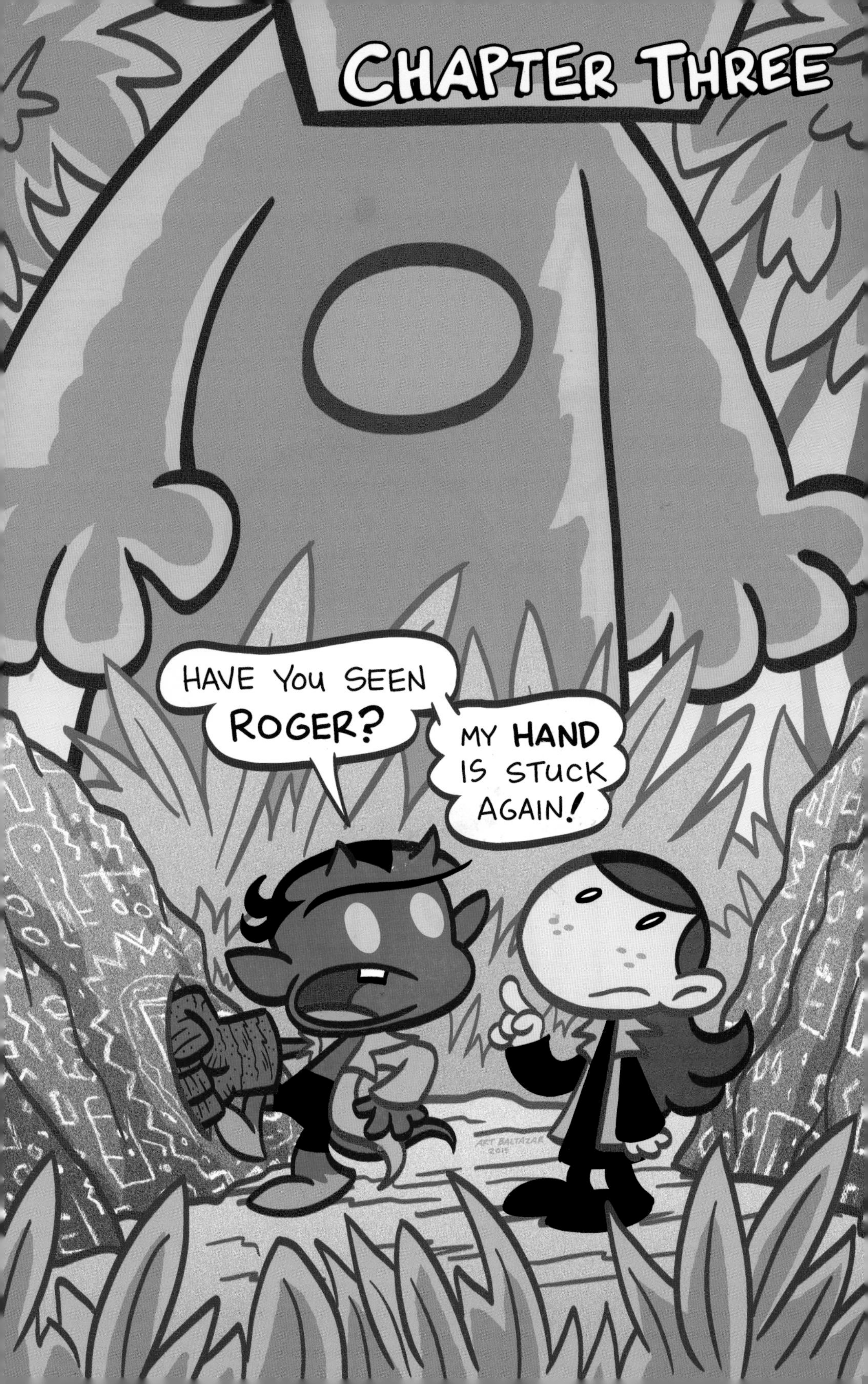
HAVE YOU SEEN ROGER?
MY HAND IS STUCK AGAIN!
ART BALTAZAR 2015

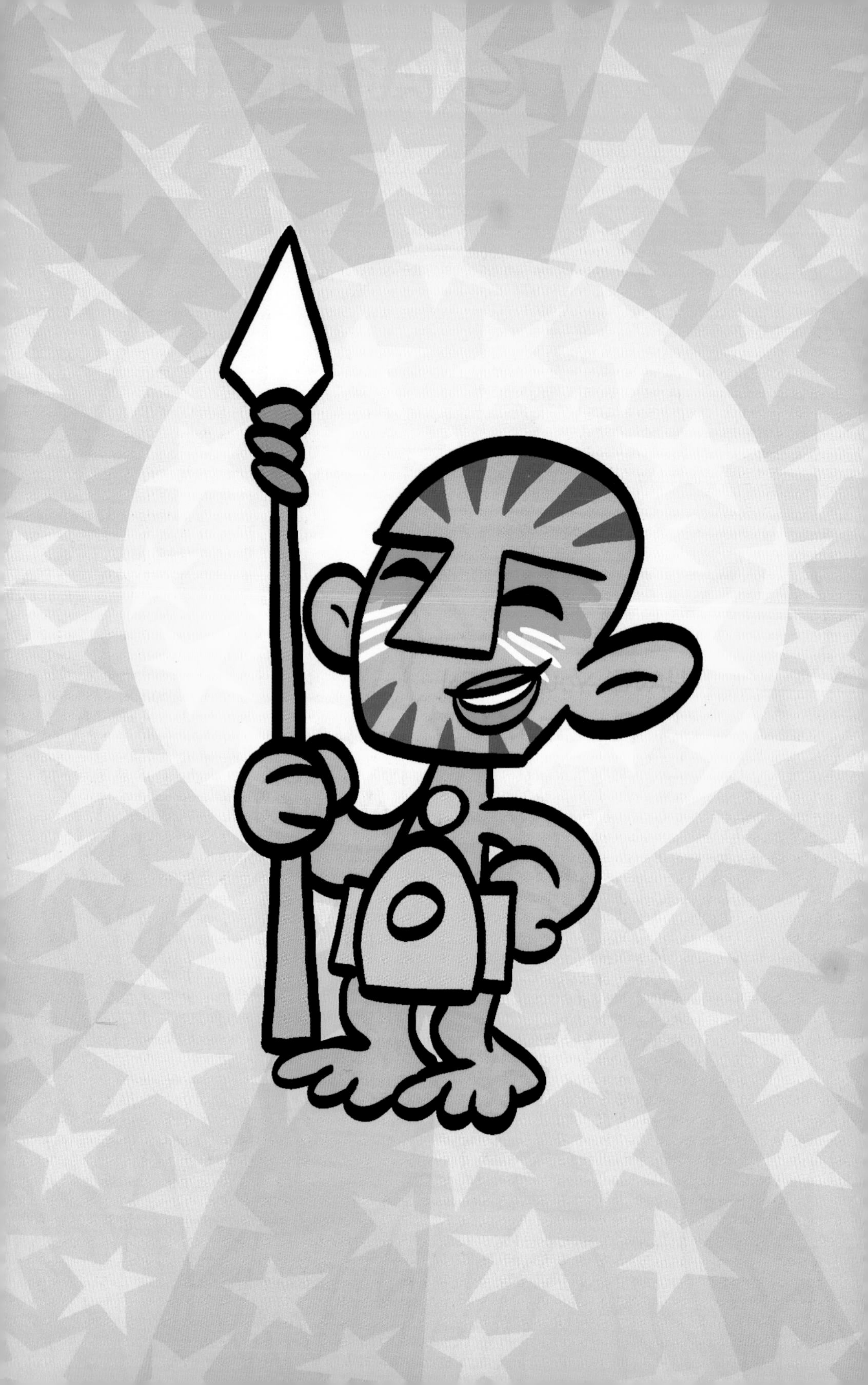

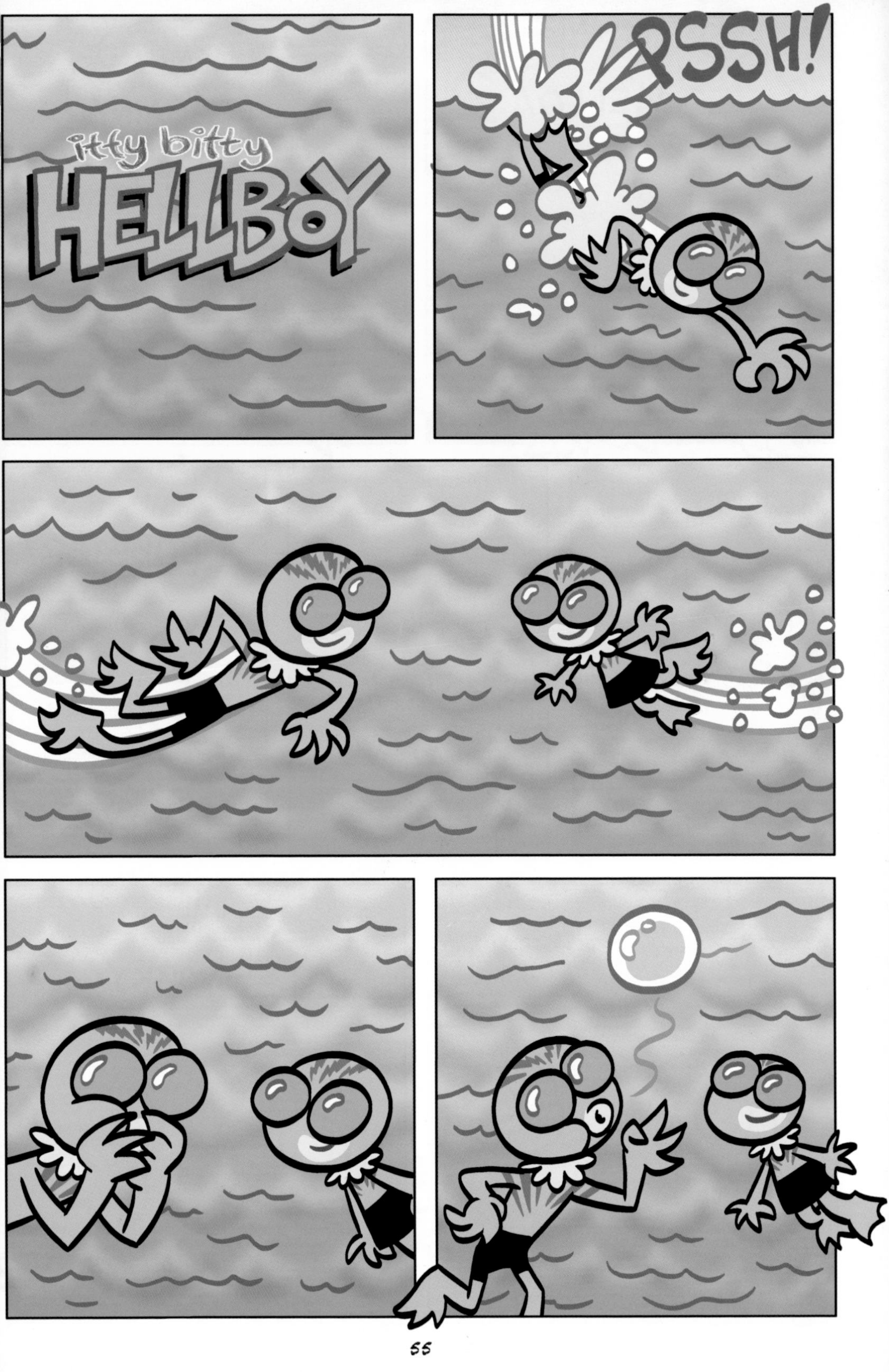
itty bitty
HELLBOY
PSSH!

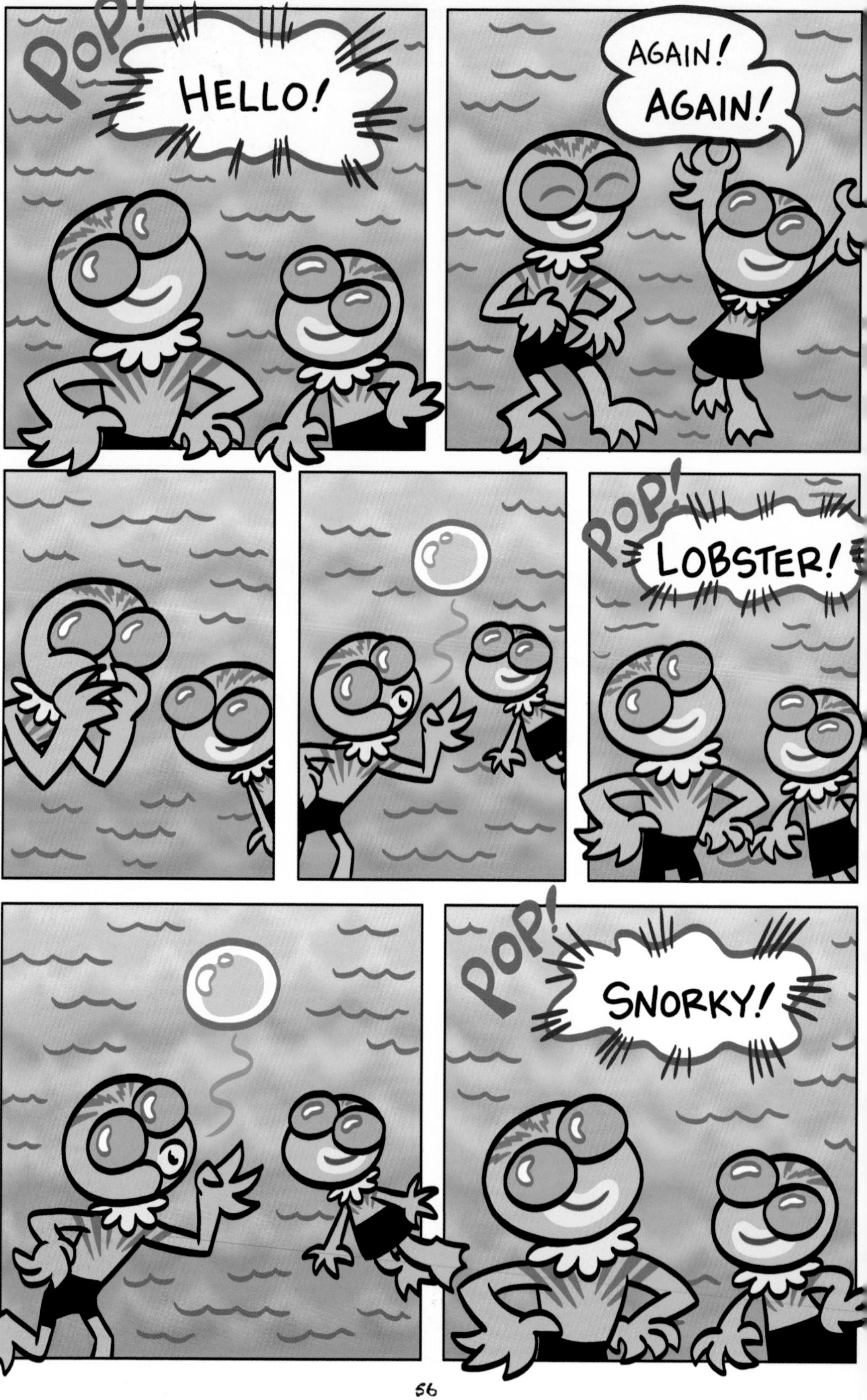
POP!
HELLO!
AGAIN!
AGAIN!
POP!
LOBSTER!
POP!
SNORKY!

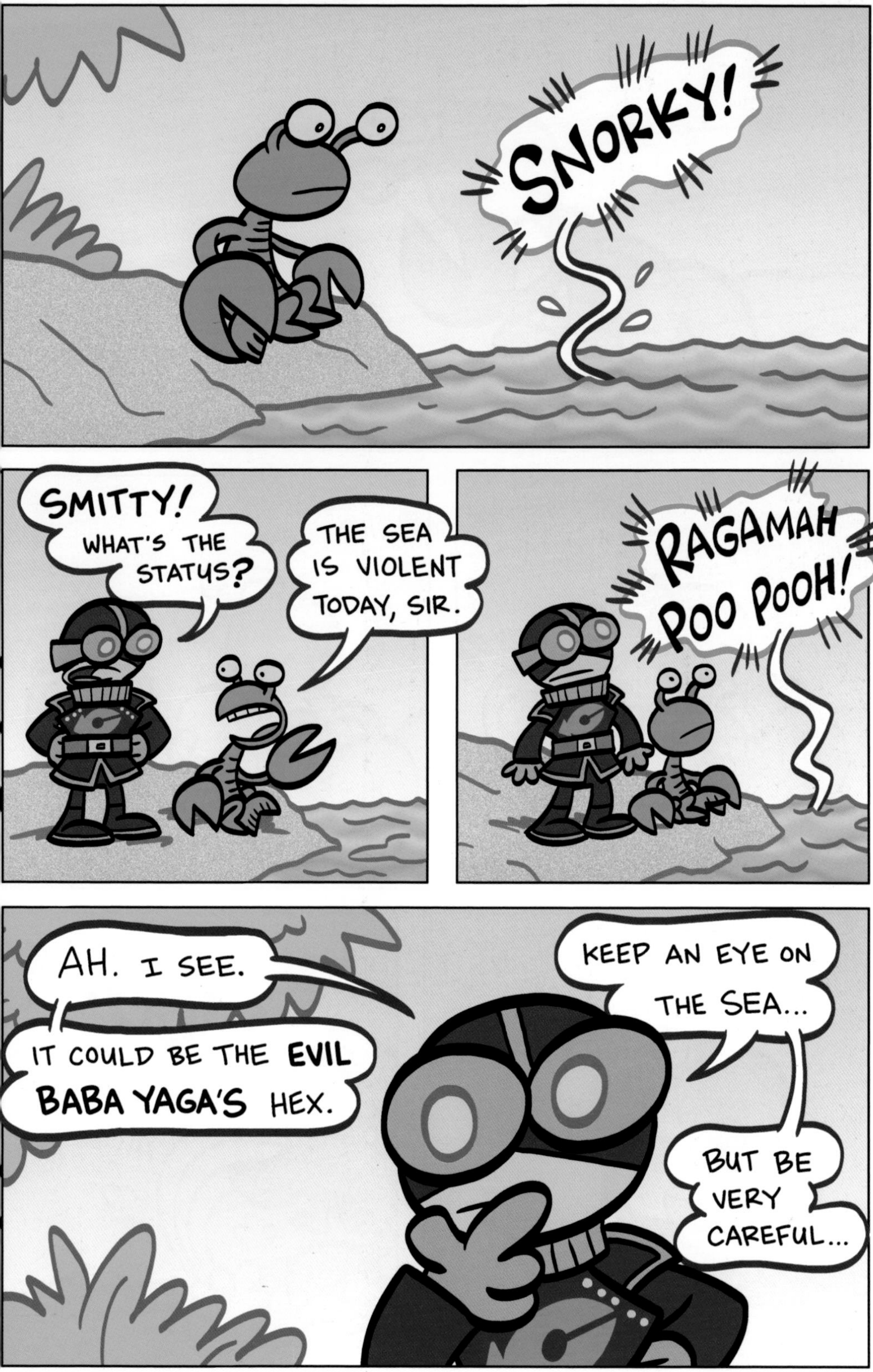
SNORKY!
SMITTY! WHAT'S THE STATUS?
THE SEA IS VIOLENT TODAY, SIR.
RAGAMAH POO POOH!
AH. I SEE.
IT COULD BE THE EVIL BABA YAGA'S HEX.
KEEP AN EYE ON THE SEA...
BUT BE VERY CAREFUL...

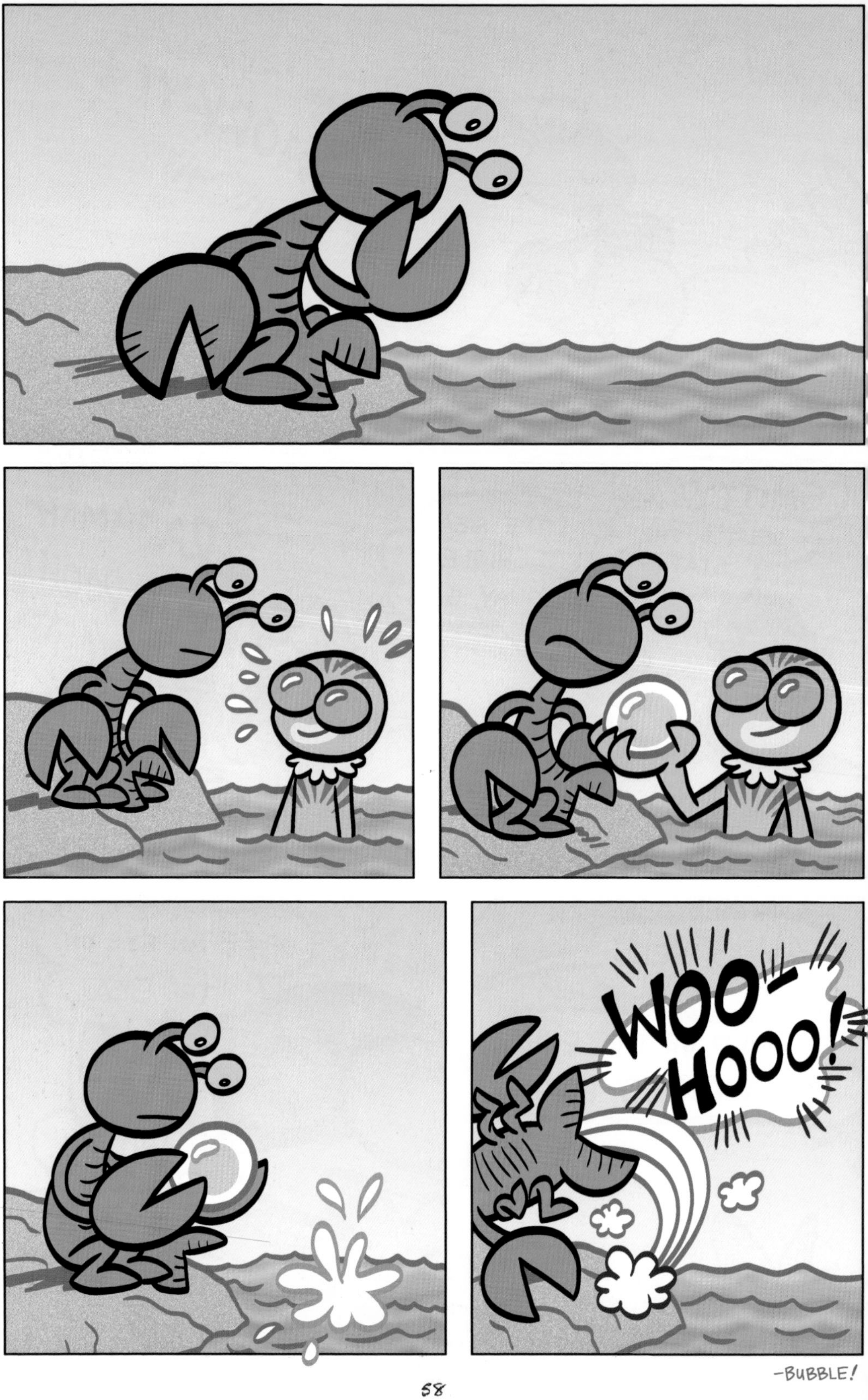
WOO-
HOOO!

—BUBBLE!

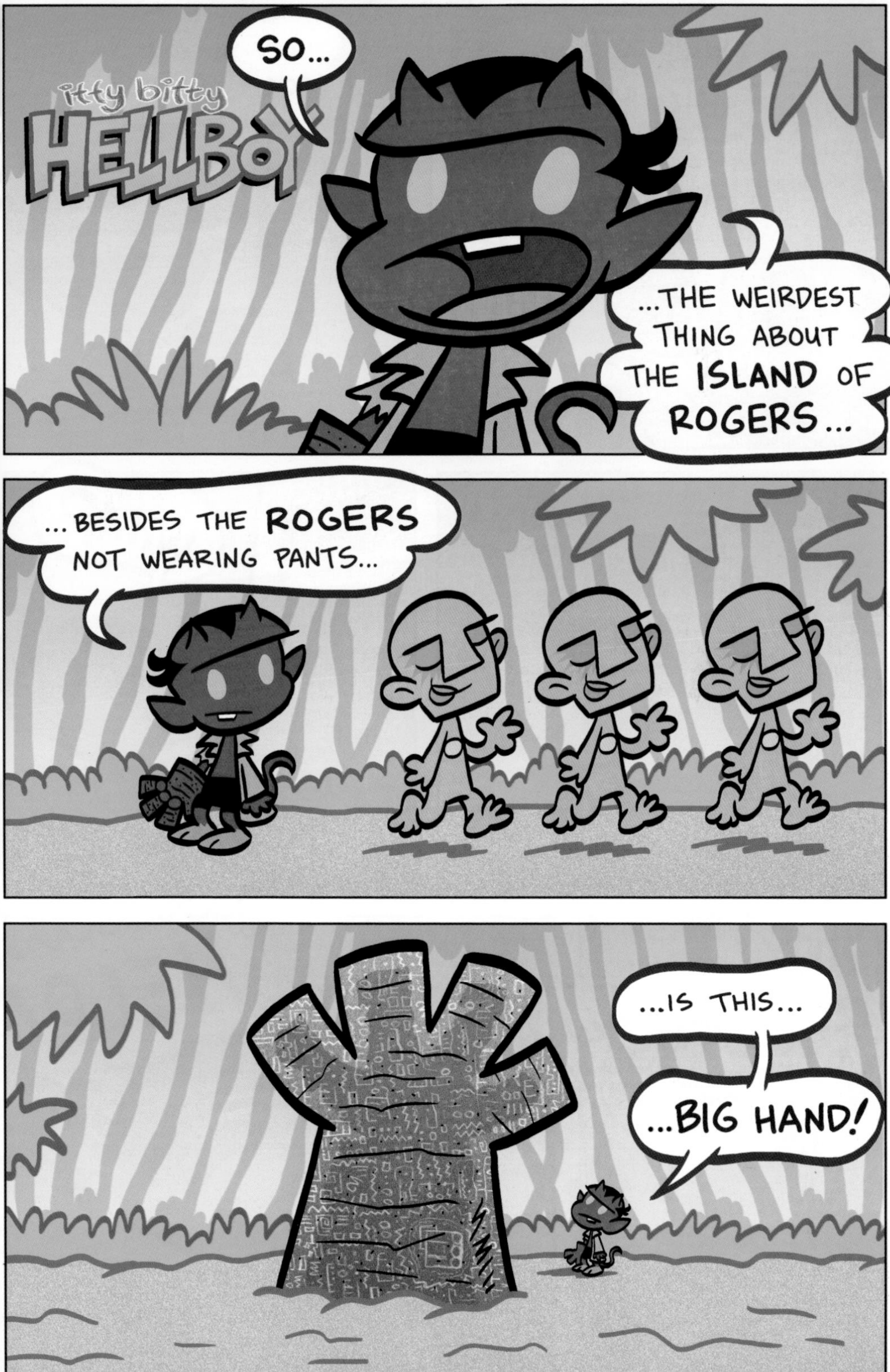
itty bitty HELLBOY
SO...
...THE WEIRDEST THING ABOUT THE ISLAND OF ROGERS...
...BESIDES THE ROGERS NOT WEARING PANTS...
...IS THIS...
...BIG HAND!

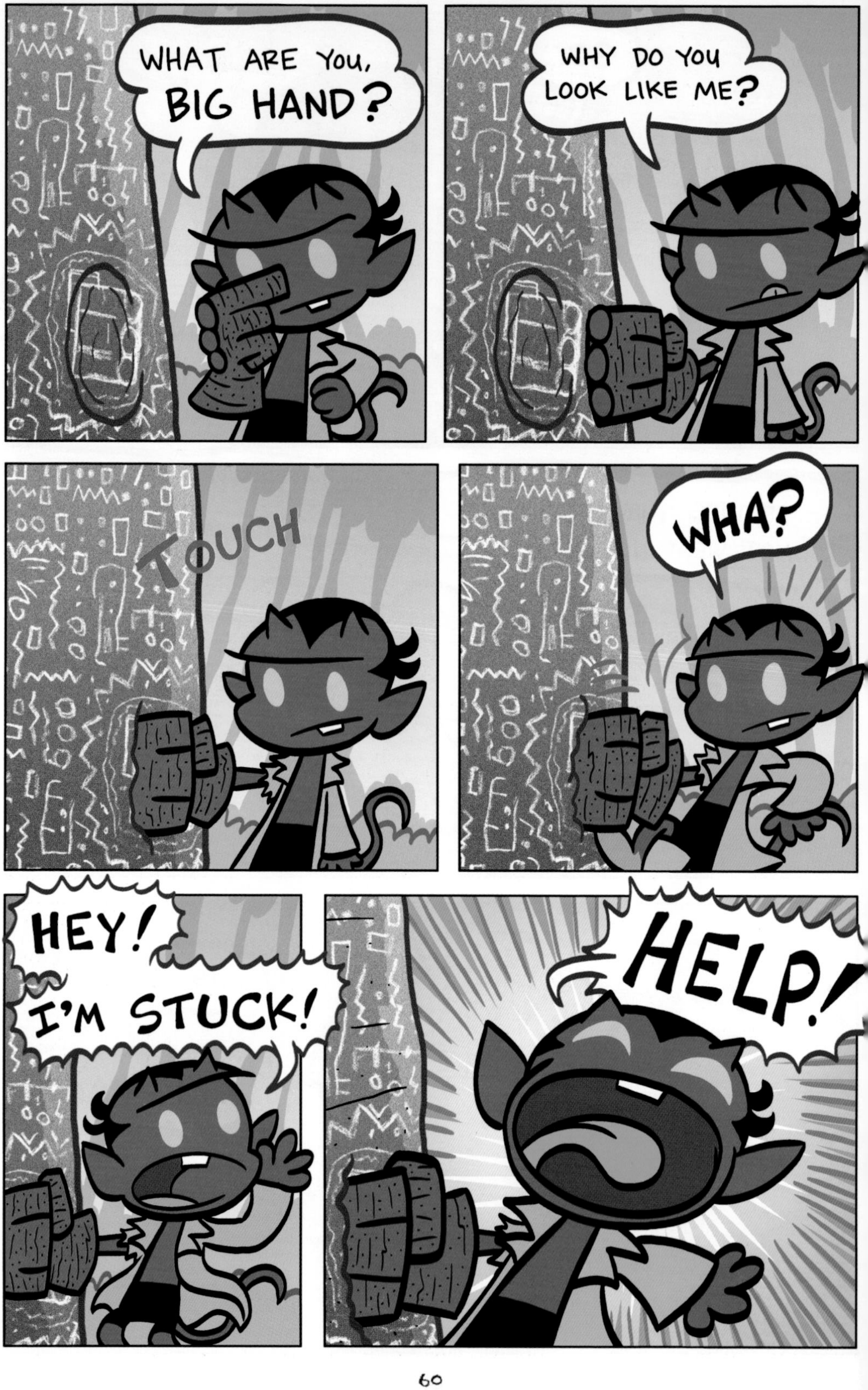
WHAT ARE YOU, BIG HAND?
WHY DO YOU LOOK LIKE ME?
TOUCH
WHA?
HEY! I'M STUCK!
HELP!

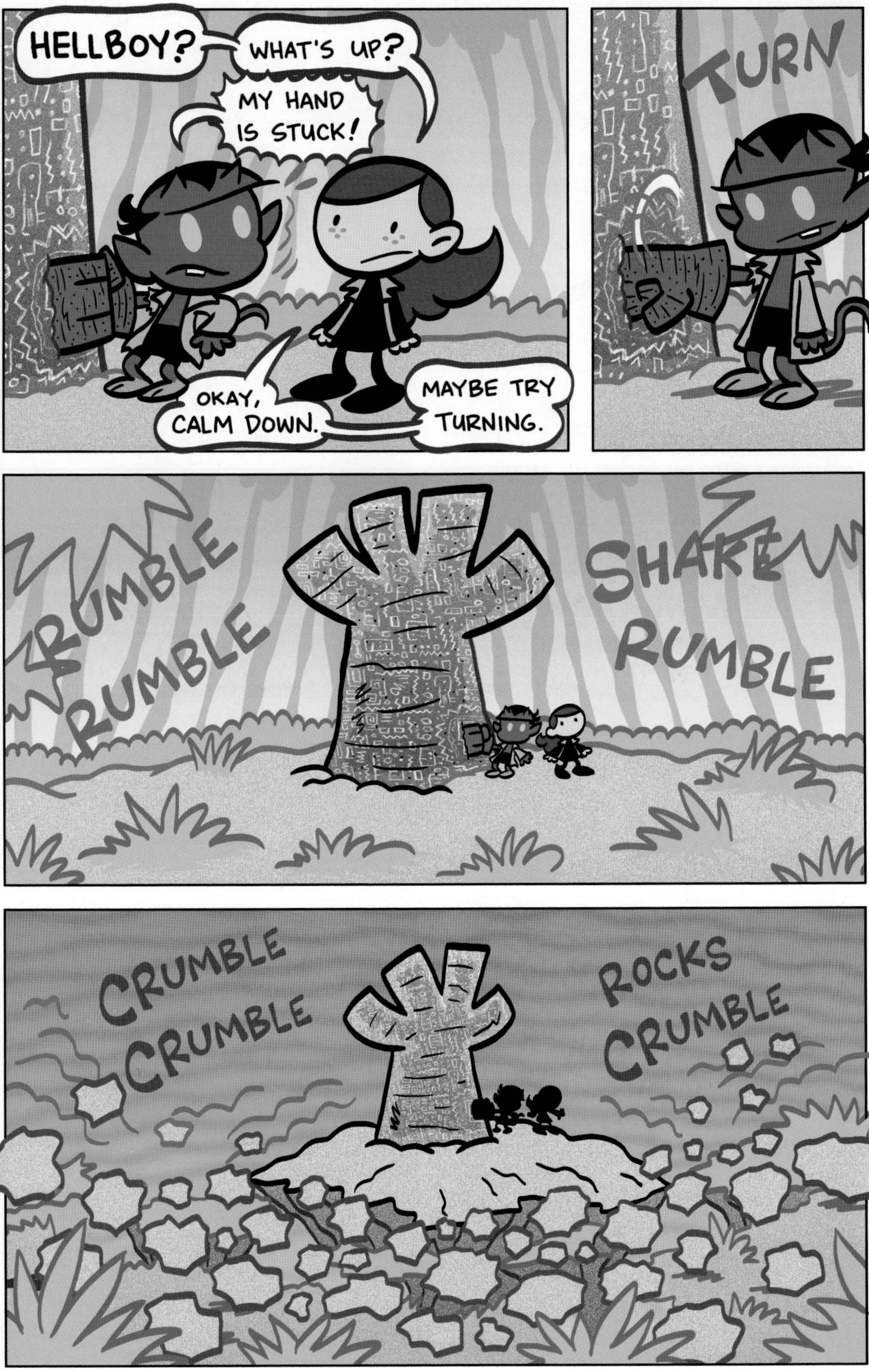
HELLBOY?
WHAT'S UP?
MY HAND IS STUCK!
OKAY, CALM DOWN.
MAYBE TRY TURNING.
TURN
RUMBLE
RUMBLE
SHAKE
RUMBLE
CRUMBLE
CRUMBLE
ROCKS
CRUMBLE

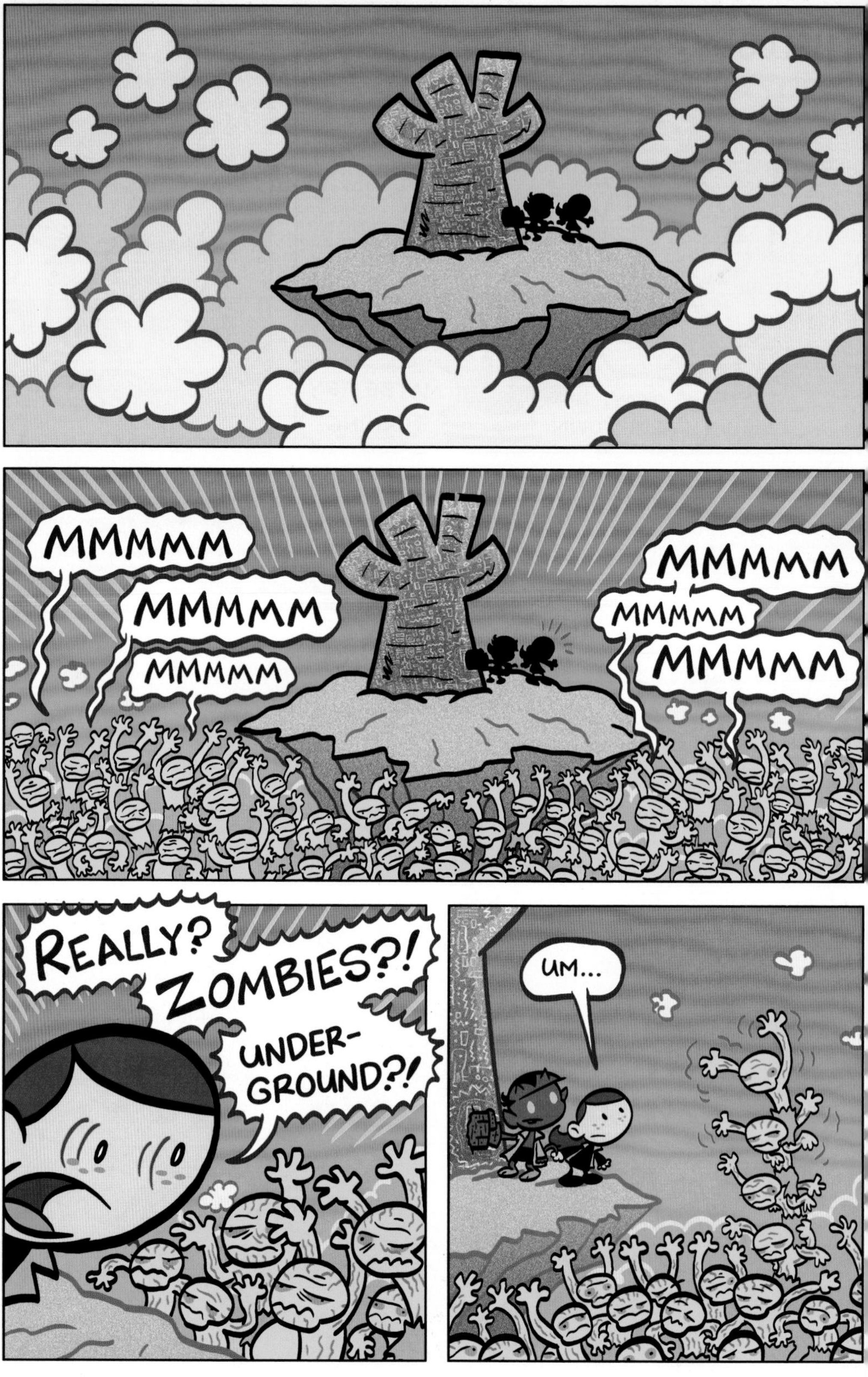
MMMMM
MMMMM
MMMMM
MMMMM
MMMMM
MMMMM
REALLY?
ZOMBIES?!
UNDER-
GROUND?!
UM...

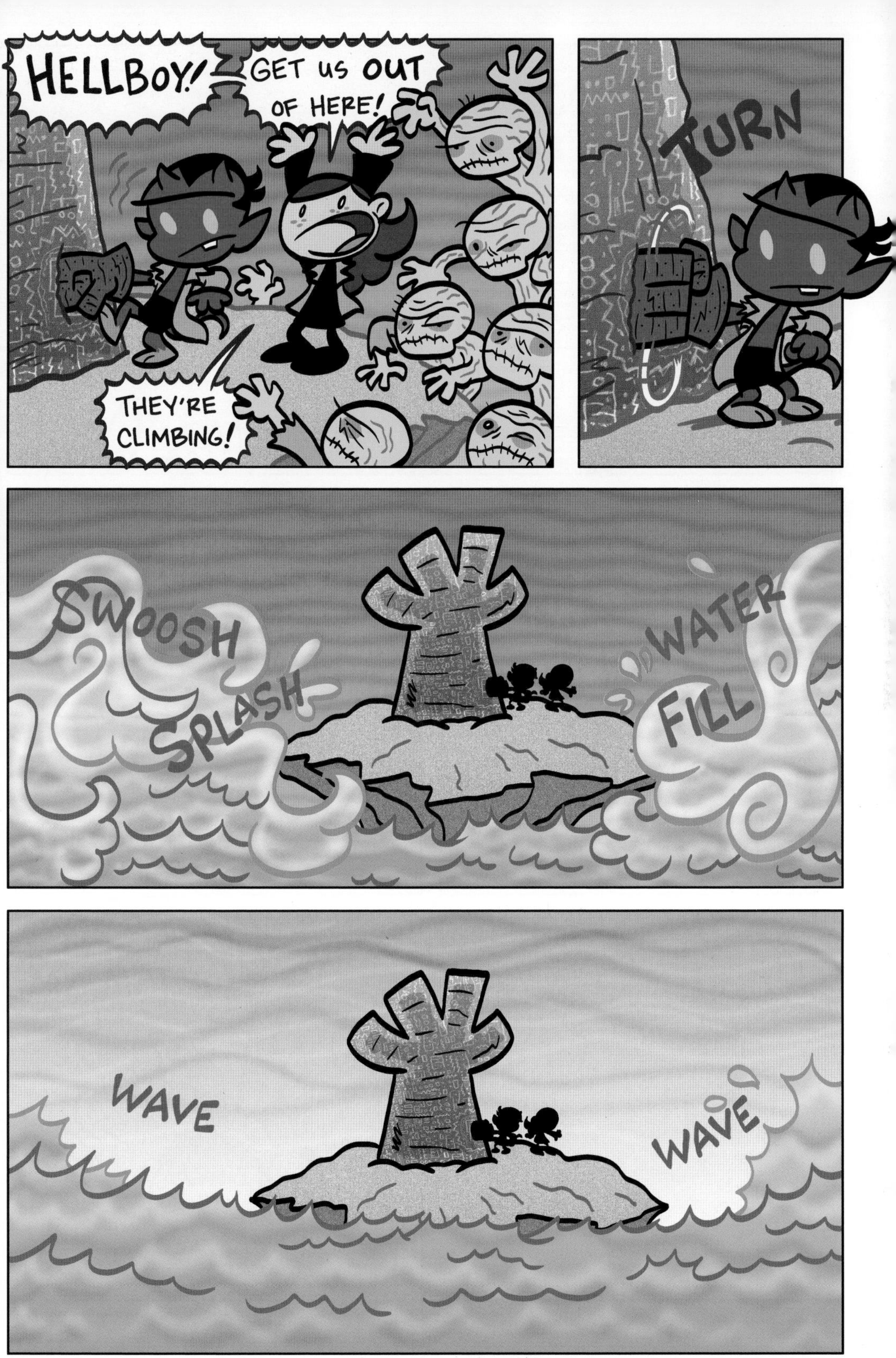
HELLBOY!
GET US OUT OF HERE!
THEY'RE CLIMBING!
TURN
SWOOSH
SPLASH
WATER
FILL
WAVE
WAVE

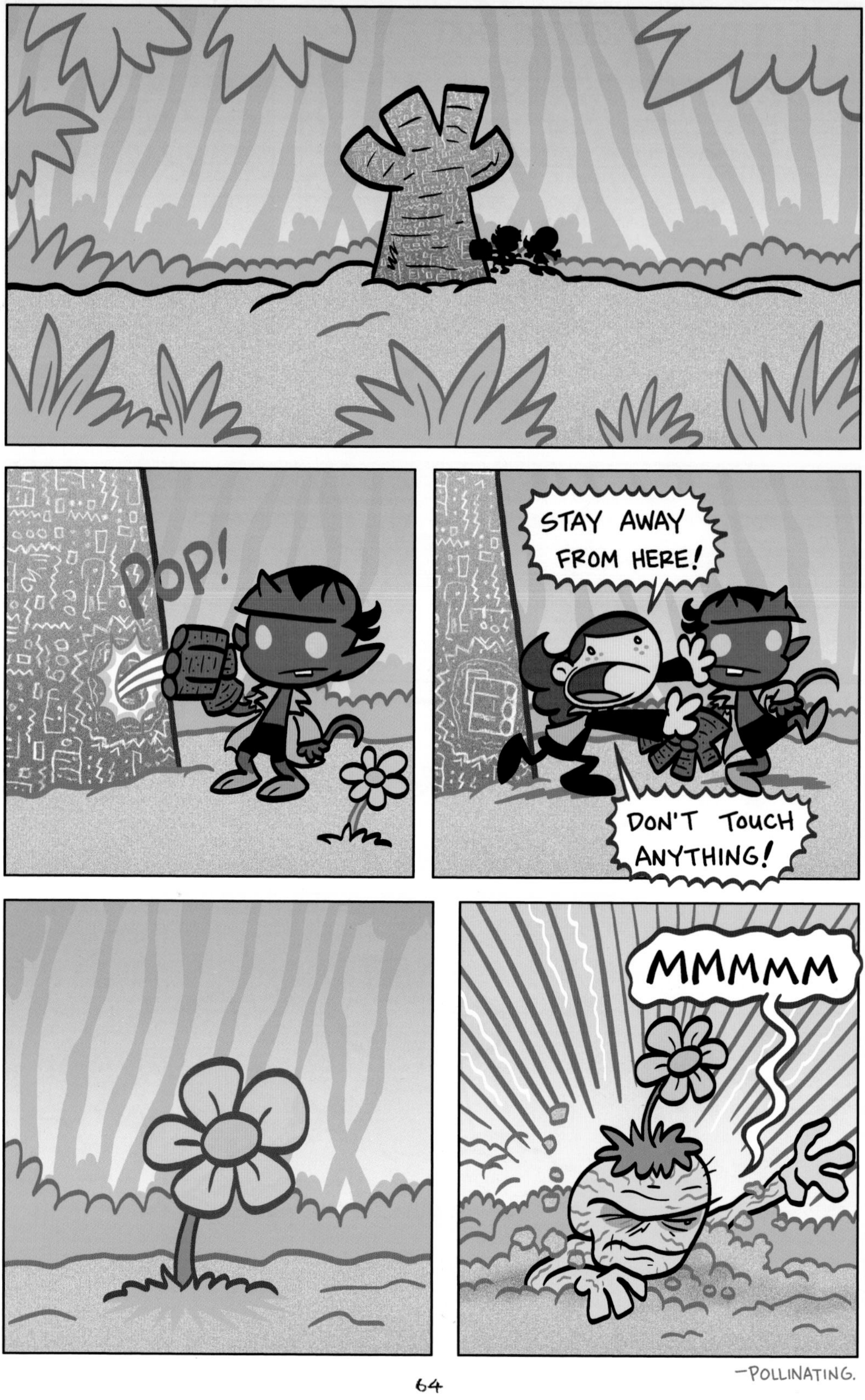
POP!
STAY AWAY FROM HERE!
DON'T TOUCH ANYTHING!
MMMMM
—POLLINATING.

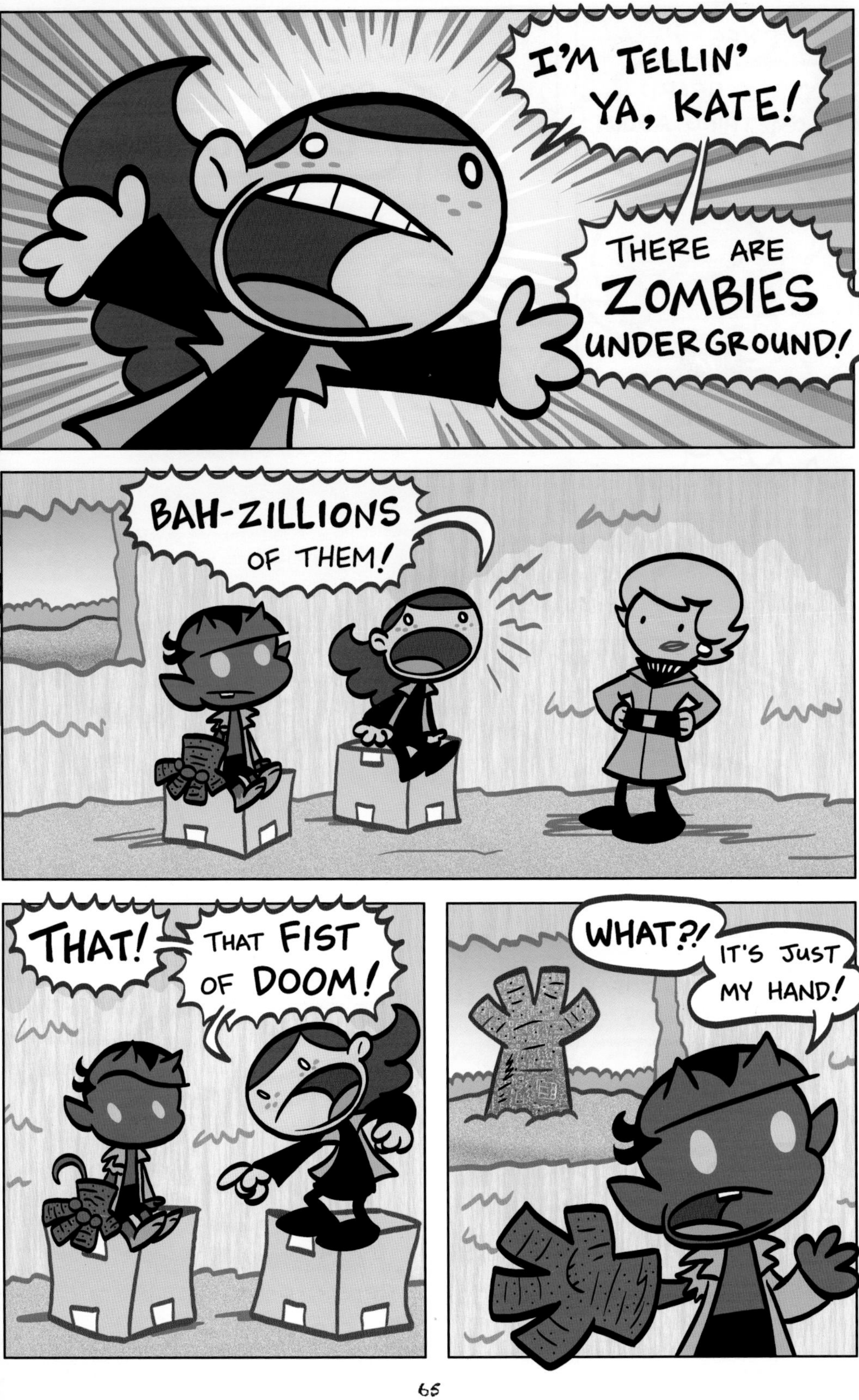
I'M TELLIN' YA, KATE!
THERE ARE ZOMBIES UNDERGROUND!
BAH-ZILLIONS OF THEM!
THAT!
THAT FIST OF DOOM!
WHAT?!
IT'S JUST MY HAND!

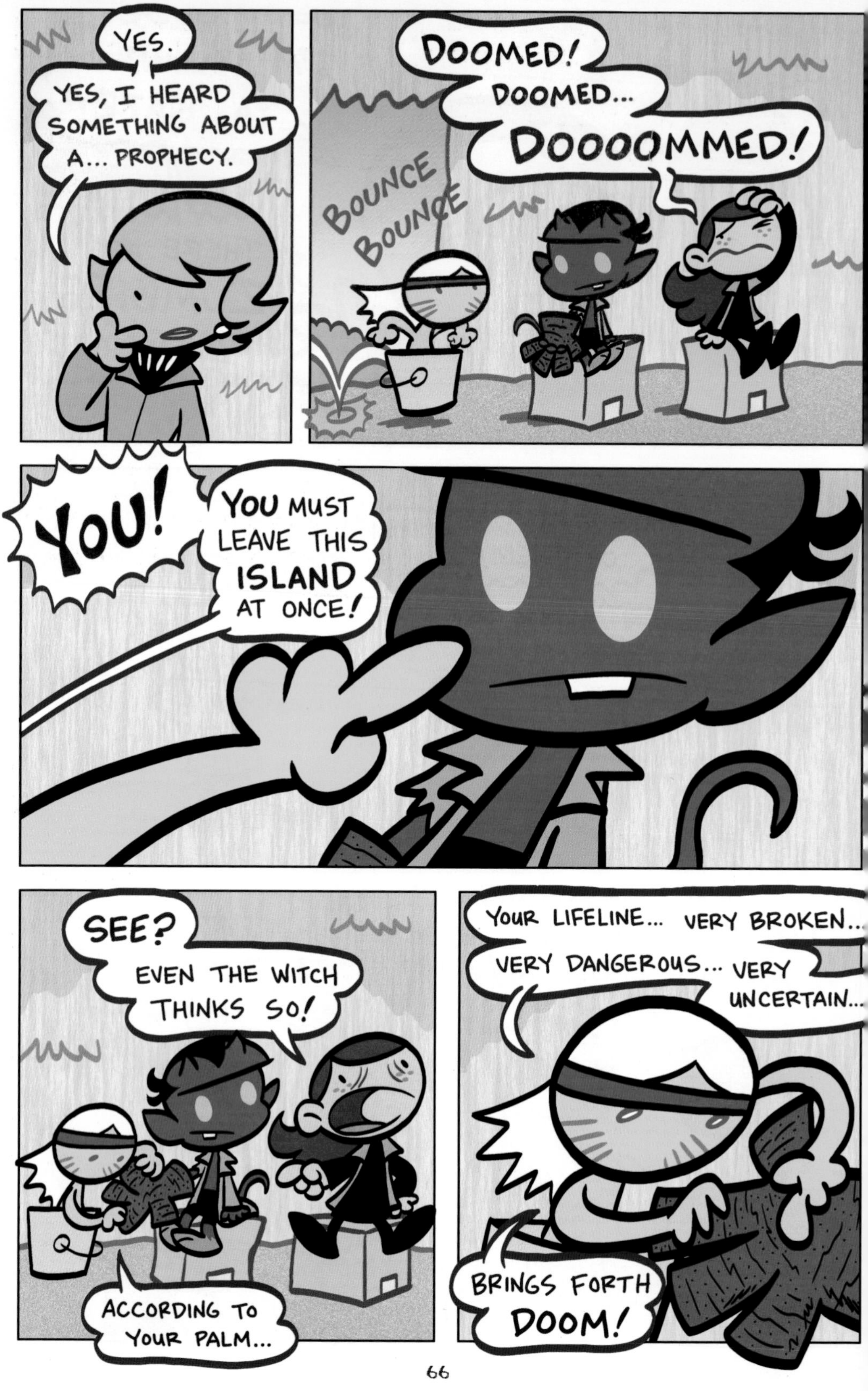
YES.
YES, I HEARD SOMETHING ABOUT A... PROPHECY.
DOOMED!
DOOMED...
DOOOOMMED!
BOUNCE BOUNCE
YOU!
YOU MUST LEAVE THIS ISLAND AT ONCE!
SEE?
EVEN THE WITCH THINKS SO!
ACCORDING TO YOUR PALM...
YOUR LIFELINE... VERY BROKEN...
VERY DANGEROUS... VERY UNCERTAIN...
BRINGS FORTH DOOM!

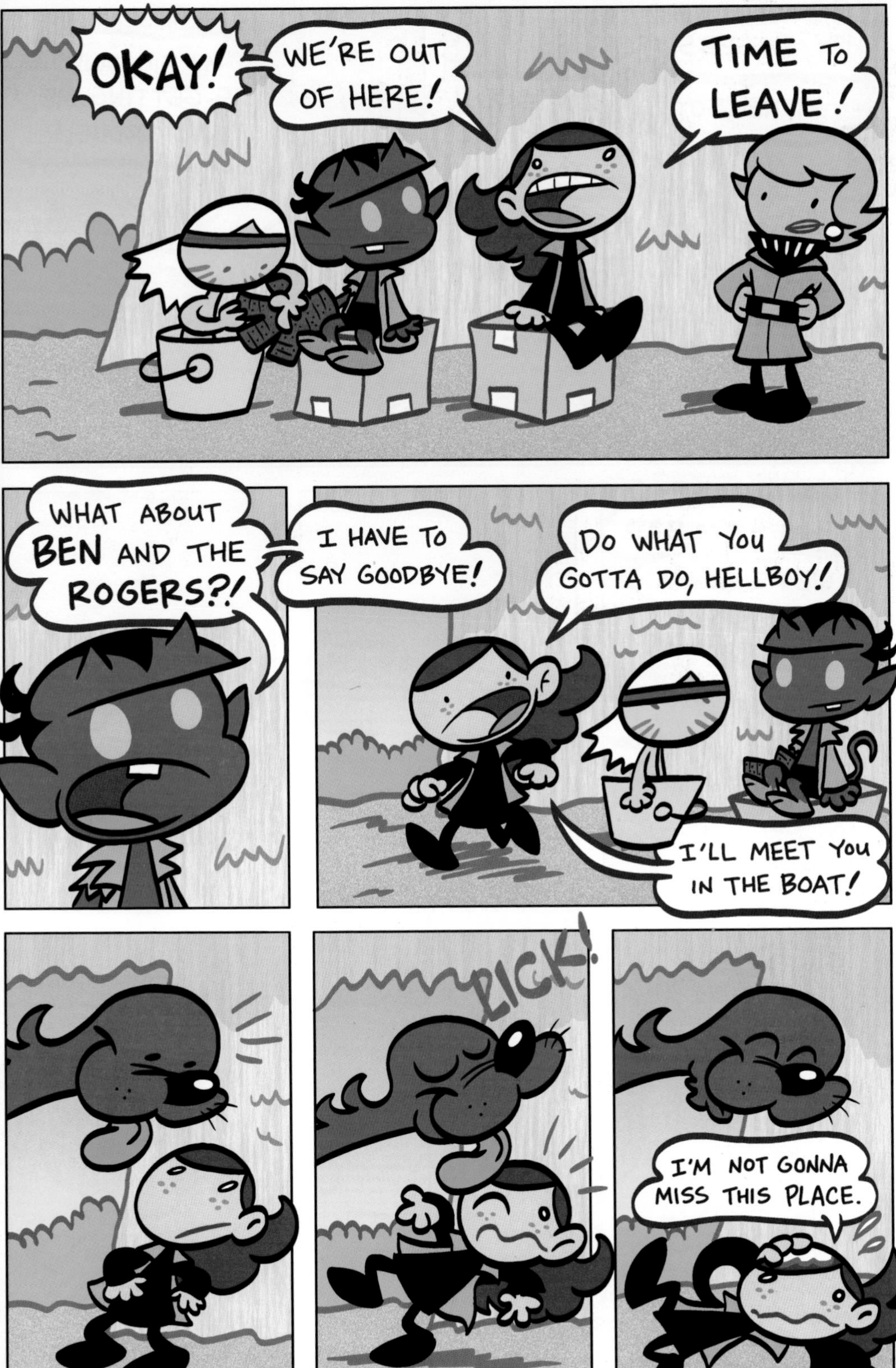
OKAY!
WE'RE OUT OF HERE!
TIME TO LEAVE!
WHAT ABOUT BEN AND THE ROGERS?!
I HAVE TO SAY GOODBYE!
DO WHAT YOU GOTTA DO, HELLBOY!
I'LL MEET YOU IN THE BOAT!
LICK!
I'M NOT GONNA MISS THIS PLACE.
-PETS!

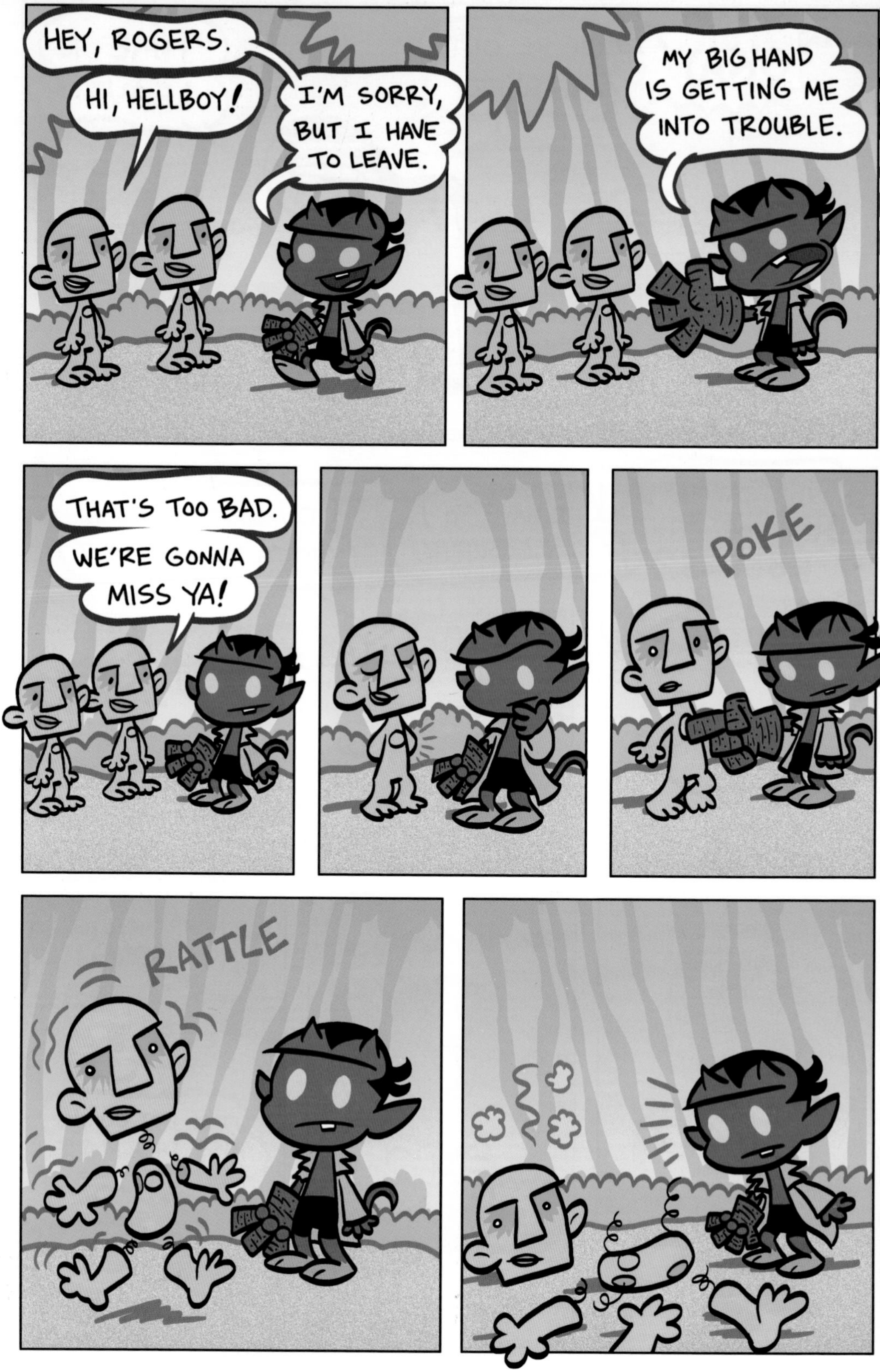
HEY, ROGERS.
HI, HELLBOY!
I'M SORRY, BUT I HAVE TO LEAVE.
MY BIG HAND IS GETTING ME INTO TROUBLE.
THAT'S TOO BAD.
WE'RE GONNA MISS YA!
POKE
RATTLE

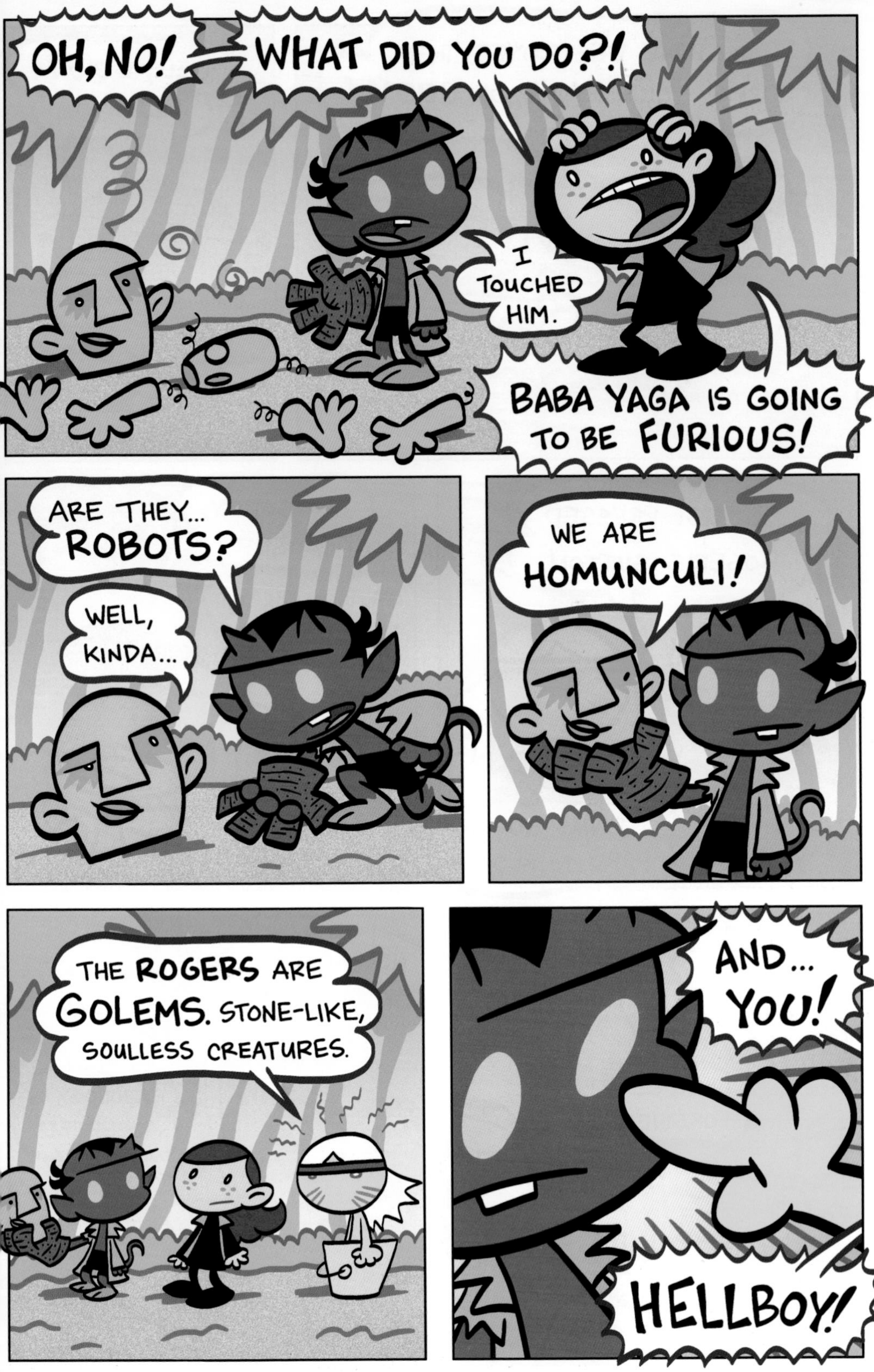
OH, NO!
WHAT DID YOU DO?!
I TOUCHED HIM.
BABA YAGA IS GOING TO BE FURIOUS!
ARE THEY... ROBOTS?
WELL, KINDA...
WE ARE HOMUNCULI!
THE ROGERS ARE GOLEMS. STONE-LIKE, SOULLESS CREATURES.
AND... YOU!
HELLBOY!

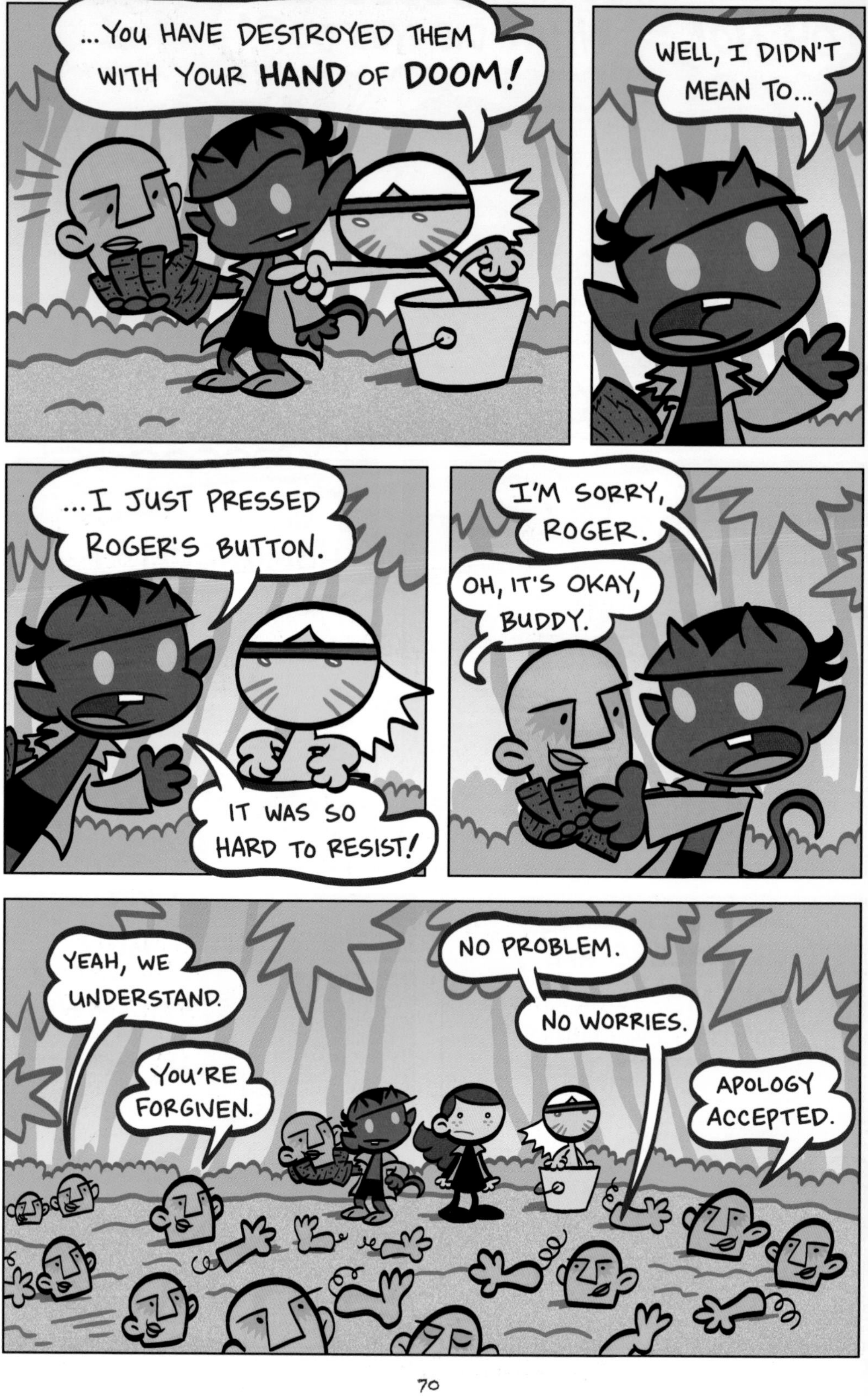
...YOU HAVE DESTROYED THEM WITH YOUR HAND OF DOOM!
WELL, I DIDN'T MEAN TO...
...I JUST PRESSED ROGER'S BUTTON.
IT WAS SO HARD TO RESIST!
I'M SORRY, ROGER.
OH, IT'S OKAY, BUDDY.
YEAH, WE UNDERSTAND.
YOU'RE FORGIVEN.
NO PROBLEM.
NO WORRIES.
APOLOGY ACCEPTED.

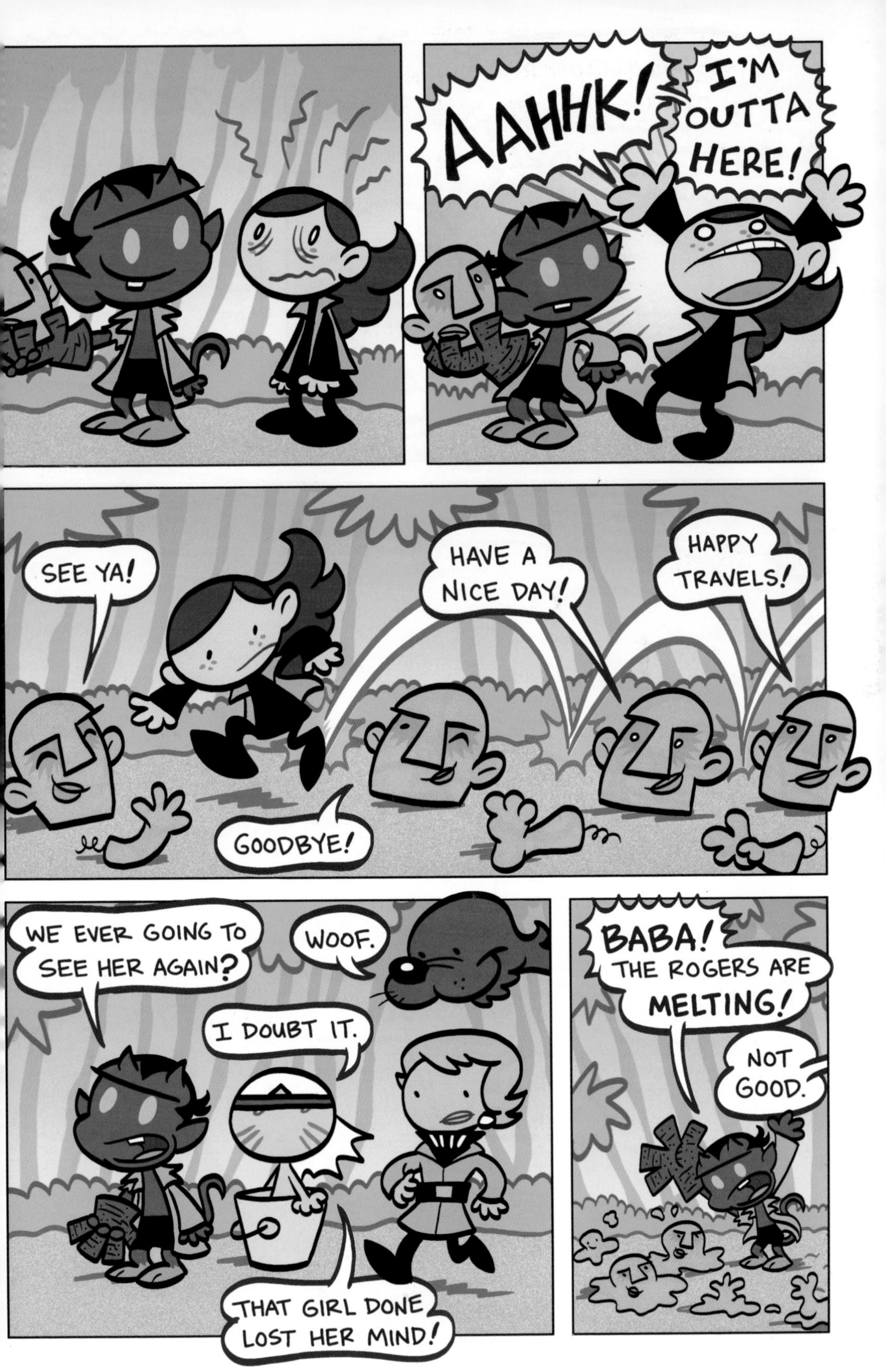
AAHHK!
I'M OUTTA HERE!
SEE YA!
GOODBYE!
HAVE A NICE DAY!
HAPPY TRAVELS!
WE EVER GOING TO SEE HER AGAIN?
WOOF.
I DOUBT IT.
THAT GIRL DONE LOST HER MIND!
BABA! THE ROGERS ARE MELTING!
NOT GOOD.

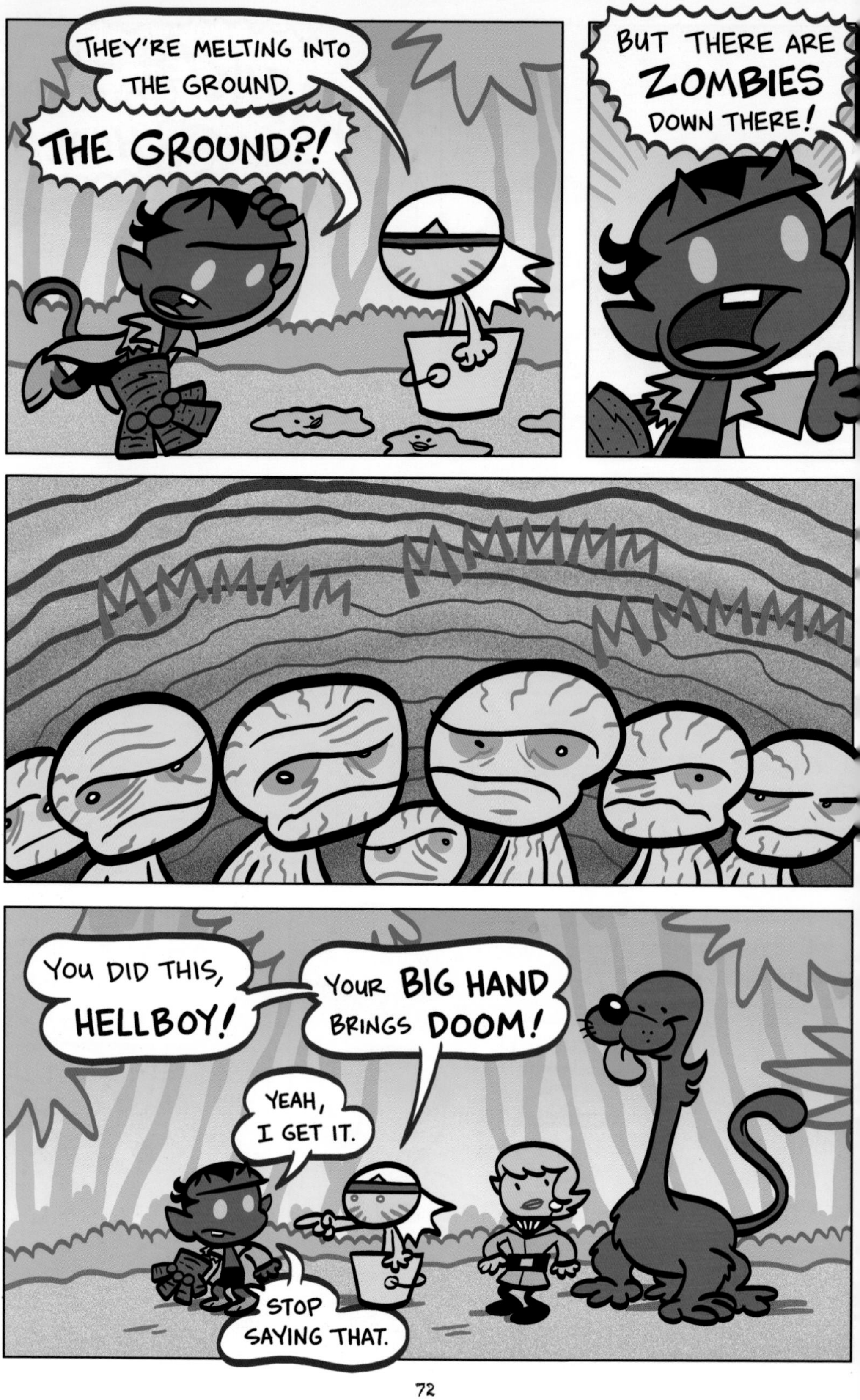
THEY'RE MELTING INTO THE GROUND.
THE GROUND?!
BUT THERE ARE ZOMBIES DOWN THERE!
MMMMMM
MMMMMMM
MMMMMMM
YOU DID THIS, HELLBOY!
YOUR BIG HAND BRINGS DOOM!
YEAH, I GET IT.
STOP SAYING THAT.

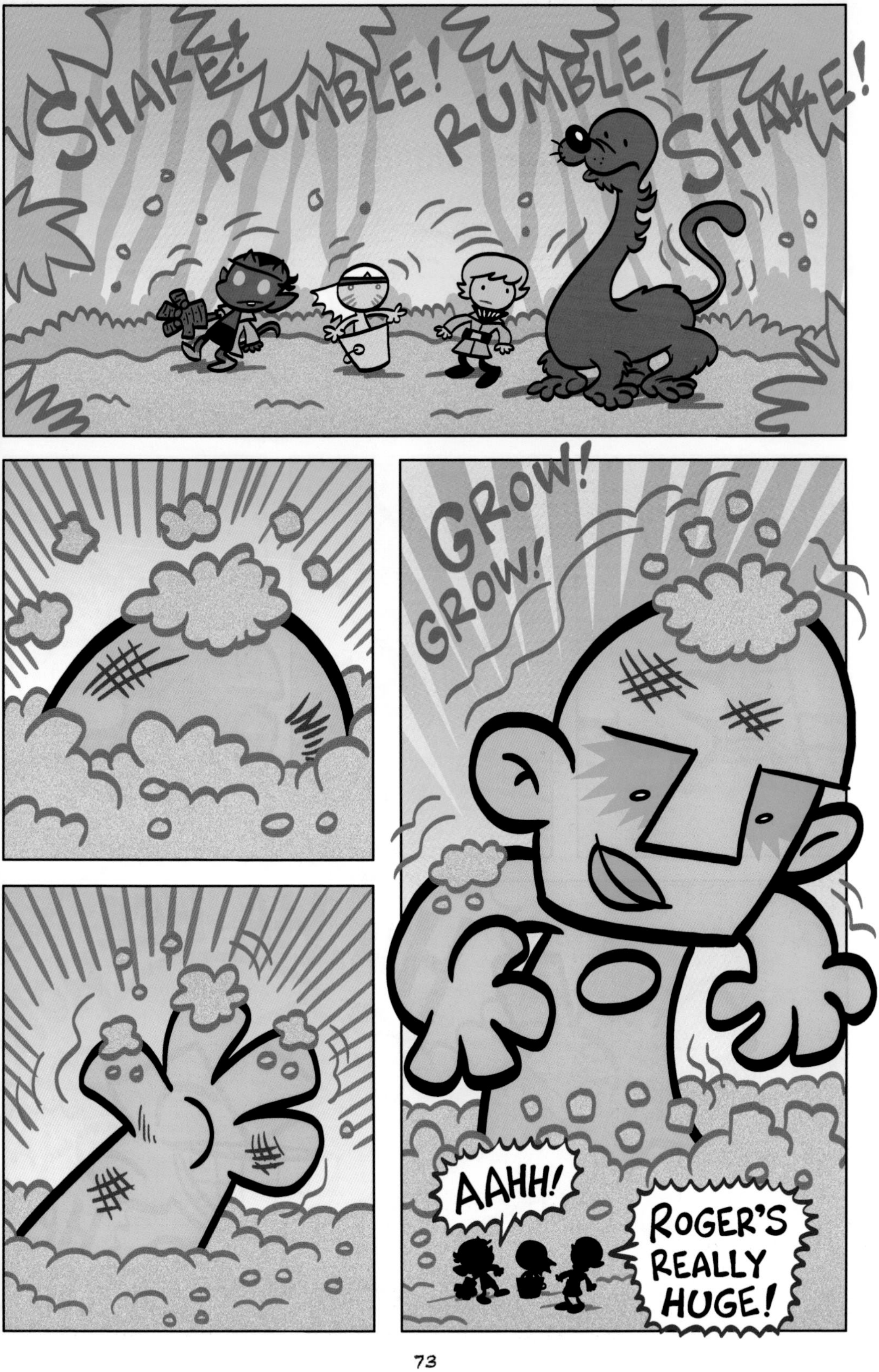
SHAKE!
RUMBLE!
RUMBLE!
SHAKE!
GROW!
GROW!
AAHH!
ROGER'S REALLY HUGE!

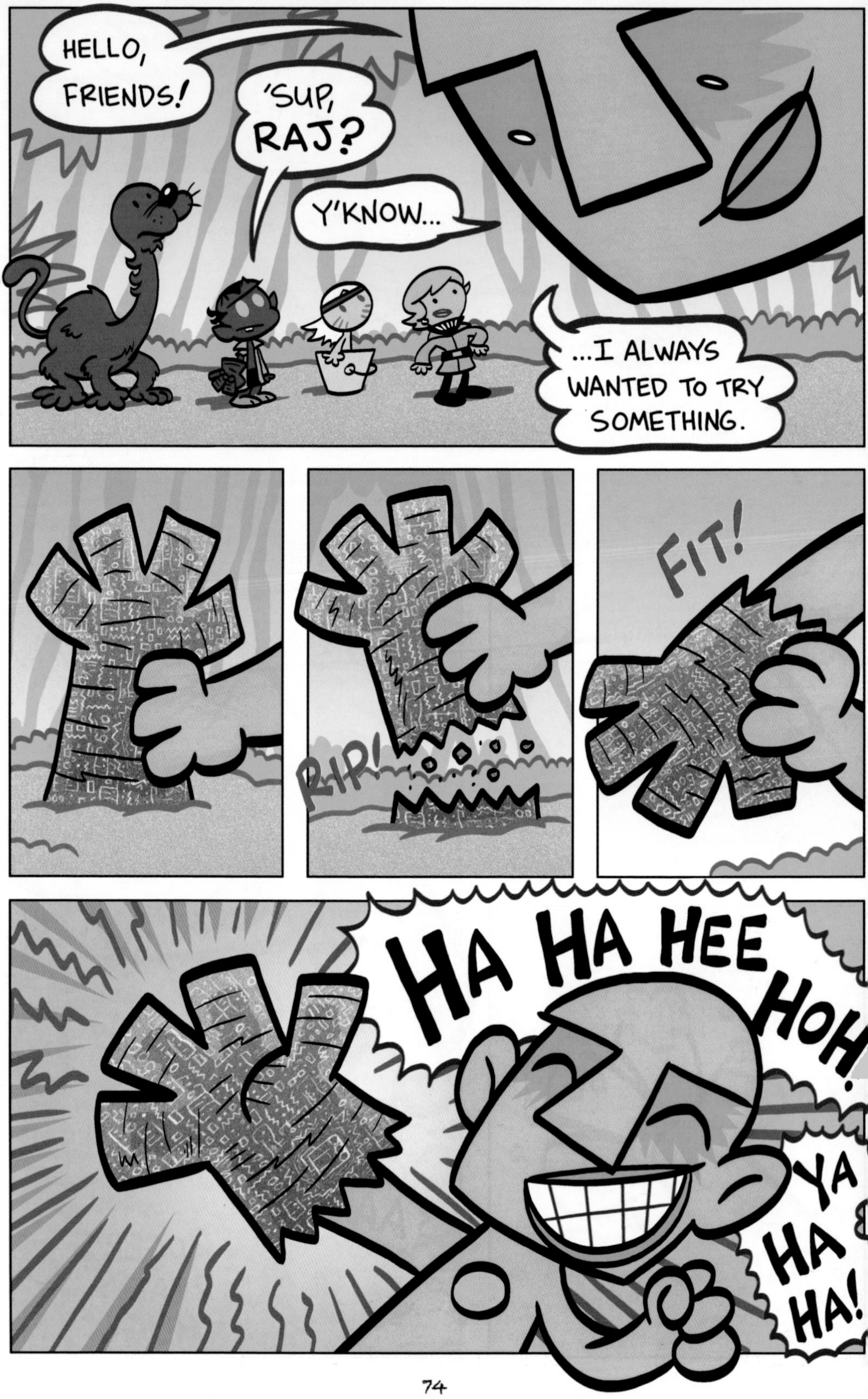
HELLO, FRIENDS!
'SUP, RAJ?
Y'KNOW...
...I ALWAYS WANTED TO TRY SOMETHING.
RIP!
FIT!
HA HA HEE HOH!
YA HA HA HA!

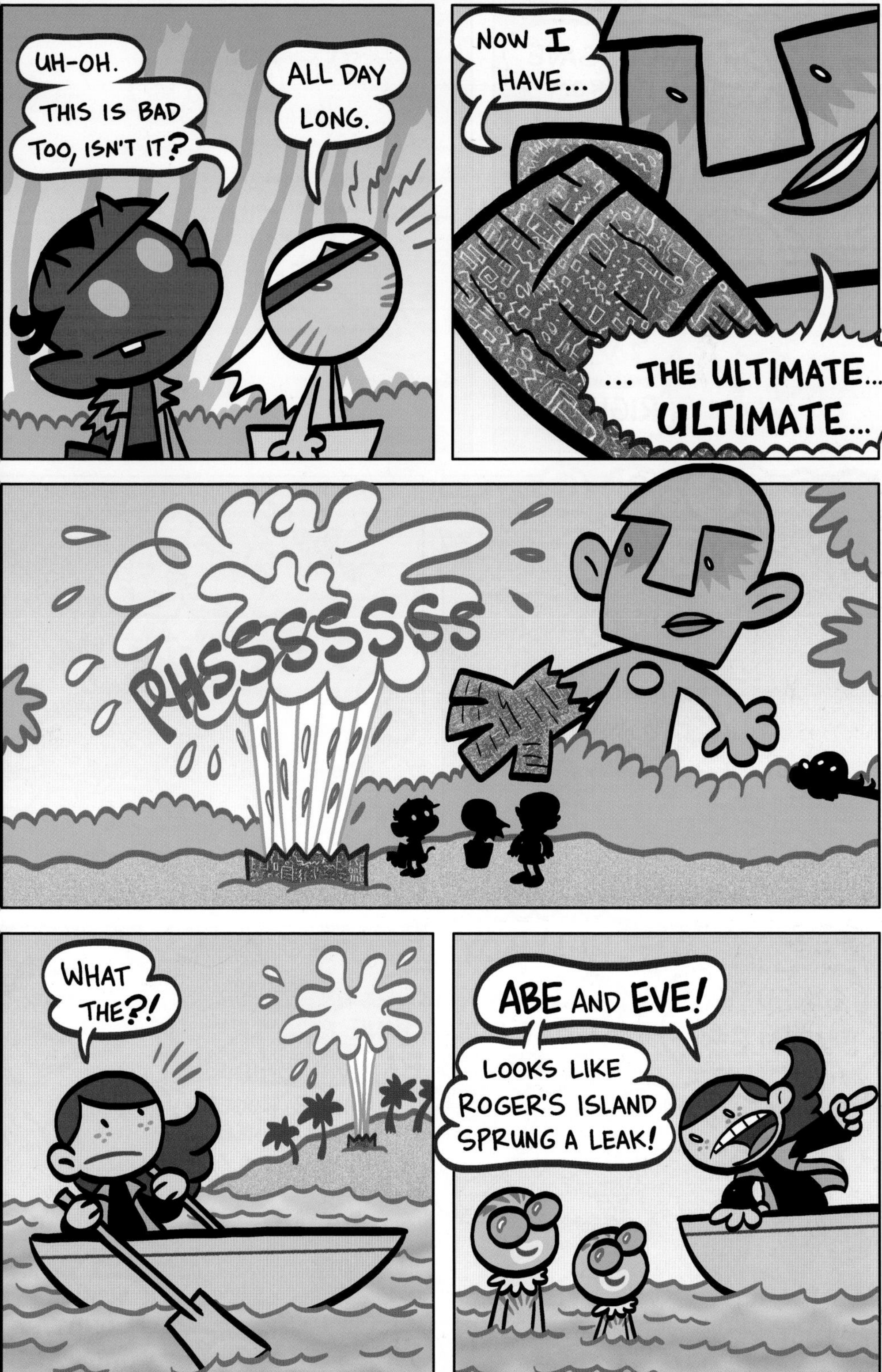
UH-OH.
THIS IS BAD TOO, ISN'T IT?
ALL DAY LONG.
NOW I HAVE...
...THE ULTIMATE... ULTIMATE...
PHSSSSSSS
WHAT THE?!
ABE AND EVE!
LOOKS LIKE ROGER'S ISLAND SPRUNG A LEAK!

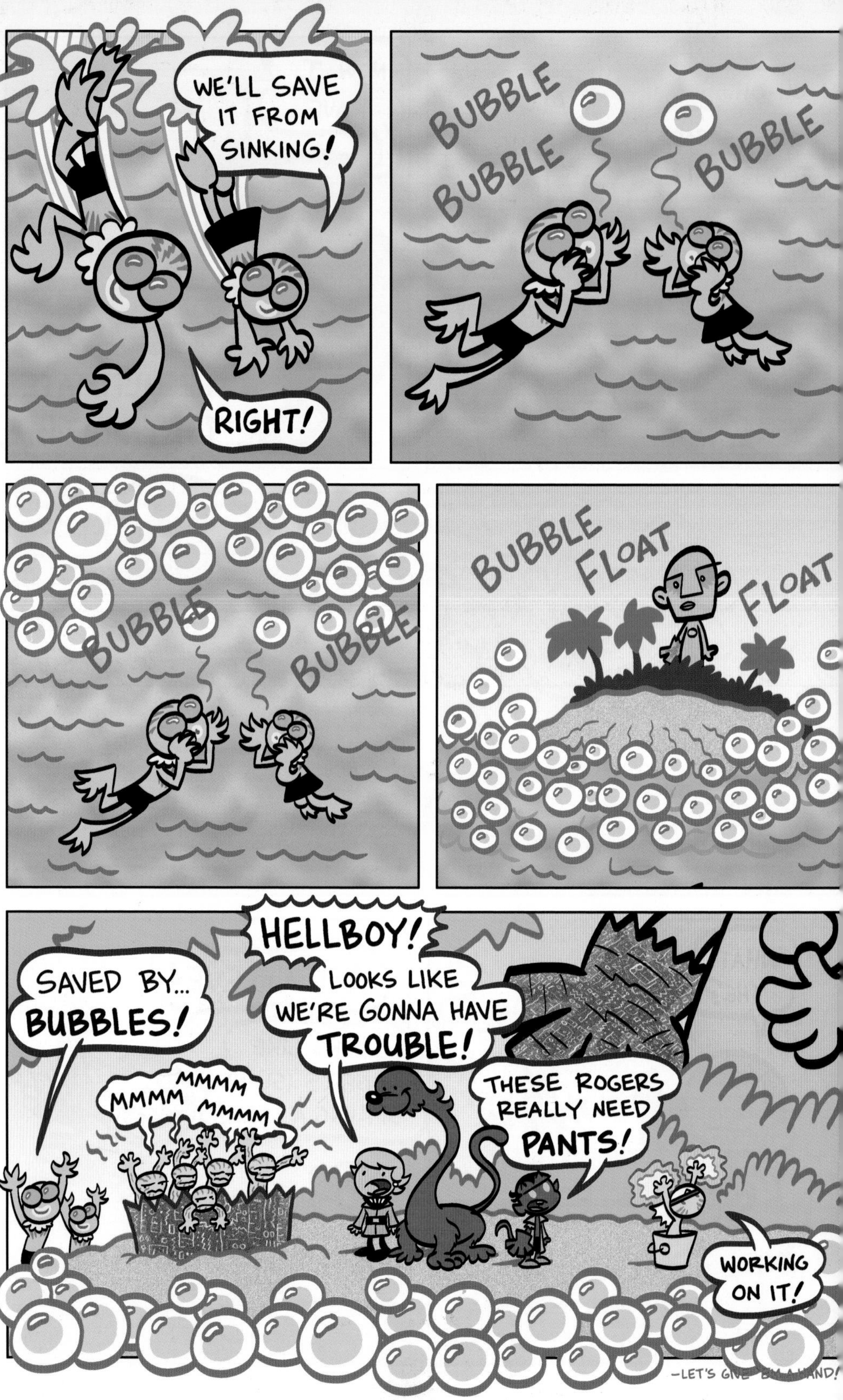
WE'LL SAVE IT FROM SINKING!
RIGHT!
BUBBLE
BUBBLE
BUBBLE
BUBBLE
BUBBLE
BUBBLE
FLOAT
FLOAT
SAVED BY... BUBBLES!
MMMM MMMM MMMM MMMM
HELLBOY!
LOOKS LIKE WE'RE GONNA HAVE TROUBLE!
THESE ROGERS REALLY NEED PANTS!
WORKING ON IT!

—LET'S GIVE 'EM A HAND!

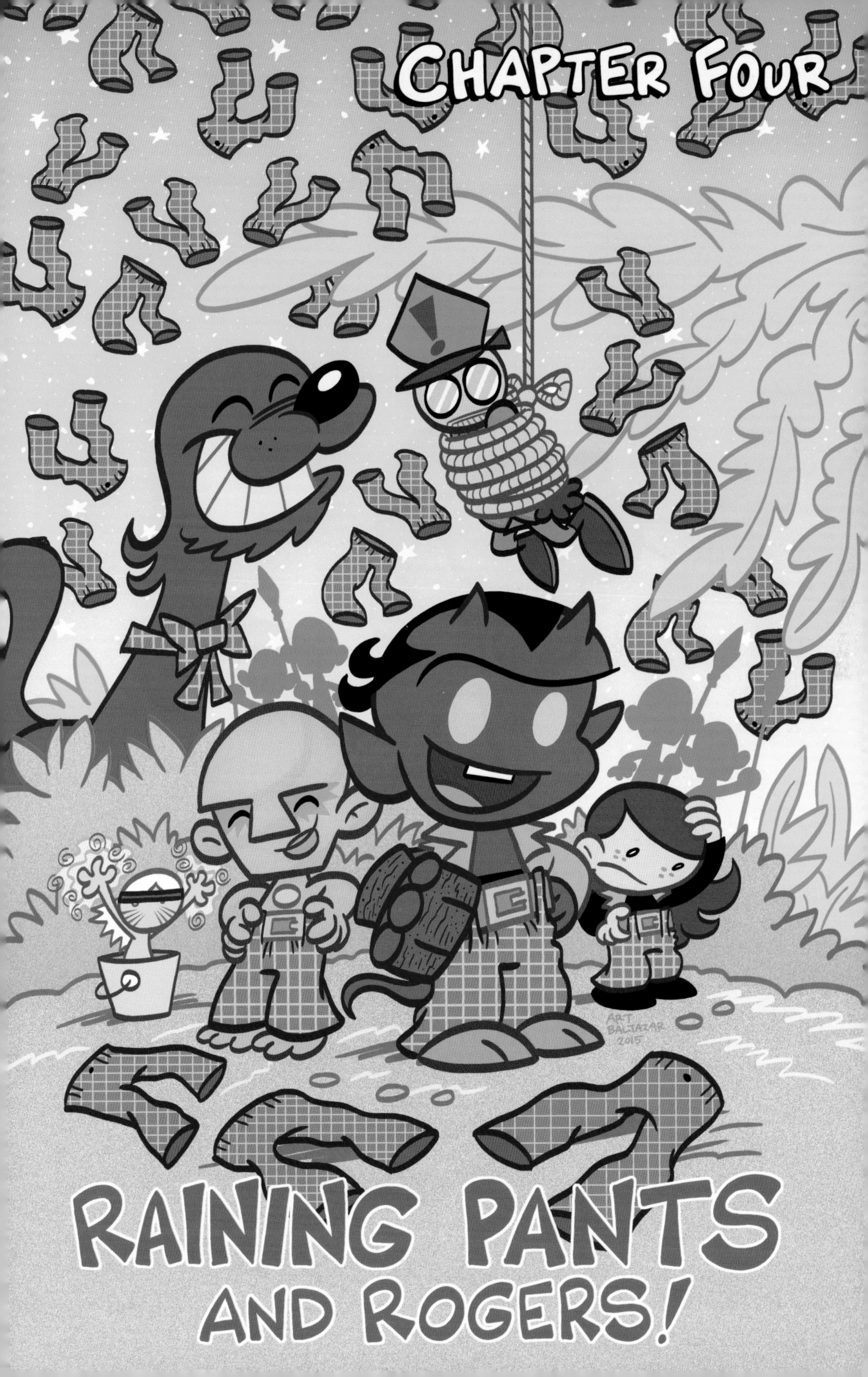
CHAPTER FOUR
RAINING PANTS
AND ROGERS!
ART BALTAZAR 2015

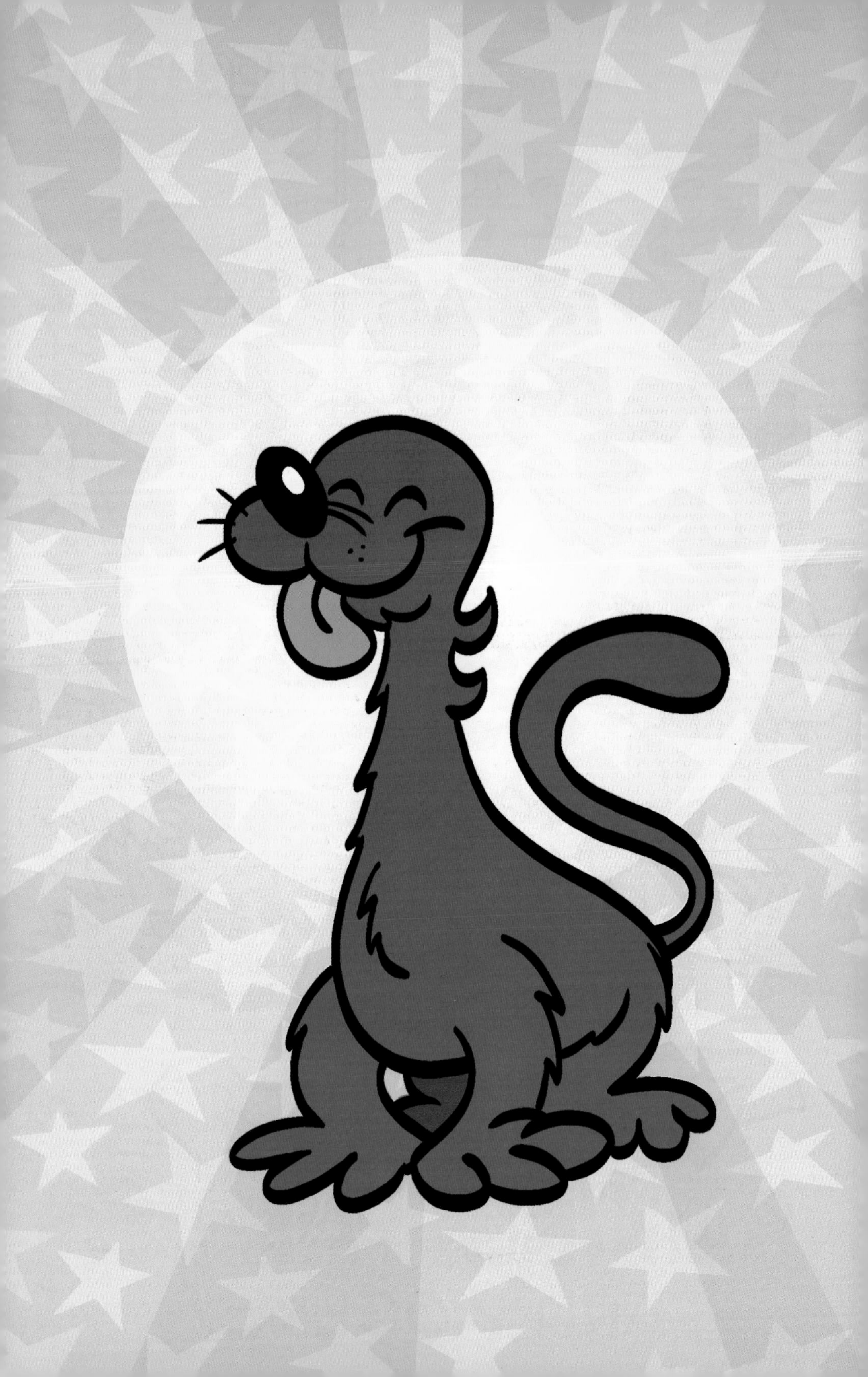

DARK HORSE COMICS PROUDLY PRESENTS...

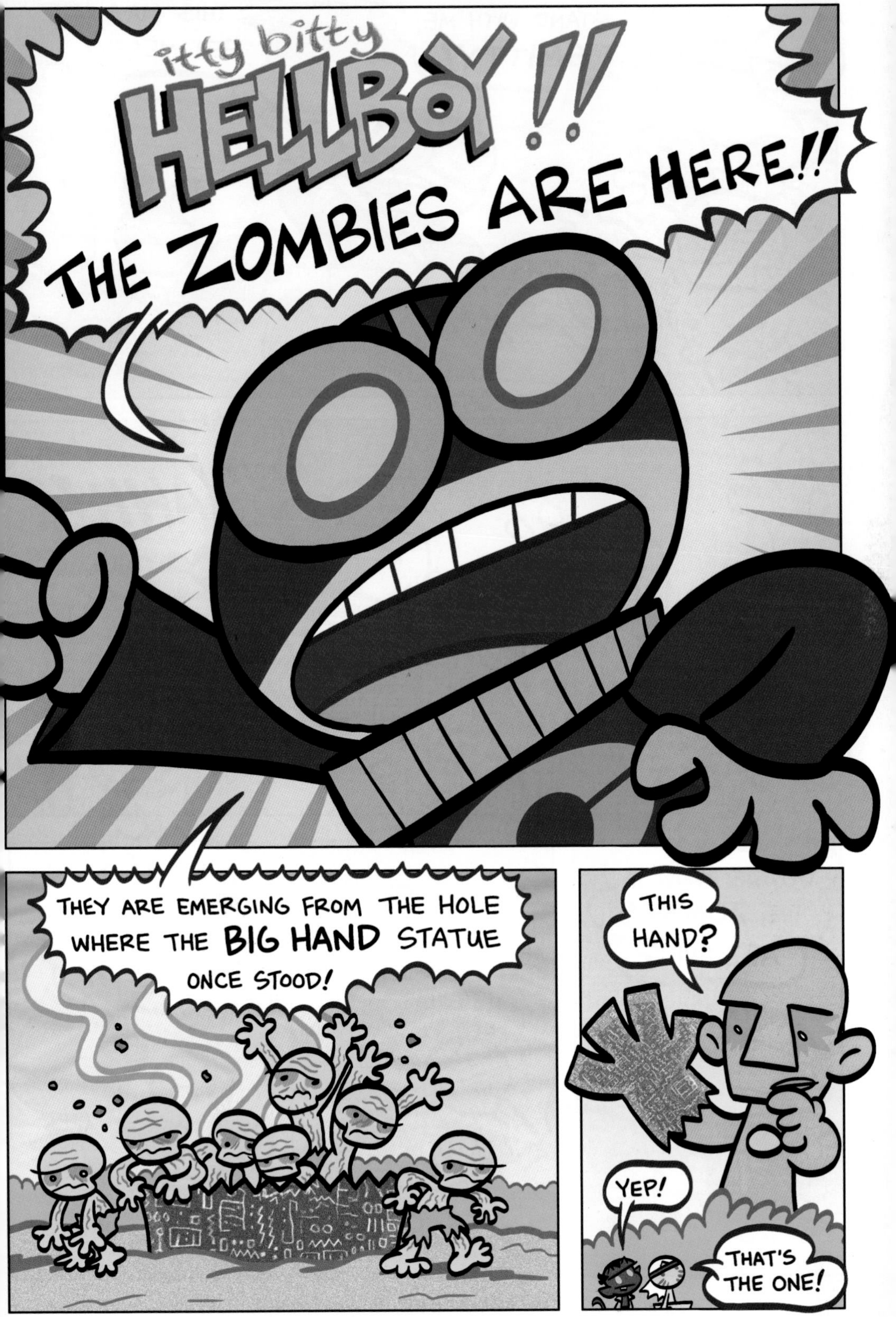
itty bitty
HELLBOY!!
THE ZOMBIES ARE HERE!!
THEY ARE EMERGING FROM THE HOLE WHERE THE BIG HAND STATUE ONCE STOOD!
THIS HAND?
YEP!
THAT'S THE ONE!

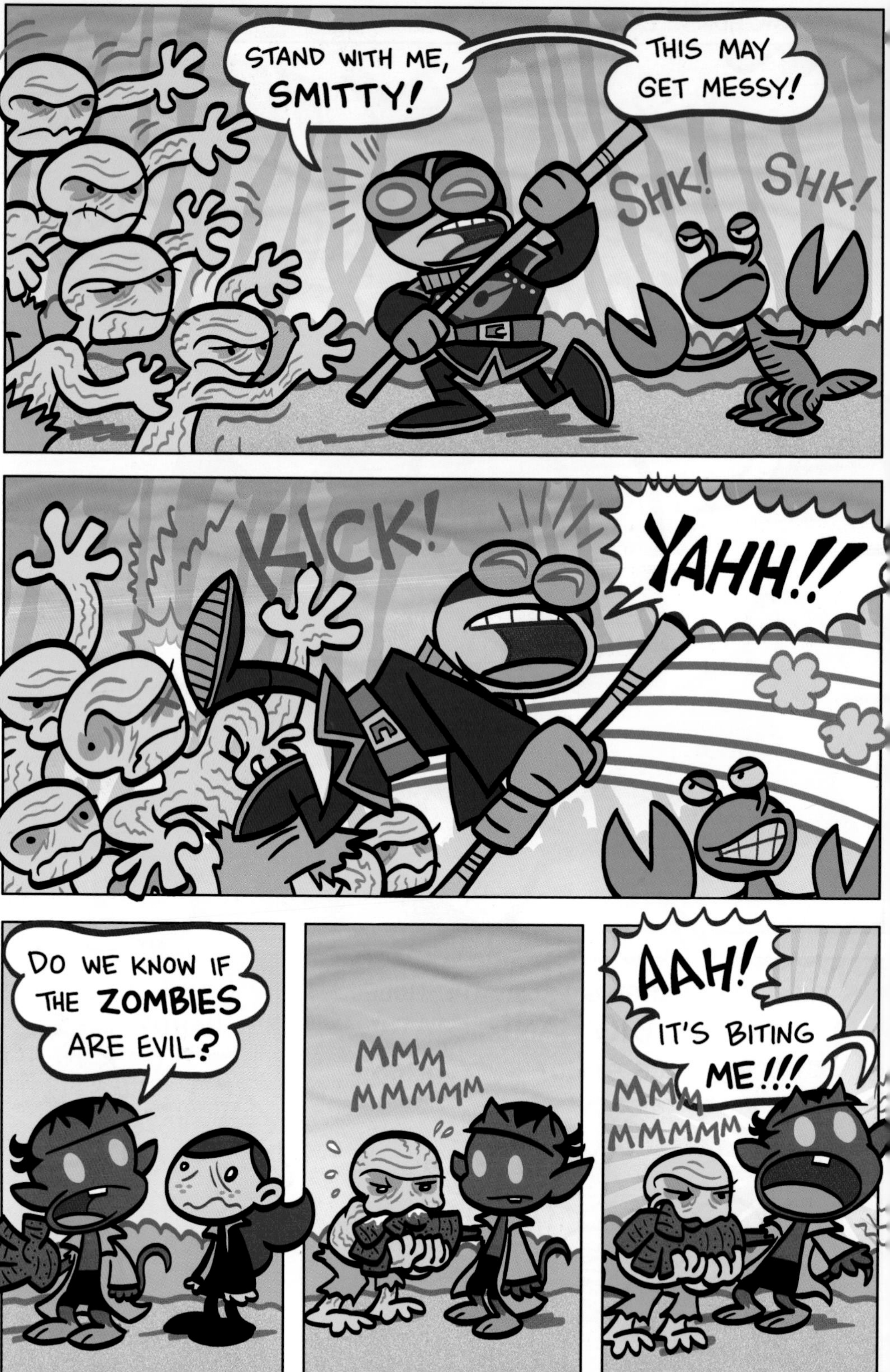
STAND WITH ME, SMITTY!
THIS MAY GET MESSY!
SHK! SHK!
KICK!
YAHH!!
DO WE KNOW IF THE ZOMBIES ARE EVIL?
MMM MMMMM
AAH!
IT'S BITING ME!!!
MMM MMMMM

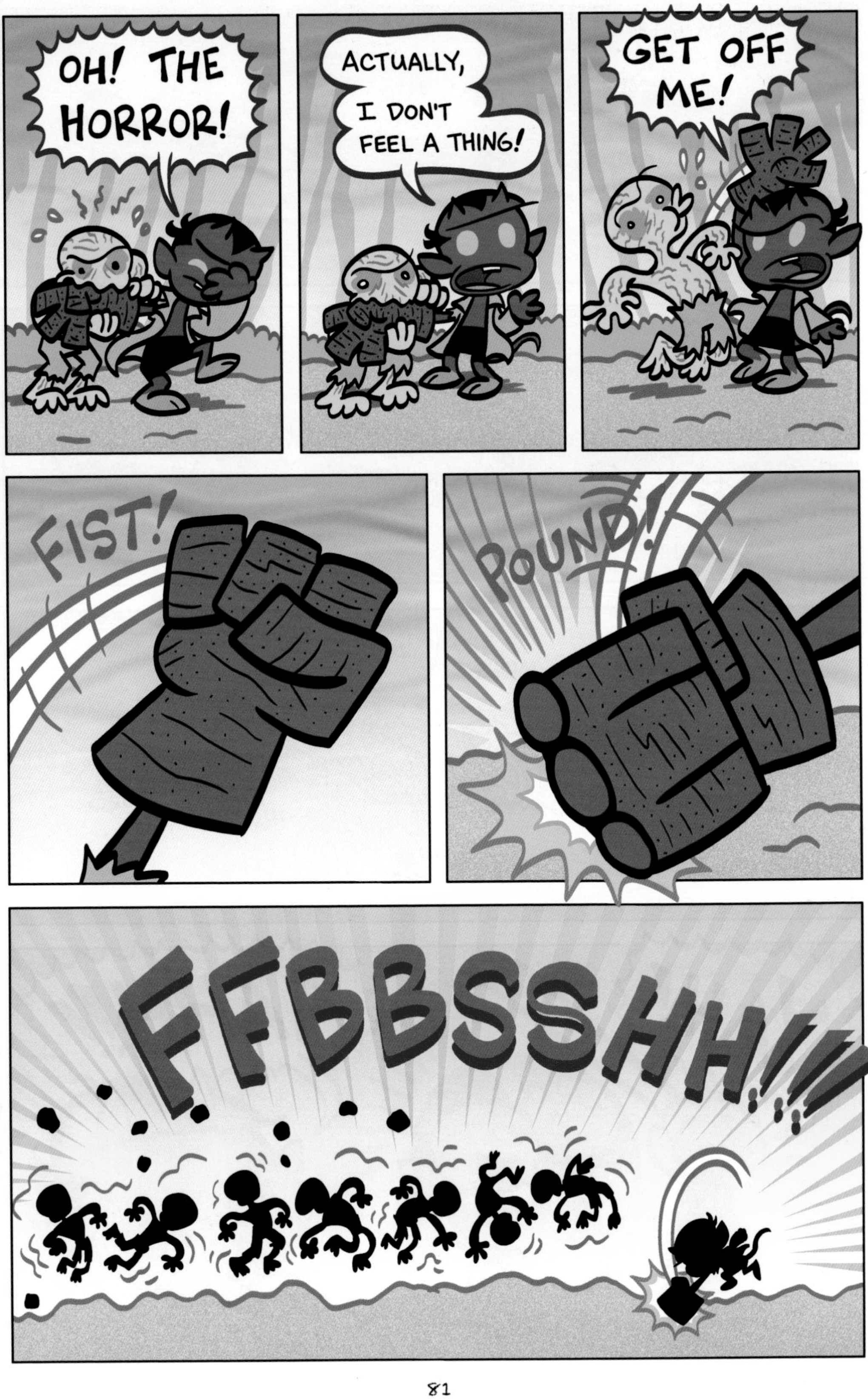
OH! THE HORROR!
ACTUALLY, I DON'T FEEL A THING!
GET OFF ME!
FIST!
POUND!
FFBBSSHH!!!

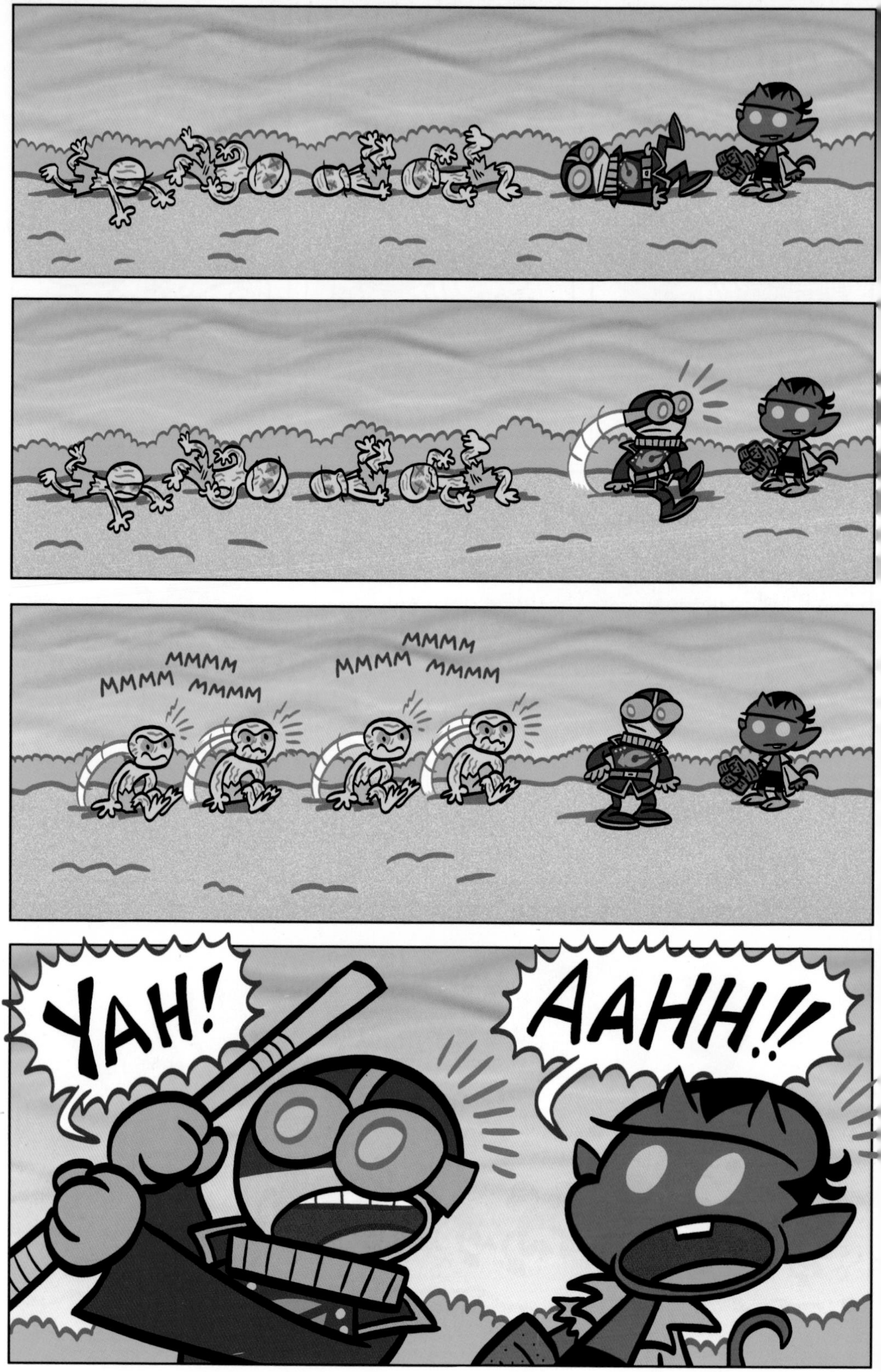
MMMM
MMMM
MMMM
MMMM
MMMM
MMMM
MMMM
YAH!
AAHH!!

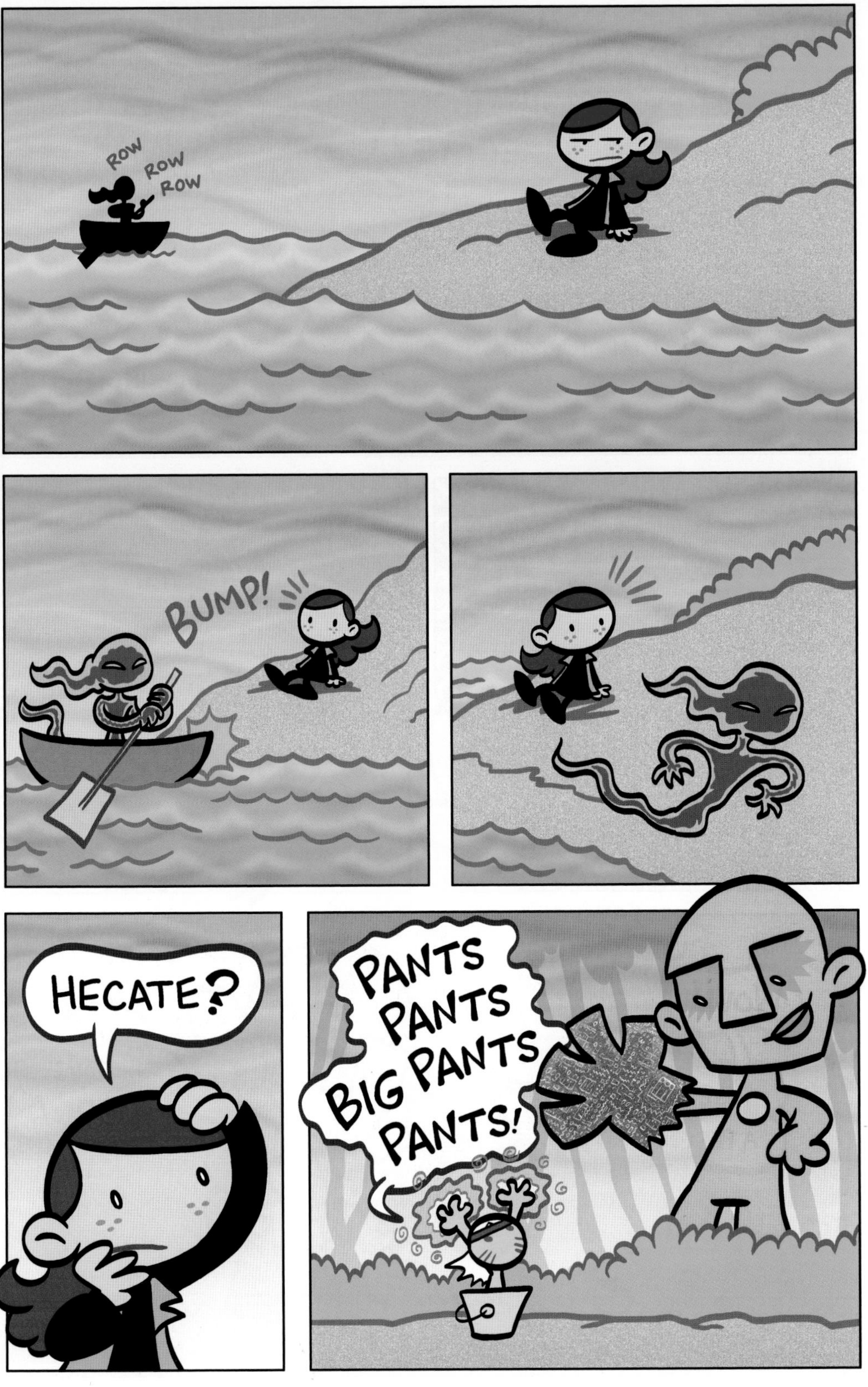
ROW
ROW
ROW
BUMP!
HECATE?
PANTS
PANTS
BIG PANTS
PANTS!

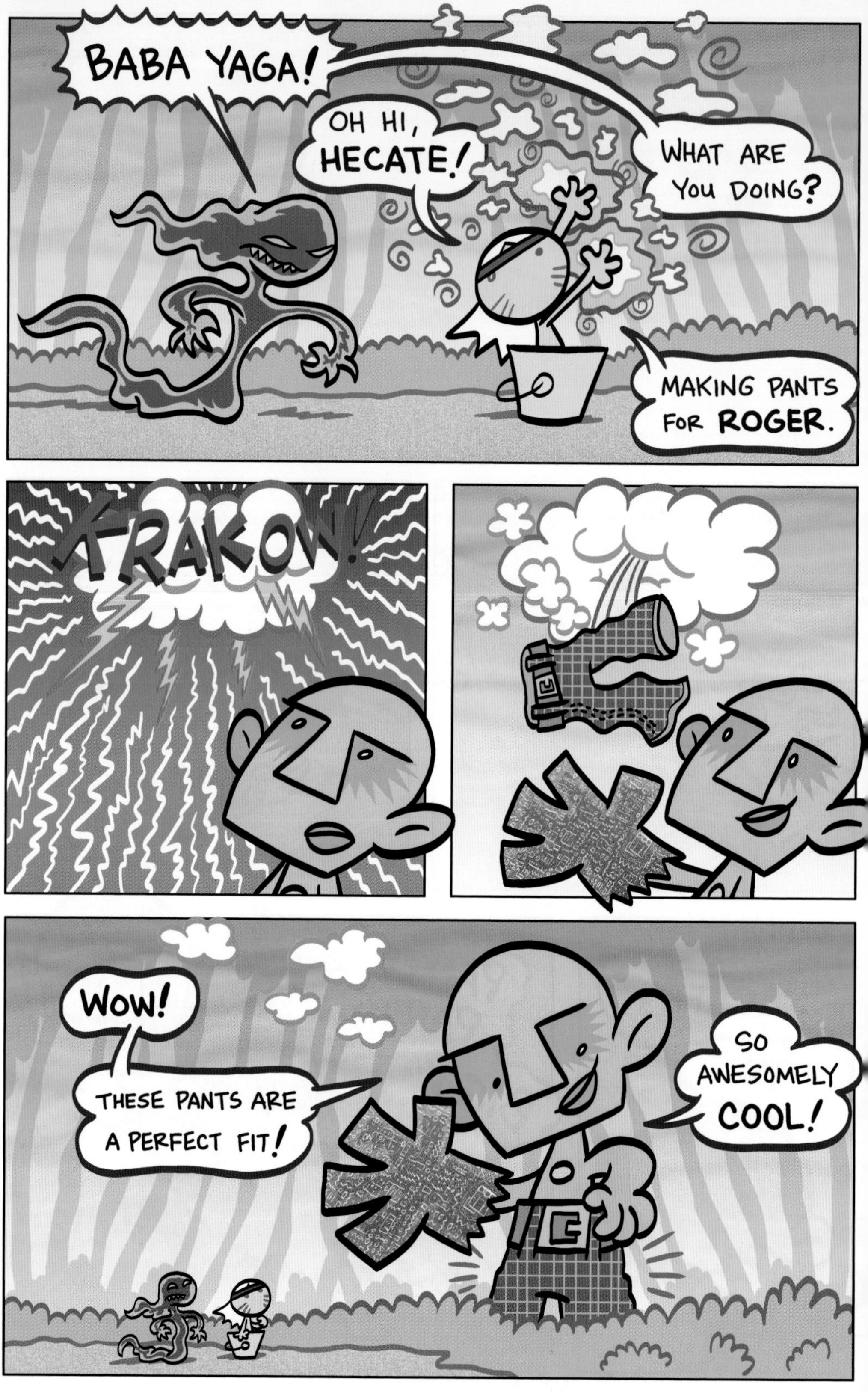
BABA YAGA!
OH HI, HECATE!
WHAT ARE YOU DOING?
MAKING PANTS FOR ROGER.
KRAKOW!
WOW!
THESE PANTS ARE A PERFECT FIT!
SO AWESOMELY COOL!

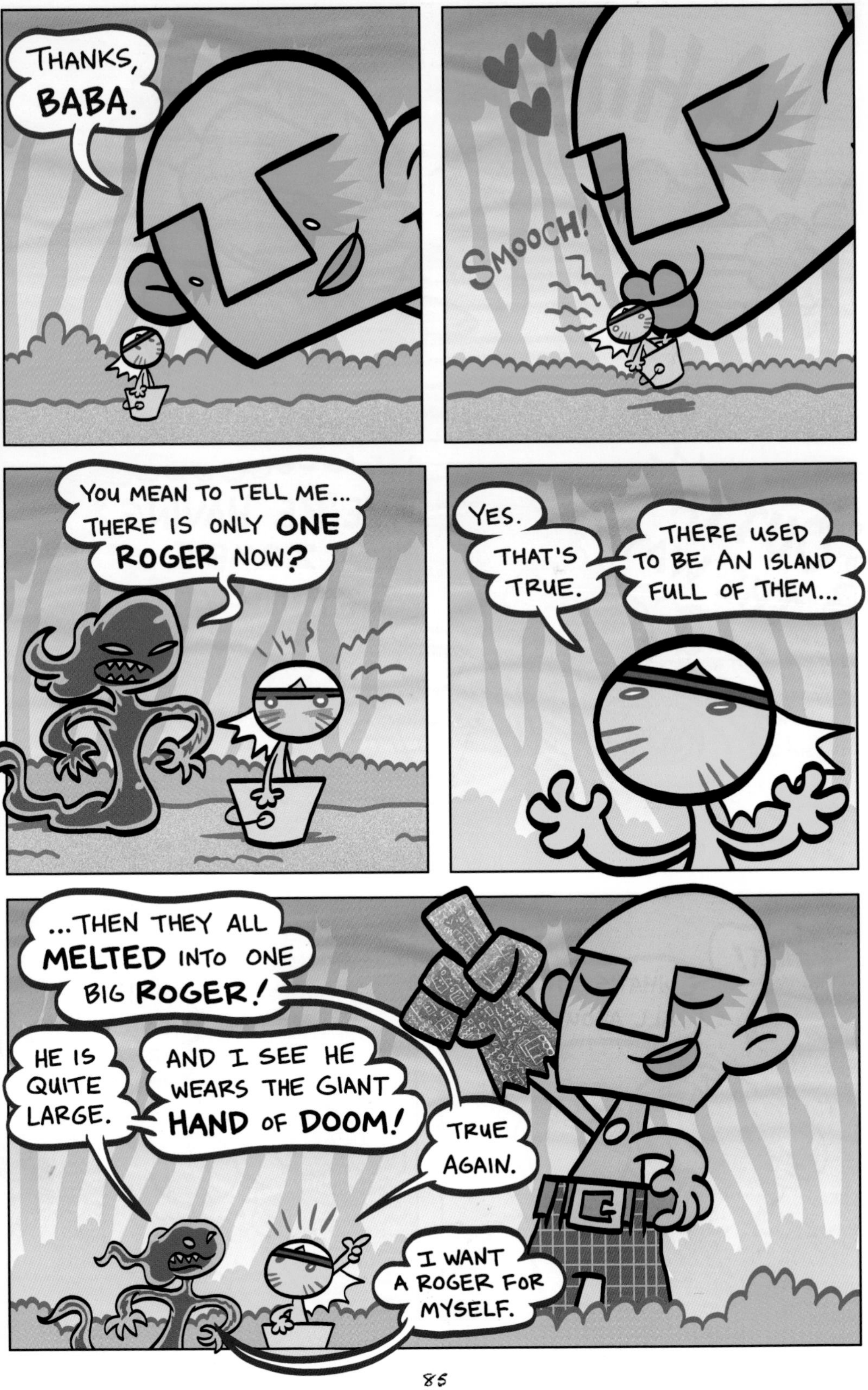
THANKS, BABA.
SMOOCH!
YOU MEAN TO TELL ME... THERE IS ONLY ONE ROGER NOW?
YES. THAT'S TRUE.
THERE USED TO BE AN ISLAND FULL OF THEM...
...THEN THEY ALL MELTED INTO ONE BIG ROGER!
HE IS QUITE LARGE.
AND I SEE HE WEARS THE GIANT HAND OF DOOM!
TRUE AGAIN.
I WANT A ROGER FOR MYSELF.

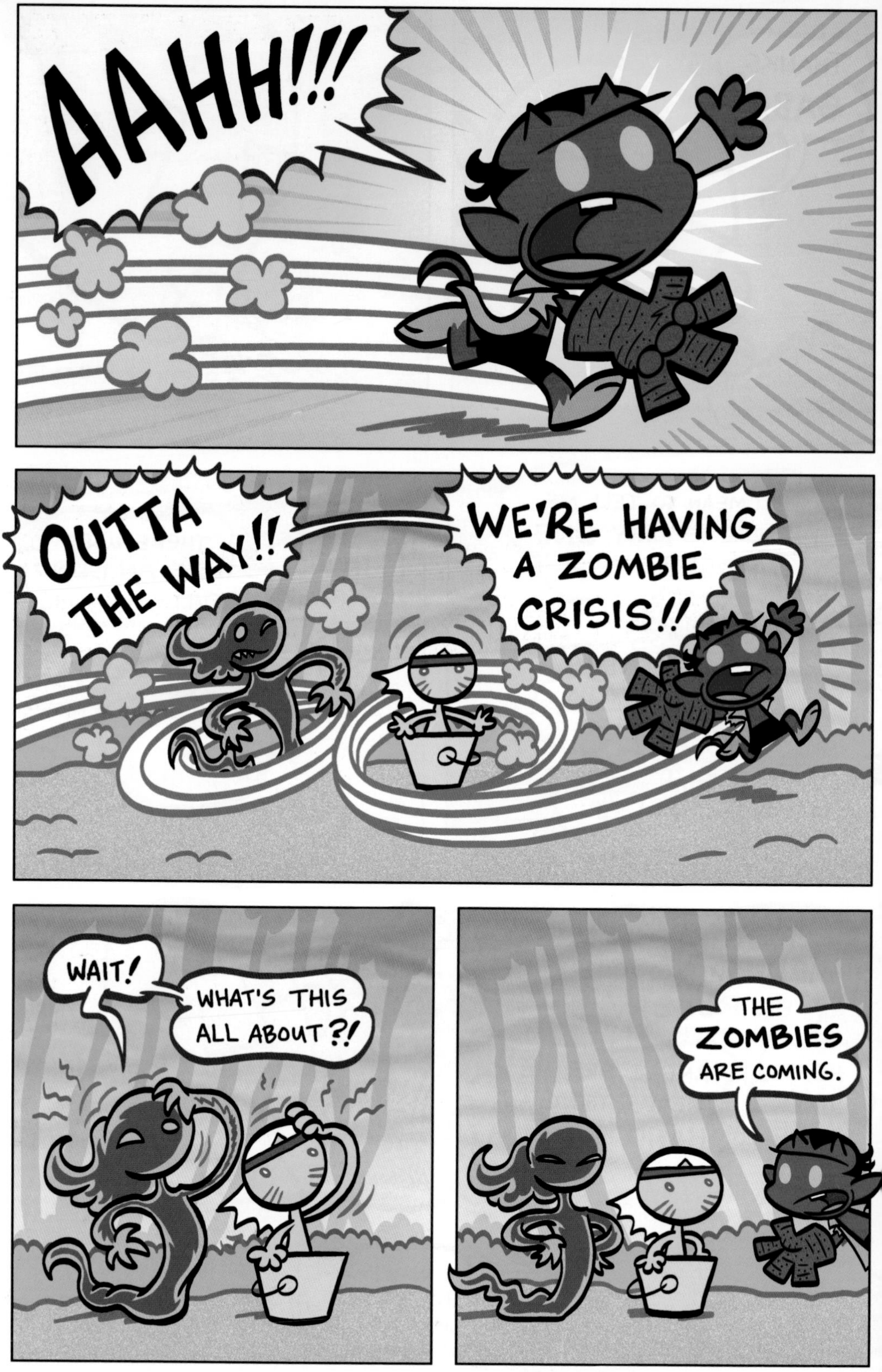
AAHH!!!
OUTTA THE WAY!!
WE'RE HAVING A ZOMBIE CRISIS!!
WAIT!
WHAT'S THIS ALL ABOUT?!
THE ZOMBIES ARE COMING.

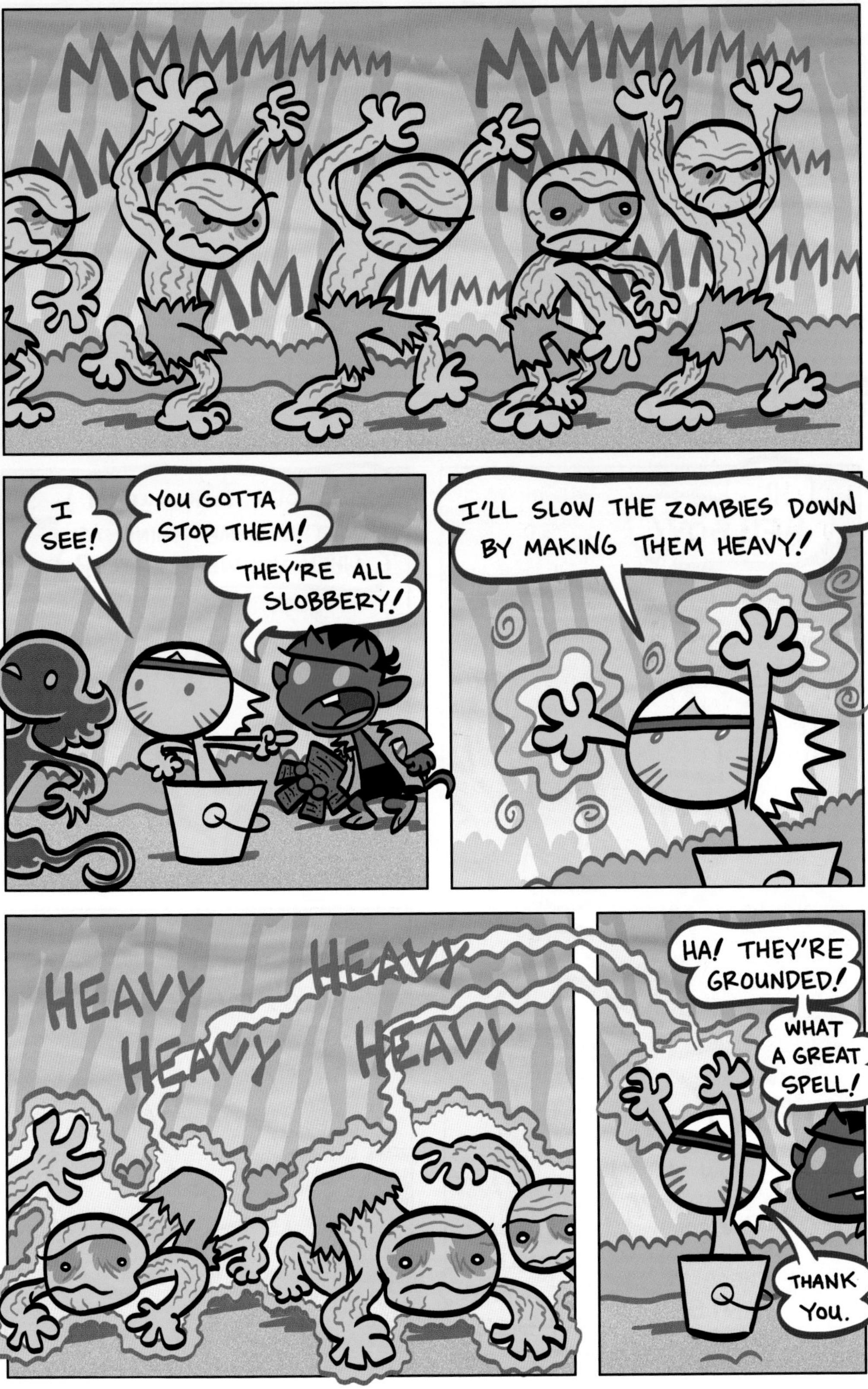
MMMMMMmm
MMMMMMmm
MMMMMmm
MMMMmm
MMMMMMm
I SEE!
YOU GOTTA STOP THEM!
THEY'RE ALL SLOBBERY!
I'LL SLOW THE ZOMBIES DOWN BY MAKING THEM HEAVY!
HEAVY
HEAVY
HEAVY
HEAVY
HA! THEY'RE GROUNDED!
WHAT A GREAT SPELL!
THANK YOU.

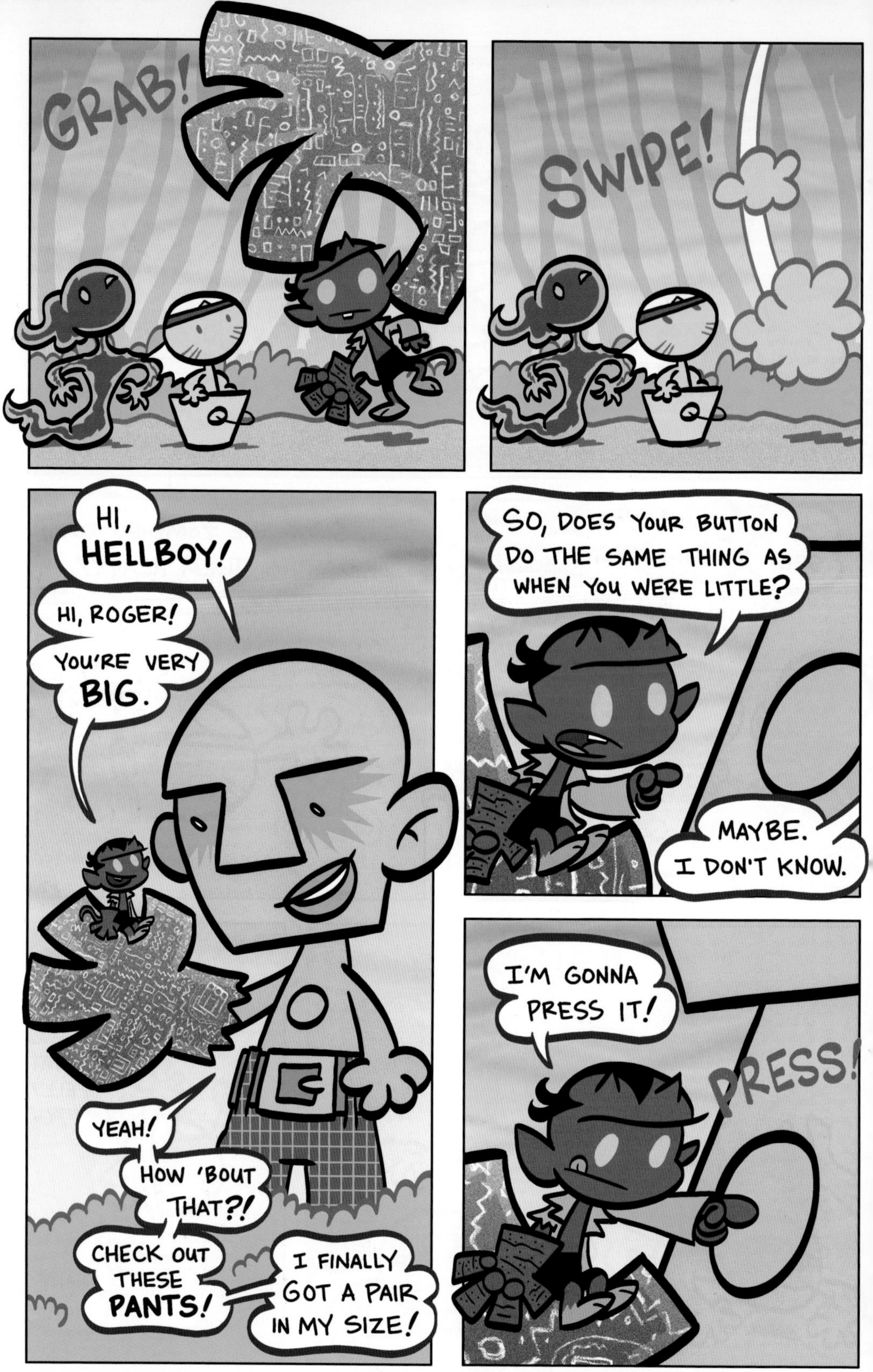
GRAB!
SWIPE!
HI, HELLBOY!
HI, ROGER!
YOU'RE VERY BIG.
YEAH!
HOW 'BOUT THAT?!
CHECK OUT THESE PANTS!
I FINALLY GOT A PAIR IN MY SIZE!
SO, DOES YOUR BUTTON DO THE SAME THING AS WHEN YOU WERE LITTLE?
MAYBE. I DON'T KNOW.
I'M GONNA PRESS IT!
PRESS!

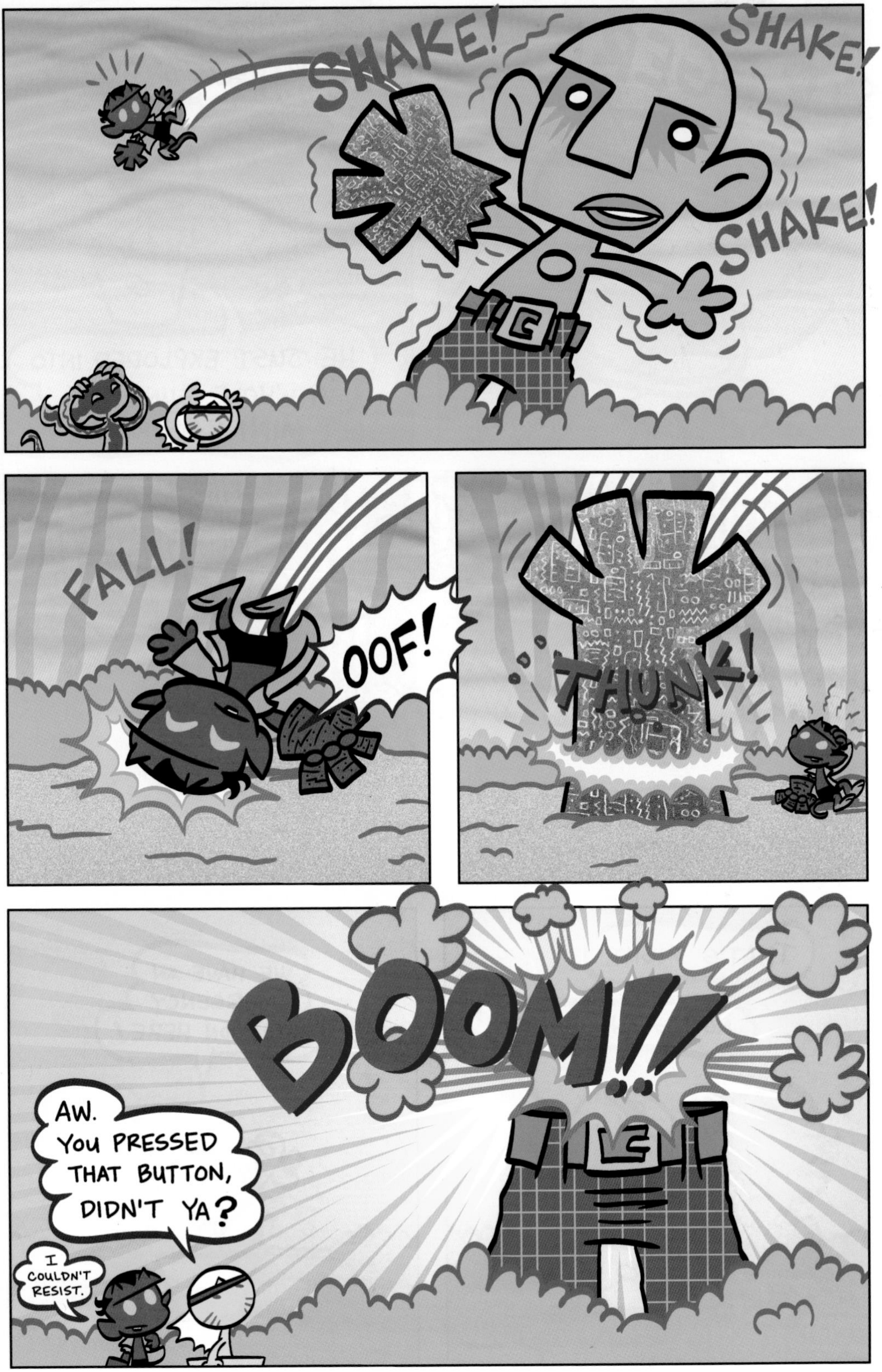
SHAKE!
SHAKE!
SHAKE!
FALL!
OOF!
THUNK!
BOOM!!!
AW. YOU PRESSED THAT BUTTON, DIDN'T YA?
I COULDN'T RESIST.

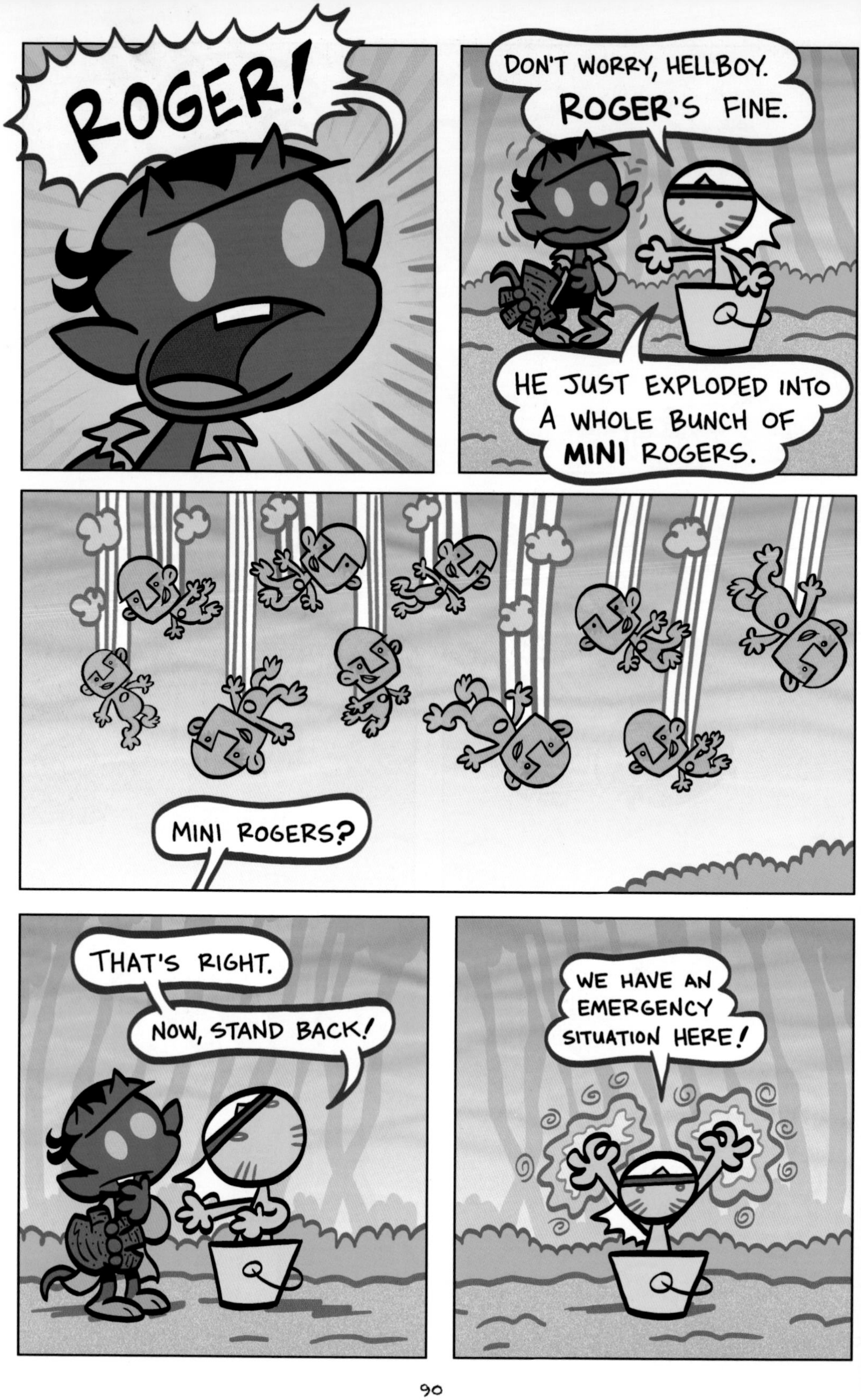
ROGER!
DON'T WORRY, HELLBOY.
ROGER'S FINE.
HE JUST EXPLODED INTO A WHOLE BUNCH OF MINI ROGERS.
MINI ROGERS?
THAT'S RIGHT.
NOW, STAND BACK!
WE HAVE AN EMERGENCY SITUATION HERE!

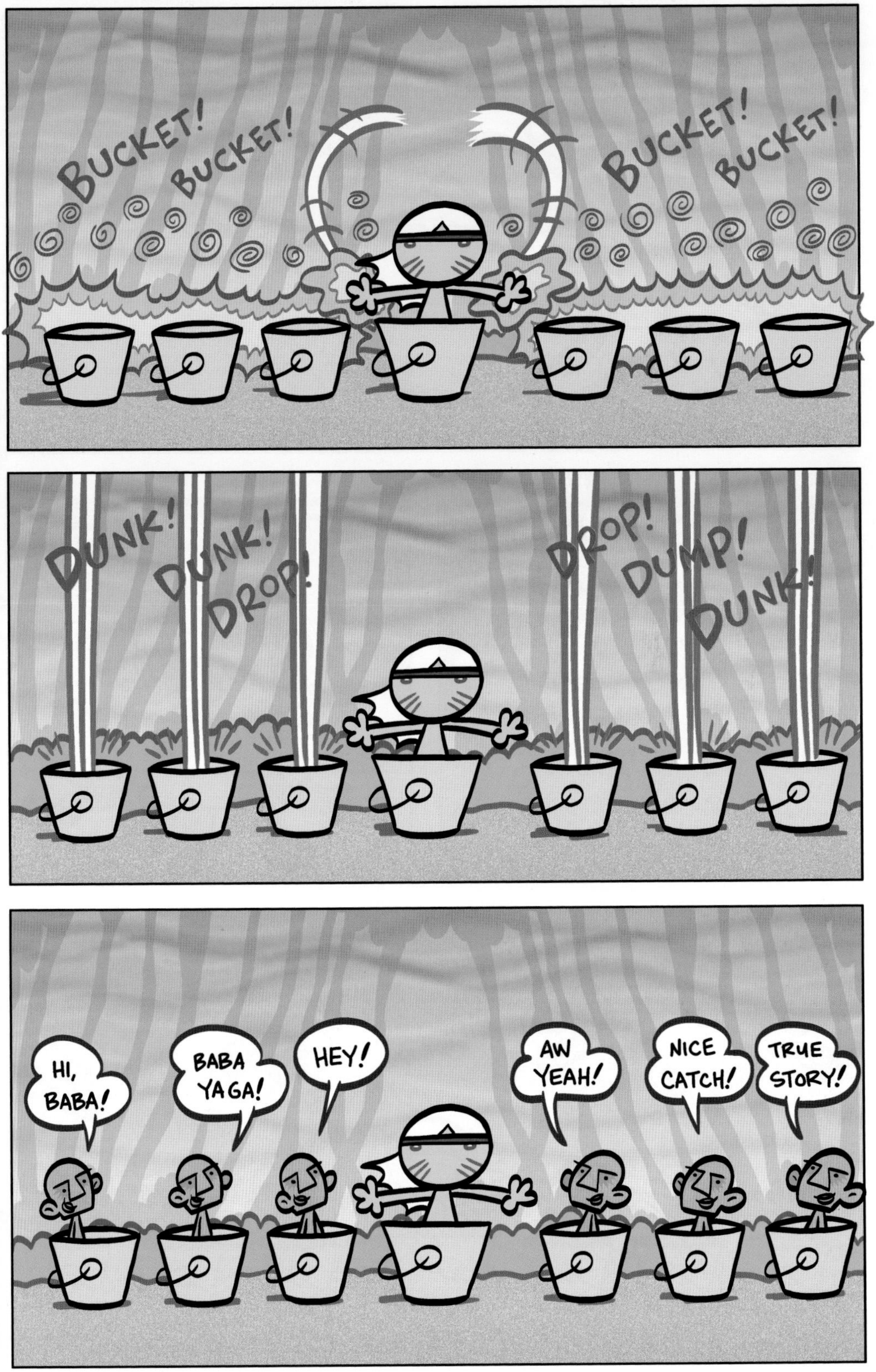
BUCKET! BUCKET!
BUCKET! BUCKET!
DUNK! DUNK! DROP!
DROP! DUMP! DUNK!
HI, BABA!
BABA YAGA!
HEY!
AW YEAH!
NICE CATCH!
TRUE STORY!

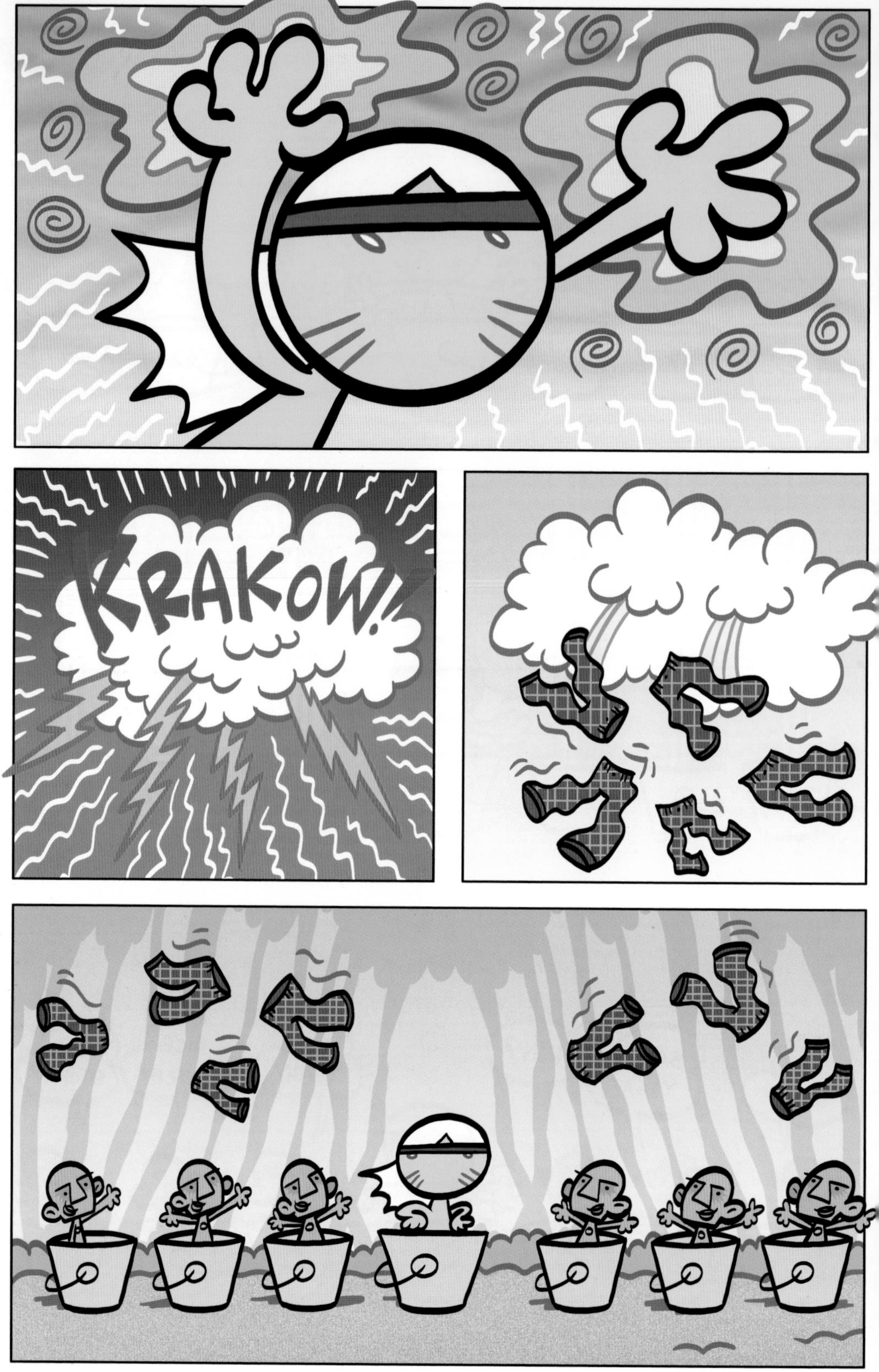
KRAKOW!

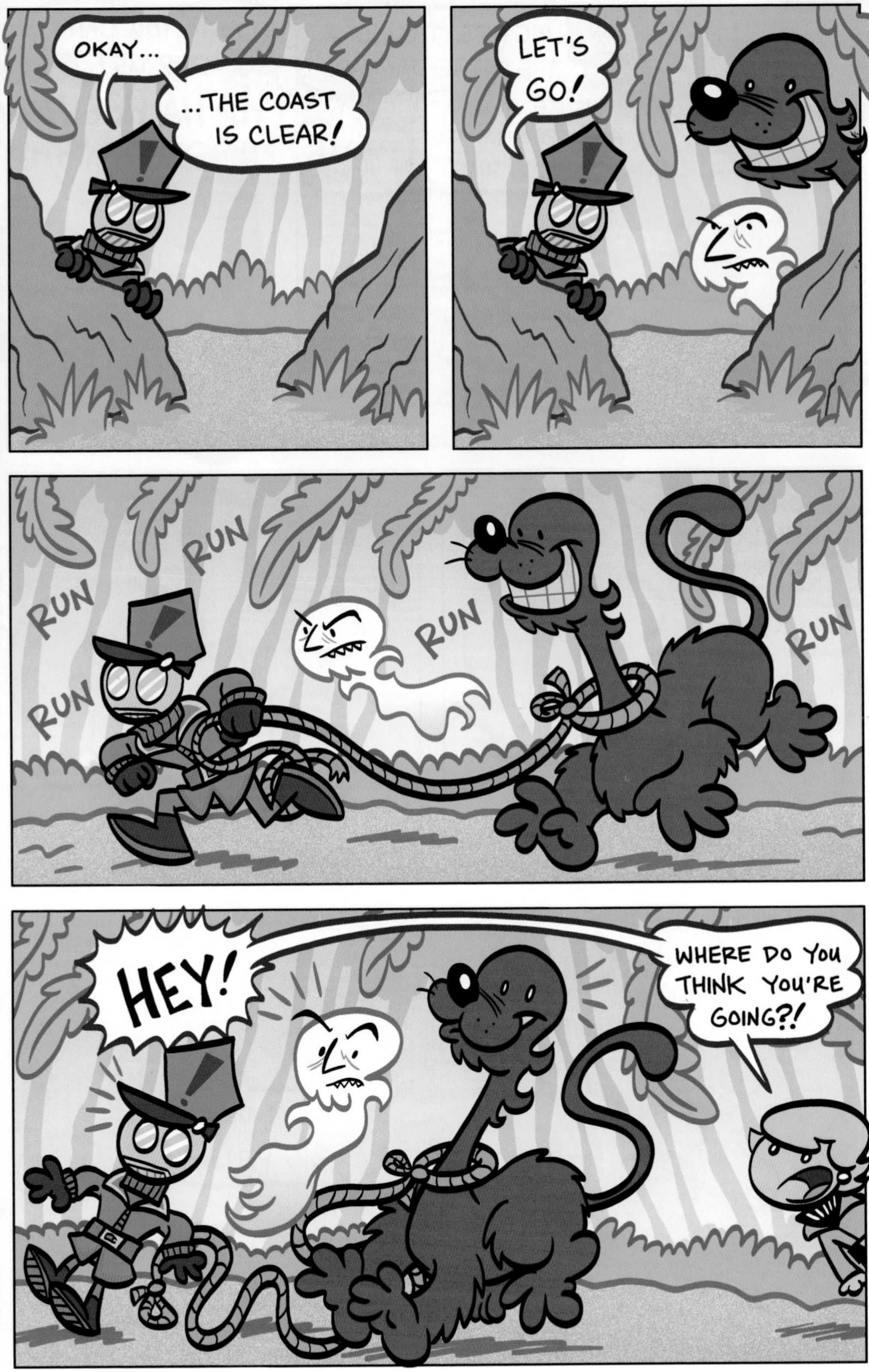
OKAY...
...THE COAST IS CLEAR!
LET'S GO!
RUN
RUN
RUN
RUN
RUN
HEY!
WHERE DO YOU THINK YOU'RE GOING?!

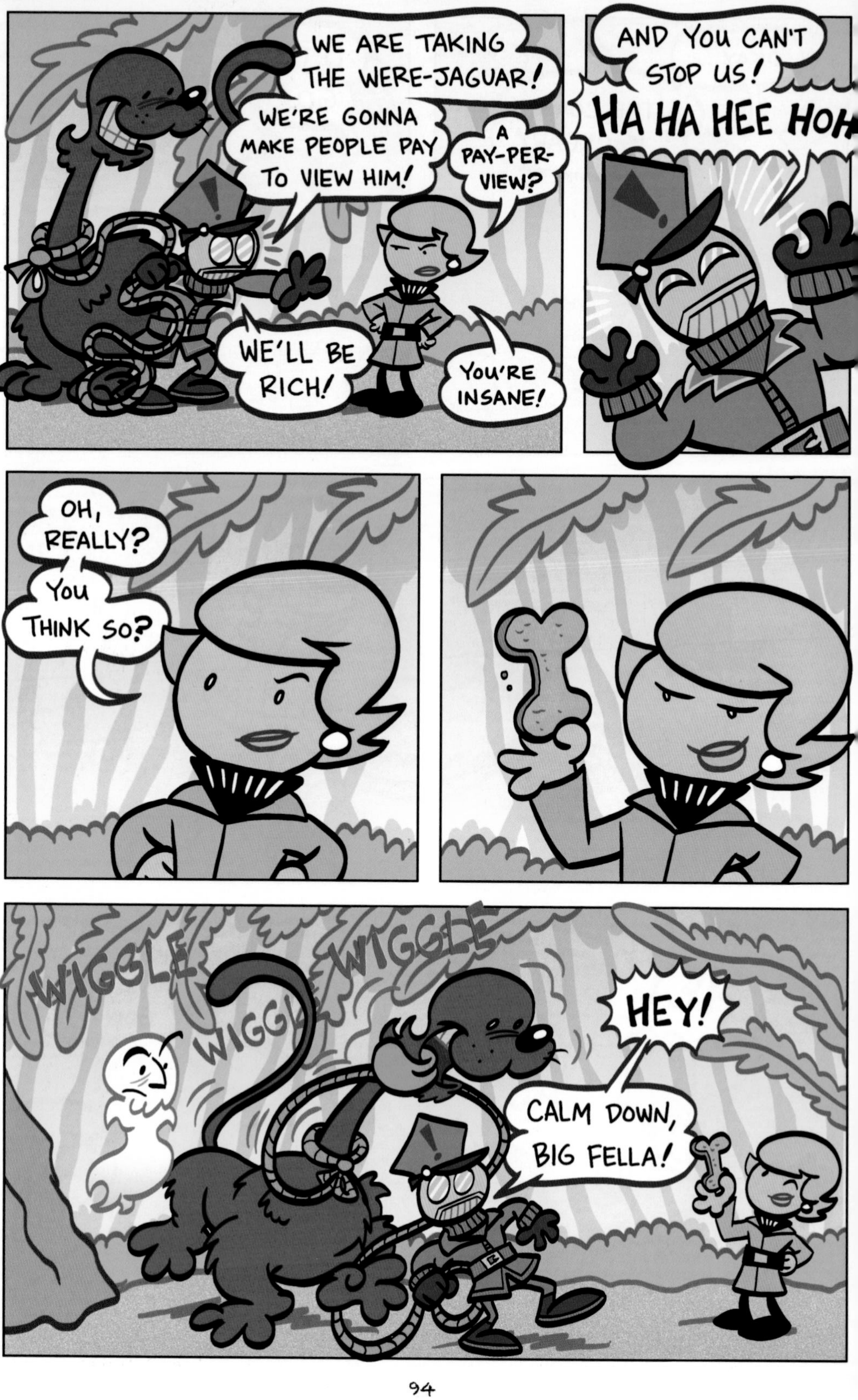
WE ARE TAKING THE WERE-JAGUAR!
WE'RE GONNA MAKE PEOPLE PAY TO VIEW HIM!
A PAY-PER-VIEW?
WE'LL BE RICH!
YOU'RE INSANE!
AND YOU CAN'T STOP US!
HA HA HEE HOH
OH, REALLY?
YOU THINK SO?
WIGGLE
WIGGLE
WIGGL
HEY!
CALM DOWN, BIG FELLA!

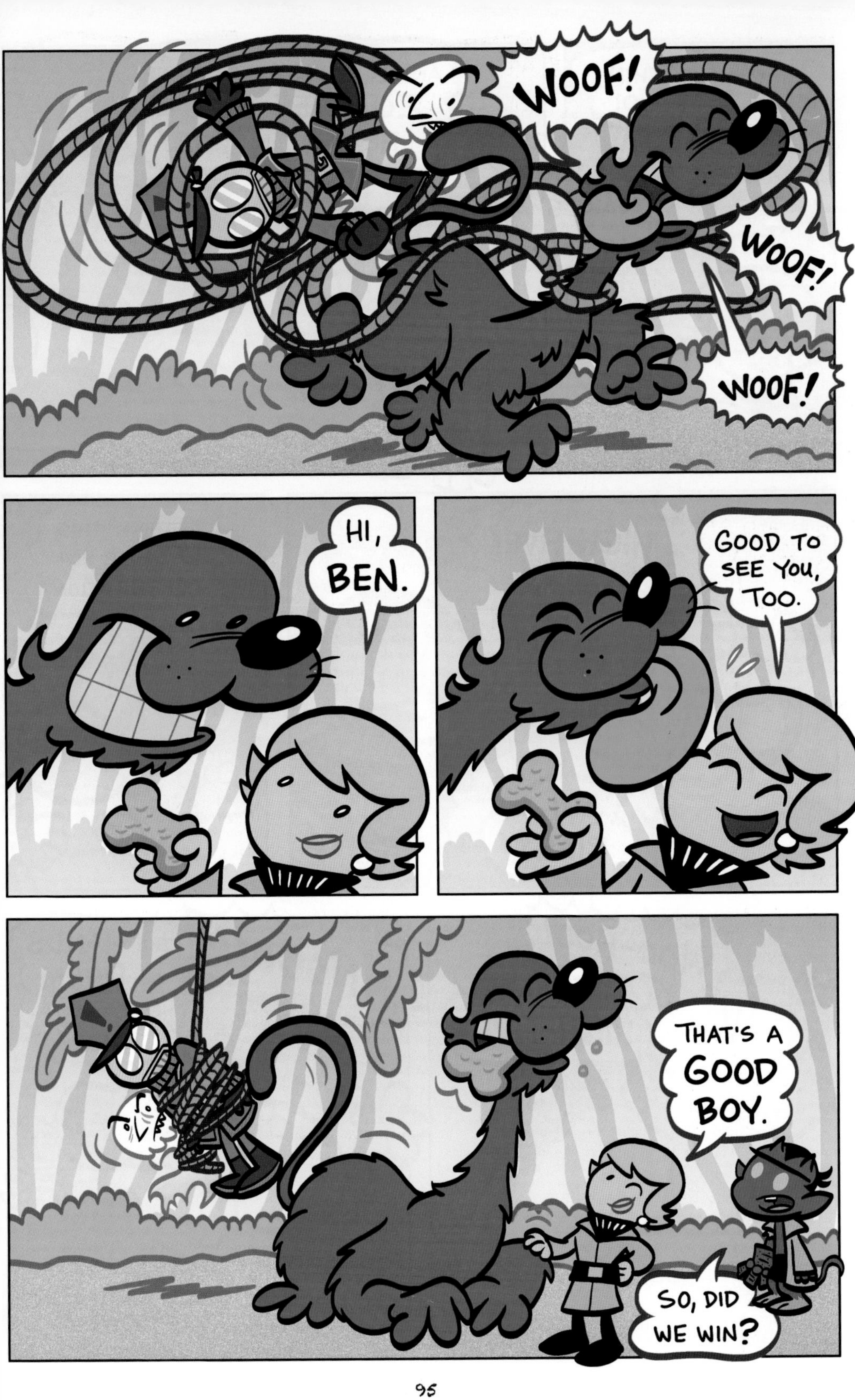
WOOF!
WOOF!
WOOF!
HI, BEN.
GOOD TO SEE YOU, TOO.
THAT'S A GOOD BOY.
SO, DID WE WIN?

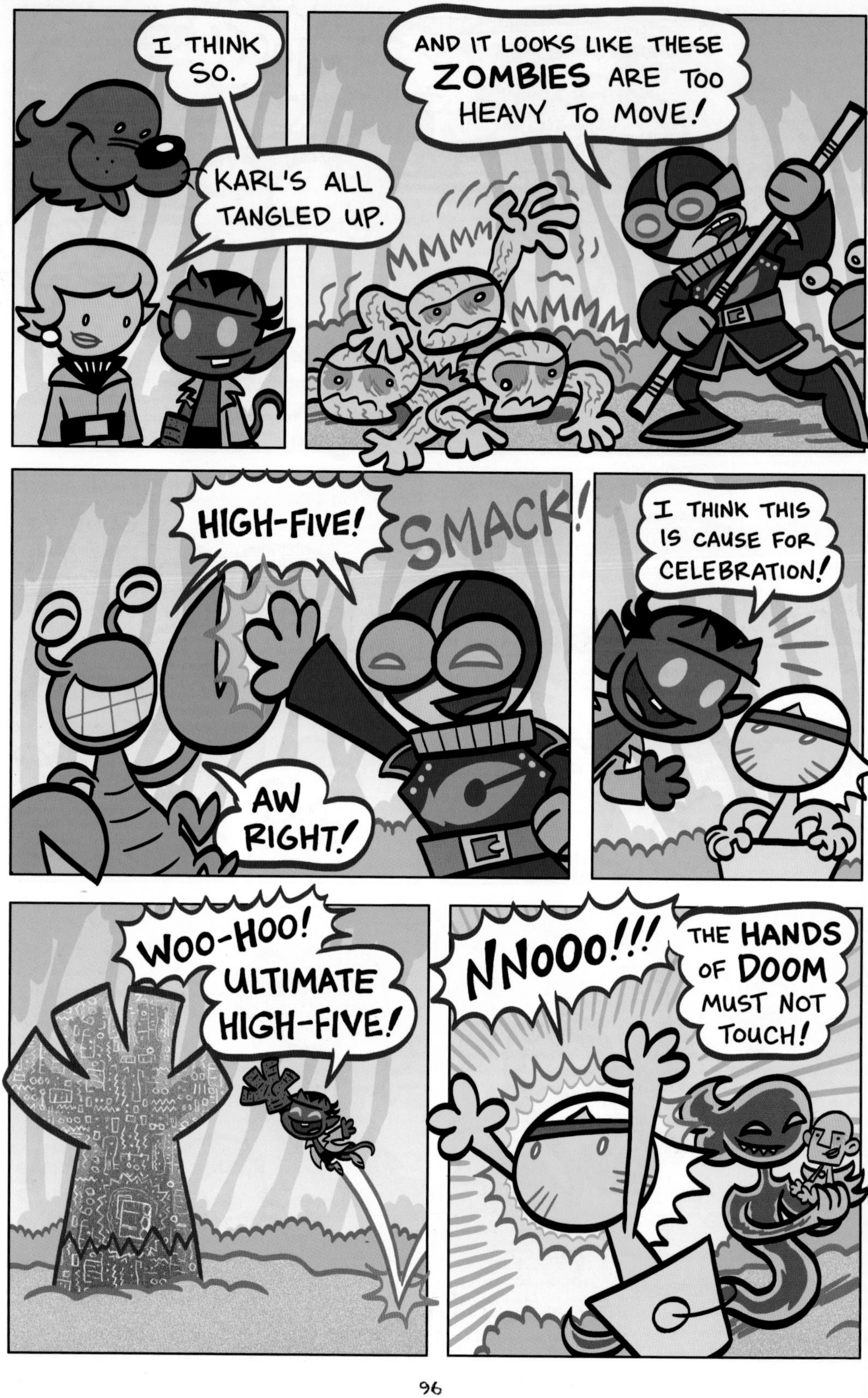

I THINK SO.
KARL'S ALL TANGLED UP.
AND IT LOOKS LIKE THESE ZOMBIES ARE TOO HEAVY TO MOVE!
MMMM
MMMM
HIGH-FIVE!
SMACK!
AW RIGHT!
I THINK THIS IS CAUSE FOR CELEBRATION!
WOO-HOO! ULTIMATE HIGH-FIVE!
NNOOO!!!
THE HANDS OF DOOM MUST NOT TOUCH!

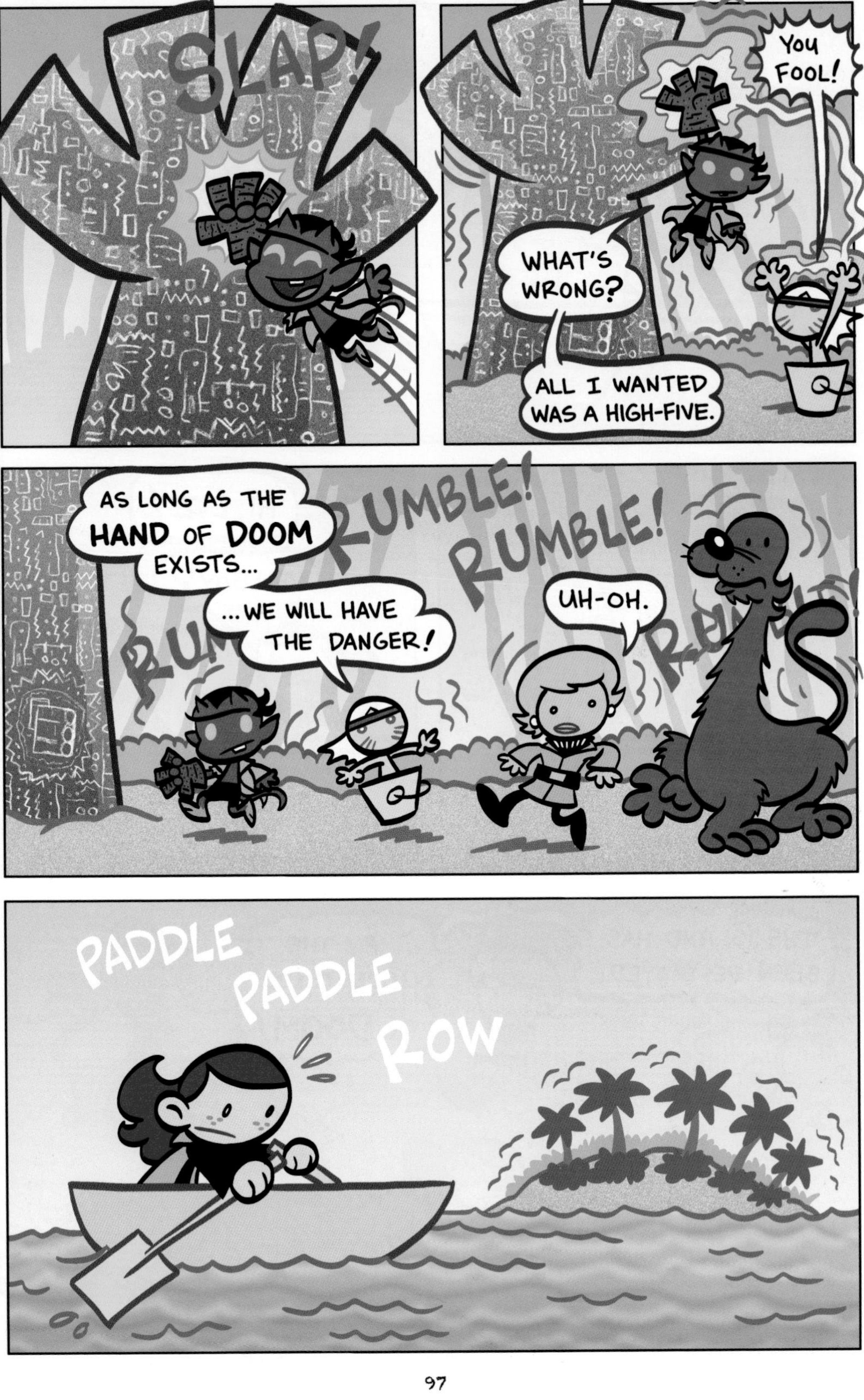

SLAP!
YOU FOOL!
WHAT'S WRONG?
ALL I WANTED WAS A HIGH-FIVE.
AS LONG AS THE HAND OF DOOM EXISTS...
...WE WILL HAVE THE DANGER!
RUMBLE! RUMBLE!
UH-OH.
PADDLE
PADDLE
ROW

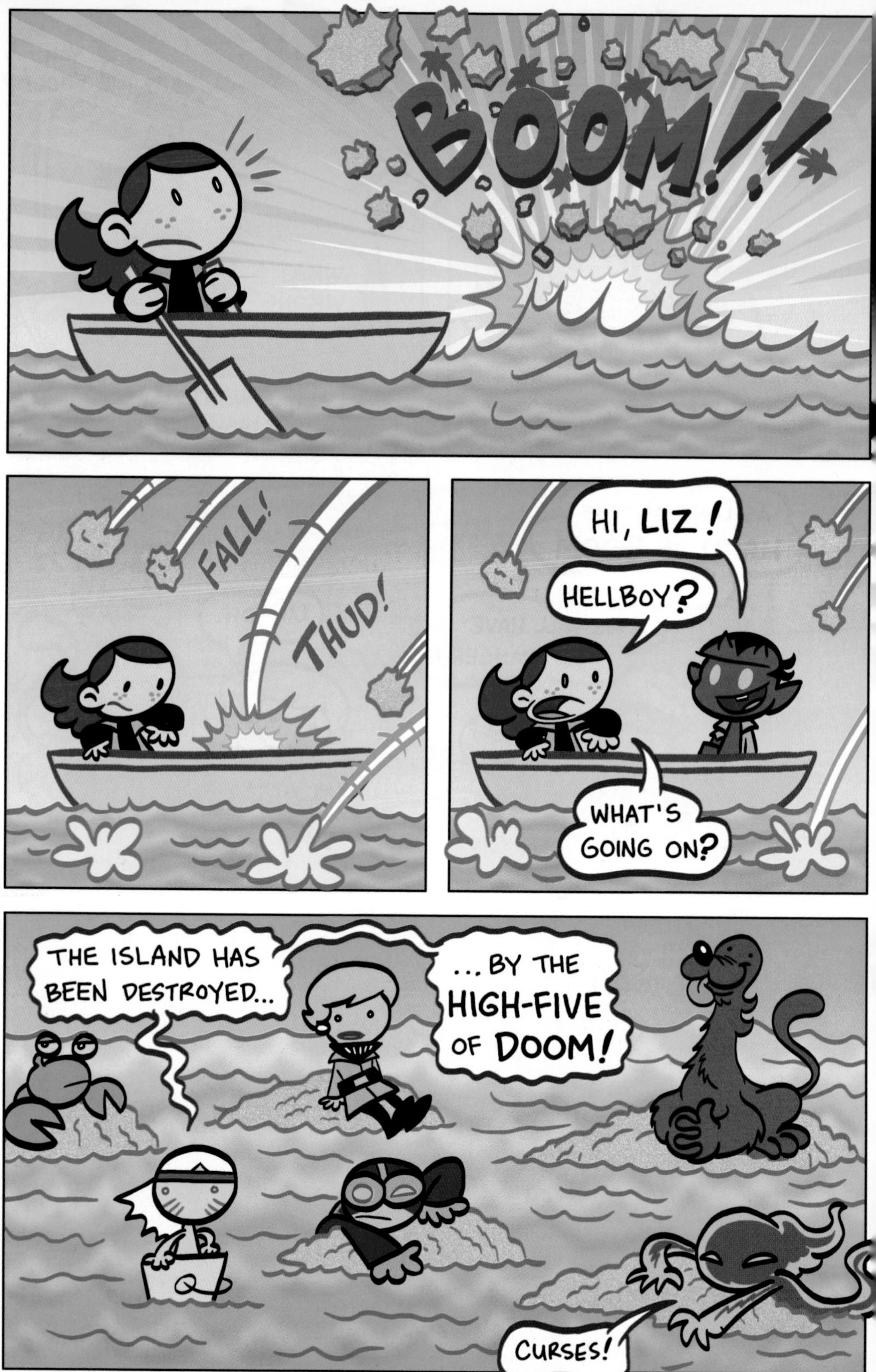
BOOM!!
FALL!
THUD!
HI, LIZ!
HELLBOY?
WHAT'S GOING ON?
THE ISLAND HAS BEEN DESTROYED...
... BY THE HIGH-FIVE OF DOOM!
CURSES!

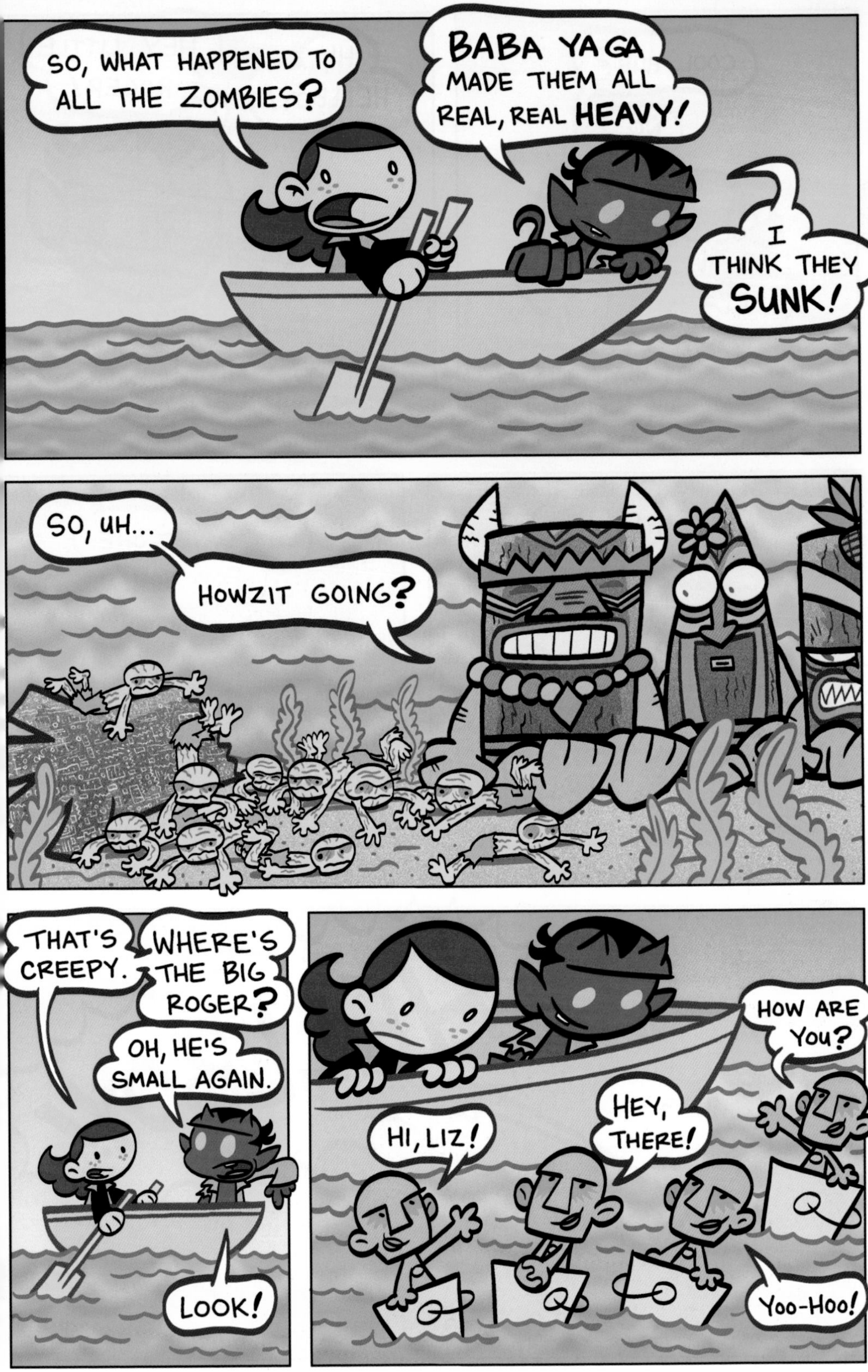
SO, WHAT HAPPENED TO ALL THE ZOMBIES?
BABA YAGA MADE THEM ALL REAL, REAL HEAVY!
I THINK THEY SUNK!
SO, UH...
HOWZIT GOING?
THAT'S CREEPY.
WHERE'S THE BIG ROGER?
OH, HE'S SMALL AGAIN.
LOOK!
HOW ARE YOU?
HEY, THERE!
HI, LIZ!
YOO-HOO!

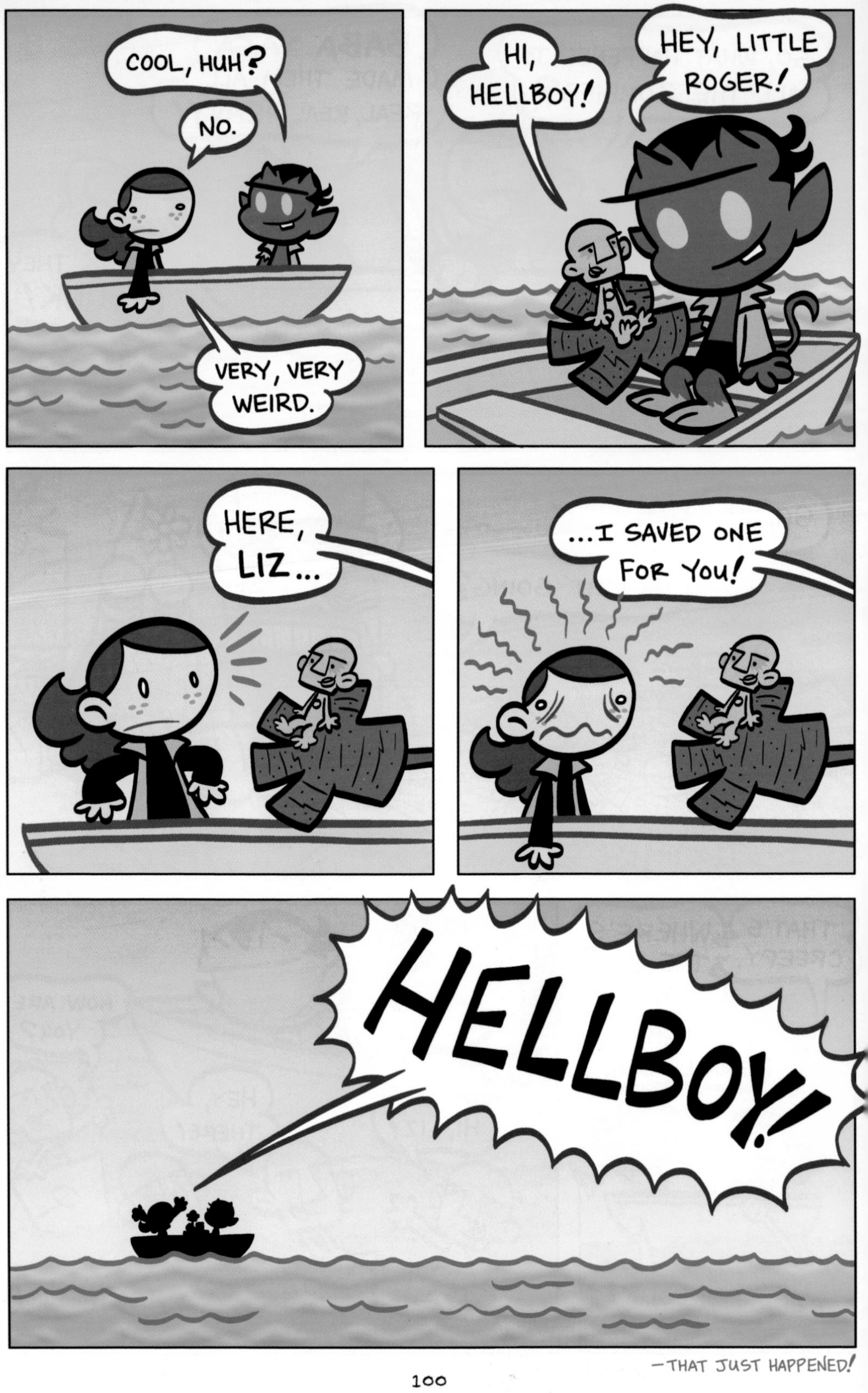
COOL, HUH?
NO.
VERY, VERY WEIRD.
HI, HELLBOY!
HEY, LITTLE ROGER!
HERE, LIZ...
...I SAVED ONE FOR YOU!
HELLBOY!

—THAT JUST HAPPENED!

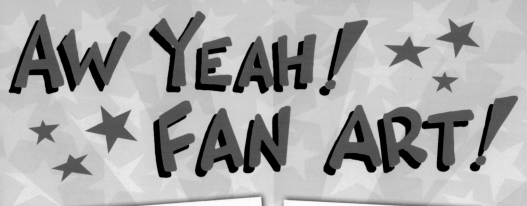

AW YEAH! FAN ART!

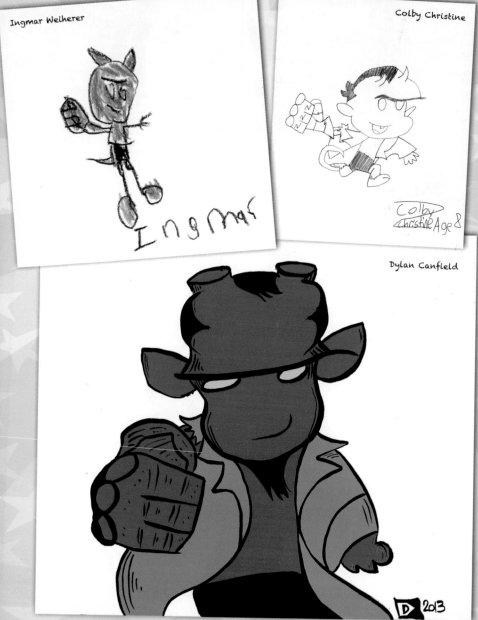

Ingmar Weiherer

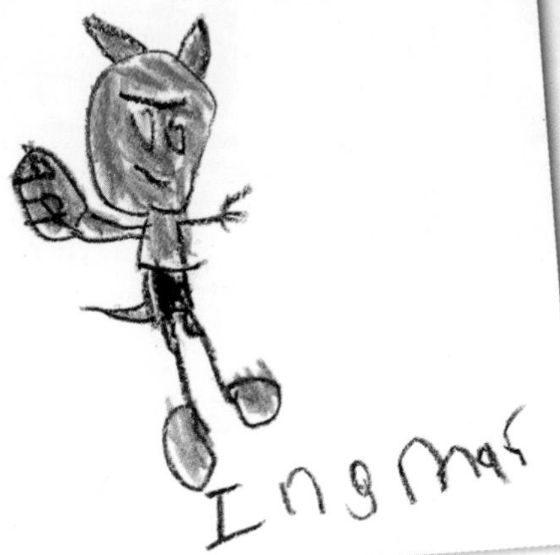
Ingmar

Colby Christine

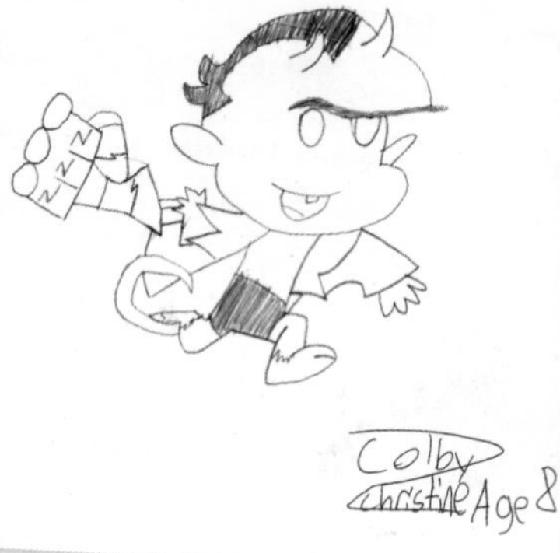
Colby Christine Age 8

Dylan Canfield

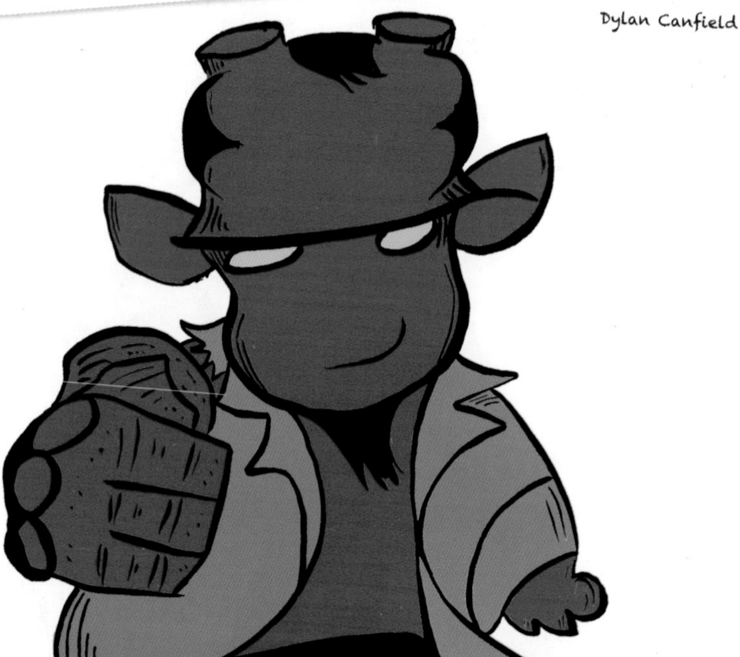
D 2013

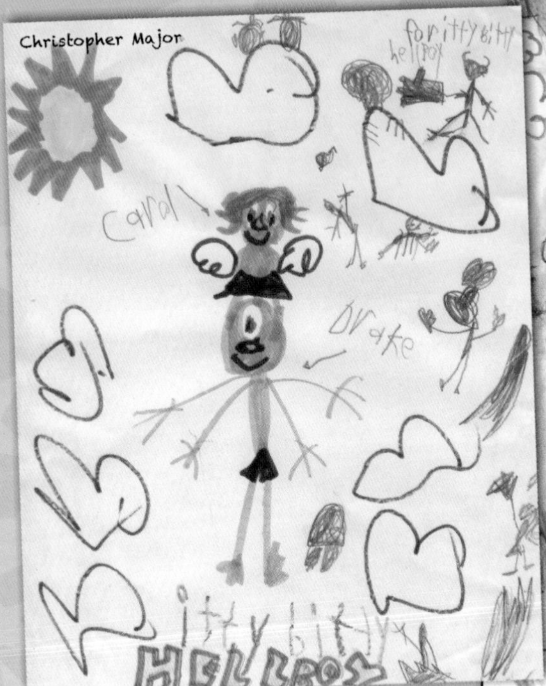
carol
drake

Christopher Major

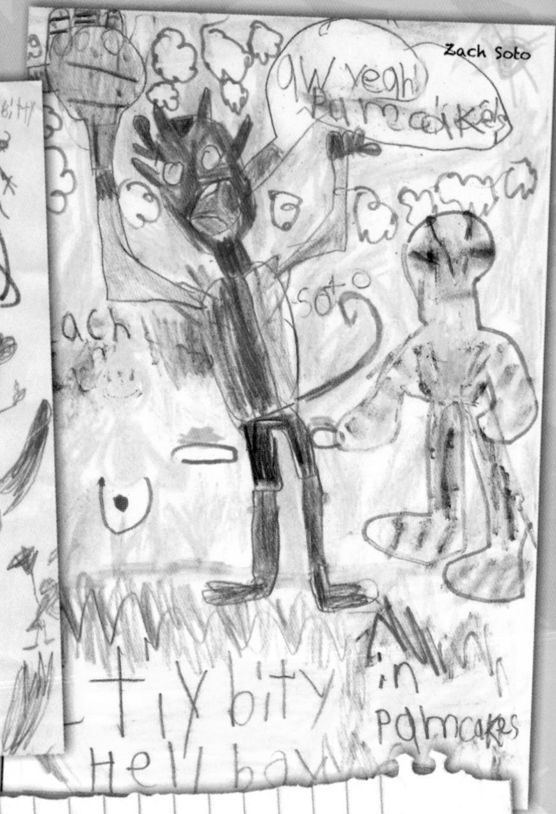
aw yeah!
soto

Zach Soto

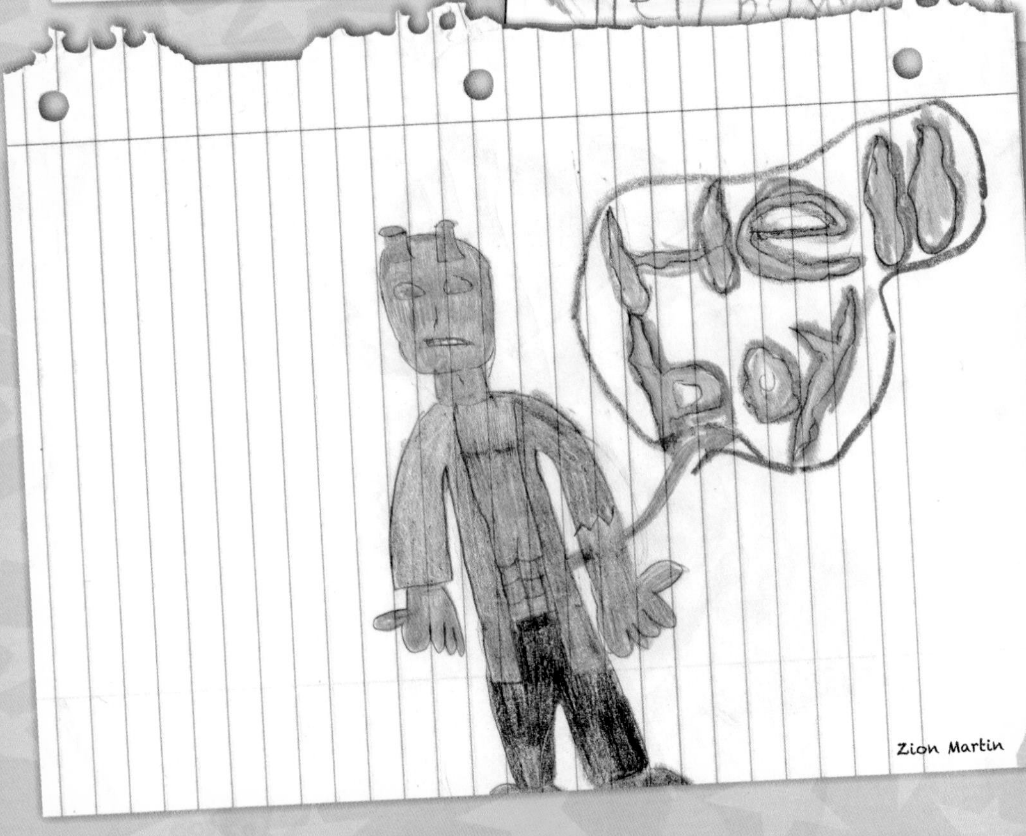

Zion Martin